SCARRED WINGS

KATERINA BRAY

SHATTERED SOULS TRILOGY

SCARRED WINGS

KATERINA BRAY

SHATTERED SOULS TRILOGY

SCARRED WINGS

KATERINA BRAY

SCARRED WINGS

Copyright © 2020 by Katerina Bray

All rights reserved. No part of this book may be used or reproduced in any form or by any electronic or mechanical means, including information storage and retrieval systems, without written permission from the publisher, except in the case of brief quotations embodied in critical articles or reviews.

This book is a work of fiction. Names, characters, businesses, organizations, places, events, and incidents either are the product of the author's imagination or are used fictitiously. Any resemblance to actual persons, living or dead, events, or locales is entirely coincidental and not intended by the author.

Printed and bound in the USA

For information, visit: WWW.KATERINABRAY.COM

Cover Design By: Dawid Boldys
Dedication Image By: Maria Zogu

ISBN: 978-0-9985247-6-4 (Hardback)
ISBN: 978-0-9985247-3-3 (Paperback)
ISBN: 978-0-9985247-4-0 (E-book)

I dedicate this to those who have loved and lost.

To those who have felt alone in times of need.

And to all those who struggle with the agony that comes with infertility.

We're never alone, even when we think we are.

Keep your head up and spread love.

12.22.18

Miracles do happen.

Serafina Gabrielle.

I may appear broken...
...but I have immmemse strength within.

To My Dearest
Readers & Supporters

With every story there's a
BEGINNING, MIDDLE, & END.
The Beginning is behind us, so I welcome you to join me for

The Middle

of the
SHATTERED SOULS TRILOGY.

Enjoy!

The Middle

"Someday, this unbearable pain will just be a distant memory, but your scars will remain as a symbol of your survival. Wear them with pride." - Katerina Bray

What defines me as a man? Is it my salary, how fancy my car is, or having the perfect house with a flawless white picket fence?

By my standards, there's no fucking way those meaningless things will define me ever again.

Yet our brainwashed society doesn't have a problem with this injustice. Which is why men doubt their true value. Have women ever appreciated men as they are? Maybe hundreds and thousands of years ago, before the bullshit ideals of today's civilization invaded their minds.

What is my problem with life?

I used to ask myself this question often, until one day, the answer hit me. Women. They're the damn problem. They need too much shit. Too many unrealistic things.

Growing up poor taught me a thing or two on the extent of work it takes to buy a damn loaf of bread, let alone material things way above your pay grade.

Although, the struggle never matters to the person requesting those unobtainable items.

The many discussions I had with my father as a five-year-old child stuck with me into adulthood. Thanks to him, I grew up knowing the difference between reality and fantasy.

Not that I didn't have moments of weakness in my younger years.

Around my eleventh birthday, my dear mother began to meddle. She was the complete opposite of my father. She loved telling me stories of Princesses and Princes falling in love, then living happily ever after.

Their contrasting opinions on the meaning and purpose of life, left me confused. Who's point of view was right? Who was I supposed to believe?

As the sweet young man I was, I wanted to make the woman I loved proud, so I took the path leading to false hope.

I followed along that road until it came to a life altering end.

That was the moment I understood the truth in my da's words. My life would've turned out much better if I'd steered clear of the pretend world I'd created in my mind.

I'm sorry mom, but you were wrong. So very wrong. Fairy tales don't exist.

1

MAESON

I only tried to end it because I'd let her down. Life wasn't worth living without her.

It's dark. The darkness is too thick.

Wake up. Wake. The. Fuck. Up.

MY EYES FLICKER. MY sight, hazy at best. My brain is muddled. The room is spinning.

She was everything. How do I move on?

Her beautiful face. That smile. Her loving heart. The reminders are everywhere. I can't escape them. For fuck's sake, let me escape them.

Yes, darkness, we meet again. Take me. Take me back. Please.

I STARE INTO HER big beautiful eyes as I hold her close to my chest. The love I see in them, breaks my soul into tiny pieces. 'I feel you leaving me,' I want to say, but don't.

Why is this happening? What will I do all alone? How will I fix this?

Who'll fix me when she's gone? The questions hit me at once, and I struggle to breathe.

Money. I need it to care for her. How will I get that kind of cash with my measly paycheck?

I dismiss the depressing thought from my mind before I peer at her again. She's fallen fast asleep.

Good. She needs it more than I do.

I pull away and lean against the wall, sliding to the floor as tears I've held back spill down my cheeks. At twenty-three, I'm not supposed to be dealing with this.

Just breathe. It'll be okay. She won't leave you.

I pledged to be the best man I could be. A promise I made in hopes she'd see my true value, yet how did she repay me?

You can still keep your promise. You'll just have to do it alone.

Unrelenting tears flow from my eyes, and for her I allow it. Only for her.

After a few minutes of releasing my pain and fears, I pick myself up and kiss her cheek, then drag my heavy body out of the room.

I head straight for the whiskey in the kitchen cabinet. I need this drink. It's not a good idea, but I haven't had one in a while.

Plus, she's sleeping, and I'll never harm her, no matter how drunk I get tonight.

Ashlie, though, she's another story.

Wake up.

No.

Stop dwelling in the past.

It's what I deserve.

Someone else needs you. Someone in the present.

She doesn't need me. She deserves better.

River meet pathetic tears.

What if she's like…

What if she's not? Take a chance.

Bloody chances are all I ever take.

Then what's another one under your belt?

Belts cause pain, and I don't need any more of that shit. I've had enough distress to last me a lifetime.

Then wake up, asshole, and find the happiness you seek. Take the tranquility she can offer you.

2

Ruby

I inhale deeply, filling my nostrils with musty unventilated air before joining the devil in his vault of pain.

"You're my favorite, you know? The rest of them aren't special like you are. They tell on me, but you won't, will you? No, because you know exactly what'll happen."

"I pro-prom-promise, I won't. I can keep secrets like you taught me," I look away from his burly face, focusing on the nasty scar on his chest.

"Good girl, Ruby. I'll take it easy on you tonight. Try not to faint this time. Just relax." His voice hurts my ears, but his fingers digging into my arm hurt worse.

"I'll try not to." My role when we're in this room is always the same. Follow the number one rule, listen well and say little to nothing.

He shoves me into his preferred position. My face to the wall, hands tied up in the air, and legs spread wide. "Remember, no screaming." His tone is harsher than before. The psychopath has officially entered the building.

I don't respond to his demand. It would go unheard anyway. He's in the zone, probably imagining the sick things he'll do to me. Nothing about this night is special or new, same damn weekly routine. The only difference is, I'm older. It's been three long years of being degraded, abused, and thrown away.

Unlike me, most fifteen-year-olds get to enjoy their lives by hanging out with their friends, shopping, and going the movies. My days are spent alone in my room, and when I'm not doing that, I'm in this basement.

Great fucking life. Great job, social services. Great job, asshole teachers. Great fucking job to those people who can help me, but won't. Everyone seems to be blind, or oblivious, or maybe they just don't care? My parents would've cared. They would've made sure this never happened.

The familiar practice crack snaps me into reality. I squeeze my eyes shut and tighten my muscles as I brace myself for what's to come.

One... Two... Slash.

Pain radiates through my body as warm blood trickles down my back. I clench my fists, preparing for the next.

One... Two... Slash.

My skin burns. Agony sets in. The scent of rusted copper permeates my nostrils.

How are my legs weak after only two lashes? I can do this.

"You're so beautiful like this. No one compares to you, Princess-Trust-Fund," He says 'Princess' with a sneer.

He's ruined one of the last precious things I hold close to my heart. The word used to have a special meaning, but now, it's the nastiest term I've ever heard. Why did I tell him what my dad called me?

Before I have a chance to start my count, the whip crashes against my raw flesh. I bite down on my lip, forcing back the scream my throat begs to release.

His putrid heavy breathing signals what's coming next. I clear my mind of my parents and anything else causing me to feel, and focus on his intake and exhale. My body, my soul, my insides, and my heart go numb. Emotions in this room are useless. They cause more pain than necessary, so I shut down... completely.

One... two... three... Crack. Pull back. Crack. Pull back. Crack. One after the other, the lashes pound onto my back. He's unstoppable.

I'm weakening quicker than usual. My knees give out when the whip lands on my side, wrapping around my belly. "Oh God!" My scream echo's throughout the room. "Please stop." The burn is unbearable, and my only reprieve to the searing fire is the blood sliding down my back, my belly, and my legs.

"No, it's perfect. Don't. Move."

How can he continue? I'm not even able to stand. Why am I surprised? No matter what state I'm in, he always makes sure to finish.

Bile rises in my throat when his hands touch the new scars. I want to shrivel away from his traveling fingers.

Too late.

He lifts me, forcing me to stand straight. The monster needs to be satisfied. It doesn't matter to him I'm shaking or I'll throw up while he's in the middle of feeding his fetish.

Mom, why didn't you tell me there are people like this in the world? I could've prepared better.

There's a familiar jingle of a belt. "It's time, Princess. Be a good girl and tell me who's your king?"

I want to scream. I want to hit him. I want to... die.

"Kill me. Please, kill me." I beg.

Deep breath. Be stronger, Ruby. You can get through this.

"How can I kill my favorite little gem?" He grabs my hips. "I'll never hurt you. I need you." He's too close. His rotten breath is suffocating.

Panic sets in, gripping my soul. I gag. "Pain. You. Cause. Pain."

His fingers glide up my torso, right on the last mark he left. He squeezes, and my vision turns white. "This kind of pain?" Harder pressure this time, and my legs collapse. "It'll be a beautiful scar soon. My marks are all over your body, and this one will be my favorite. It wraps around you like I do." He digs in further, gripping tight, and that's when I feel...

Nothing. I feel nothing.

"RUBY WAKE UP. PLEASE, wake up."

The voice slurred. Alcohol filled. Dangerous.

Best to keep quiet. He's worse if interrupted. "No, I don't feel you here. Leave me alone."

"You need to open your eyes, damn it." He shakes my shoulders twice. "What's happening? Wake up."

He never talks during this part. He always lets me be when I'm in my safe place. What's different today?

"Are you finished? "Only then."

He's testing me.

"What the fuck are you saying? Wake the hell up NOW!"

His voice sounds weird. It's not the same. Did he say you or ye? Is this a new game?

"Ruby, open those beautiful amber eyes for me. Please, my Princess. Leave that place you're in. Come back to reality. You're safe here." He caresses my hair.

Feels nice. So nice. I miss being touched like this. Doesn't hurt at all.

"It's safe? Promise?" My eyelids flutter.

A big black shadow hovers over me. "I promise."

Green eyes, dimples, pearly white teeth, and black hair come into view. I recognize this man. He's not the one in my nightmares of the past. He's the one in my hopes for the present.

"Maeson Lachlan Alexander." I smile and close my eyes again. The shattering pain in my soul eases. "My prince."

His hand freezes in my hair, and a rush of breath escapes his lungs. "Yes, and you, Ruby Bennett, are *my* Princess."

His words soothe my reopened wound. A sense of peace appeases my broken heart before I drift back to sleep.

I hope I remember this tomorrow. Please let me remember.

3

MAESON

How do I bring her back to me? She's lost somewhere deep in her mind. This is the third time she's shut down since I arrived three hours ago.

When she spoke, she said things a terrified little girl would say. One broken to the point of no return. Shattered into multiple parts of herself only to avoid reality. To escape the fucking victimizing prick. To protect her true self from being completely eviscerated.

What brought it on, though? She was fine earlier. Wasn't she? I might still be drunk, but not inebriated to the point of memory loss. I'm just missing a few pieces to the puzzle named Ruby Bennett.

There's so much more to learn about her, but I'm not sure I can handle it.

Not true. I can handle her past, present, and future. I just don't think I can deal with knowing I can't fix her. I fix everything. Well, except for myself, but that's beside the point.

How can one person be this traumatized and go on?

How did you do it, dumbass?

Well, I almost didn't. That's the point. Ruby's been dealing with everything that's happened on her own. When I'd gone too far, the people who cared about me stepped in. Who's stepping in for her?

Nobody.

My heart aches for her and the terror she's survived. Maybe it's too late for anyone to save or to fix her? Although, plenty of people said the same about me, yet it didn't stop them from standing by my side as I fell apart. She doesn't need a saving grace. She needs more than that. Ruby needs to know what it feels like to be cared for again. She needs people who are willing to stand by her in times of need, even if it's just Molly and me.

Two people are better than none at all.

A soft moan escapes her lips.

I stop pacing and rush to her side. "Ruby? You with me?"

She moans again.

"Please wake up. I promise you it's safe. I'm not the man you think I am. You're dreaming, Princess." I stroke her arm, before moving to her mangled curls, twirling them around my fingers.

Her eyes open slightly. "Maeson?"

Hope flourishes in my heart. "Yes. It's me. I'm right here." I sit at edge of her bed.

"Sorry. So sorry. I don't know what happened. All I did was lay down. I must've passed out. Didn't mean to scare you." She pushes against the pillows, but the attempt to lift herself fails, and she sinks back with a sigh.

"You did nothing wrong to be sorry about." I cover her shaky hands with mine. "Are you alright?"

"Yeah. This happens randomly. I'm here but not, you know? It's weird. I heard you trying to help. I appreciate it." Ruby's sad smile makes my chest constrict.

Her lips are puffy from sleep, her hair is more wild than usual, and her eyes are swollen from crying. Even in this state of disarray she beautiful beyond measure.

"I've never seen it happen before, so I wasn't prepared. Shit, I thought you were dying when I first walked in. Just know that as long as you let me, I'll always try to help and be there for you." I squeeze her hand.

"Nope, not dying. Not yet anyway. You're stuck with me until you throw me away and replace me with a new woman. Someone less… me."

"Don't say such stupid things! Why assume I'll discard you and not the other way around?"

"Because I'm such a—"

"No excuses. The roles could be reversed, you just won't admit it. But I digress, so less talk about what could or might happen, and more on what's going on with you."

"Nothing. Same old. We just found out my best friend, also known as your friend and employee, is having a baby with your best friend who's more like a brother to you." She shrugs. "Good times."

I almost laugh at the adorable way she summarized the drama of our day. Although, I didn't miss how she purposely avoided my actual question. "Yeah, unexpected for sure. The lies didn't help my reaction, but I wasn't asking about those two." I lift her chin, forcing her to meet my eyes. She can avoid all she wants with other people, but that shit won't work with me anymore.

"Oh, you meant me? I'm fine."

"Bullshit. This kind of nightmare wasn't *fine* and neither are you."

"I can handle it."

"I'm not so sure about that, but since you just woke up, I won't push any further." I stand. "Would you like a drink?"

"Yes, please. Jack and Coke." She covers her face as a giggle escapes her delectable lips.

"Alcohol already?" I check my watch—five in the morning. "Hell no, to the Jack. How about a Coke instead?"

"Fine, Dad."

When I deepen my smile, she inhales deeply.

Oh, yeah, I still got it.

"I'm thirsty. Hurry up with my drink, and quit showing off."

"Of course, your majesty." With a laugh, I bend at the hip and lower my head.

"Oh, and Maeson… when you come back, it's your turn to fill me in on that scar you're hiding underneath those tattoos. Think I didn't notice, did you?"

Yeah, I actually did.

Unable to face her, I stare at the open doorway and straighten. "Not up for discussion."

Not today, not tomorrow, and probably never.

4

Ruby

Not up for discussion, my ass. He will disclose more information about himself. I'm not taking no for an answer. The time is now.

I trudge out of my bedroom. I've spent enough time in this room with the lingering presence of my haunting past. If I focus on Maeson's secrets, it'll help me forget my own. At least for a little while. "You're not getting off that easy, Old Man." I walk into the kitchen with a smirk.

"I sure am, *Child*." He points to a steaming cup of tea on the counter.

"The request I made was for Jack and Coke. You denied the jack, and now you took away the option of a soda only to swap it with tea? Don't I have the right to drink what I want?"

"Sure, when I'm not around. I made the tea to soothe you, not because I'd purposely vetoed the other options. Thought it'd help more." He sets a small round glass container next to the floral tea cup. "Sugar?"

"Yes. And lemon, please."

Maeson grabs one from the fridge and drops a thin slice into my drink.

I take a tentative sip. "Not the worst I've had. Thanks."

"The pleasure is mine." He smiles as he pours some for himself.

"Why'd you get so mad about Molly being pregnant? Was it because it's with Jax?"

He slices his head downward and to the left.

"Then why?"

"Because they lied to me. They purposely hid being in a relationship from me. I despise lies."

"Who doesn't? Personally, I think you were too harsh. They didn't have to tell you the moment they started dating. Maybe they were afraid of your reaction and that's why they kept it from you. Poor Molly was devastated you stormed out like you did."

"I know."

"Did you apologize to her then?"

A slice of his head in negation is his answer.

"Why the hell not? Don't look so perturbed. Your reasoning is ridiculous. She looks up to you and sees you as the big brother who'd always defend her. All you managed to do was let her down."

"Did you know?" He shoots me a deadly glare.

"What? Are you insane? I was as shocked as you. Besides, if I did, I wouldn't have told you. It wasn't my secret to spill."

"You're right." He lowers his eyes. "Ruby?"

The hushed sound of my name spilling from his lips gives me goosebumps. "Yeah?"

Maeson hangs his head. "This will sound stupid, but I flipped out because I felt betrayed. Especially, when I tell them everything."

"Bullshit you do. You hid your accent from Molly as if she'd change her opinion of you. Then you lied about us being together until it was too obvious to hide. So, don't judge others when you're no saint."

"Fine, fine." He waves his hand in the air. "Point made, okay? I feel like an asshole as it is. Don't rub it in."

"Someone has to make you face the facts. You're not mister high and mighty all the time. People have lives to live whether you like it or not, and you not being privy to every single detail about theirs isn't a big deal. I barely know shit about you, but you don't see me pissing circles around you, do you?"

"No, you haven't pushed on that. But what can I do about it now? My reaction can't be taken back." He rubs a hand over the scruff on his face.

"It can't, but you can call Molly to tell her you're an asshole for overreacting."

"I will."

"You better." I finish my tea and smile wryly.

"Since you've ripped me a new one, is there anything else on your mind?"

"Nope. I've said my spiel."

He smiles, but it doesn't reach his eyes. "I'm such a dick." He picks up my empty mug and rinses it.

"Not all the time." The headache I've been ignoring hits me full force, and I press two fingers against my temple before sliding from my seat to lay on the couch.

Real sleep without a damn nightmare would do me some good. Maybe with Maeson here, it can happen. I close my eyes, searching for some sort of peace within myself.

"What exactly transpired in that foster home you grew up in?" Maeson's voice washes over me, his warm breath against my ear.

"A lot."

"But what precisely and why?"

What does he want me to do? Spell it out for him? Break it down piece by piece? Deep breath. It's time.

"You already know about the whip, but what you don't know is it was part of this fucked-up fetish he liked to take out on his foster kids since his wife wouldn't allow it done to her. Not that I blame the bitch." I shrug, but don't open my eyes, afraid of the expression I might find on his face.

"What kind of fetish?" He spits the last word out with disgust.

"You're going to make me say it out loud?"

"Only if you're ready to."

Deep breath.

"Whipping us was his hobby, and if we cried, he did it longer. Once he had his fun, he took us... sex... sexually." Copper pennies, mildew, rotten breath. The scents of my past... The reminders. I lean over the edge of the couch and gag.

Just breathe, Ruby. Just breathe.

Maeson pulls me into his arms. "Bloody hell! I thought... I didn't think he..." The veins in his neck bulge and red blotches appear on his face. "How'd he get away with doing such vile shit to children?"

Deep... breath...

"The wife protected him at every turn." I heave once more and Maeson softly brushes my hair back. "We were too scared to tell anyone." My body trembles as the words tumble from my mouth and the memories invade my mind.

Maeson's fist clenches and unclenches. "I hope the woman rots in fucking hell for standing by silently while children were... What kind of a bloody fucking mother is that?"

"The worst kind."

"Such abhorrent creatures. I couldn't imagine..." He curls his lip. "How'd they get caught?"

How indeed? That was one of the proudest days of my life.

"A few weeks before I moved out for college, I'd had enough and left an anonymous tip on the child and youth services line. I told them to search the basement and to look at the kids' bodies. Which thankfully they did, and after a long drawn out trial, both were sentenced to life."

Justice was served that day.

"The bastard lasted a few weeks before the other inmates killed him, but the bitch made it few months longer. The cunning psychopath she found safety from her cell mates in solitary. Until she was released, then they took action."

"Piece of shit excuses for human beings. I hope they suffered before they got the end they deserved." Maeson's eyes shine as he strokes my face. "I'm truly sorry for everything you've been through. How you've managed to continue living is beyond my comprehension, but I'm grateful you did. It's refreshing to meet someone who knows the agony brought on by real life struggles."

"What do you mean?"

"You're not alone in a painful past, my dear. When you say, *'I don't understand,'* I do, just not to the same extent you've suffered. I was lucky enough to have my loving parents around until I left home."

"Then how can you possibly identify?"

"I've felt the pain that comes with loving and losing, Ruby. My mother, I lost before I had the chance to say goodbye. Then, while dealing with her loss, I foolishly jumped into a relationship with someone who was vindictive and manipulative. She used me for everything she could get her hands on, and ultimately, broke my trust and faith in women."

"She ruined you for all others? Like my ex did?"

"You could say that."

"How?"

"A story for another day."

"No way! You know my deepest most painful past, yet you can't tell me about a lousy ex-girlfriend? Bullshit! Talk or leave."

"You think it's that simple?" Maeson's green eyes darken.

I meet his gaze. "It's not, but you bear no issue nosing in on my life. It's your turn, Maeson Lachlan Alexander."

"Fine." He shuts his eyes and takes a deep breath. "I met her shortly after I returned from my mother's funeral. I was in a rut and my funds were running low. My options for work were slim to none. It was a low point in my life, and she accepted my situation. So, we casually dated until I couldn't afford to attend college anymore. Then she asked me to move in with her since our relationship was blooming. Bored yet?" He smiles sadly.

"Not at all! You're not getting off the hook that easy."

"I had to try." There's a glimpse of his dimples before he turns serious again. "I held many odd jobs until I paid her back. I was the man. I was supposed to take care of her, not the other way around. Bloody fuck, I was so disgusted with myself." He shoves off of the couch and stomps to the windows. "Eventually,

I saved enough money for a better place for us. Things were great for a wee bit after the move. I was too blind to see the red flags. I fell too deeply to realize she was lying the first night she didn't come home. The tramp said she was with her girlfriends, and I let it go like a fucking fool."

I nod. "I know what you mean. Been in that position many times, but it's not your fault. You placed your trust in someone who didn't deserve it."

Maeson doesn't acknowledge my words, instead, he continues to maniacally pace, lost in his own world as he tugs on his hair. "Nights in a row. Came home drunk. High. Both. Dumbass. Didn't give up. Why? Loves to blame." His gaze lands on me. "I digress." He squeezes his eyes shut. "Can we stop now?"

"If that's what you want, I won't push. It's not like you're my boyfriend or anything. We just have sex. No emotions involved, so you don't owe me your life story."

I'm such a liar. Why pretend? It's better this way, that's why.

"Guilt trip?" He laughs. "No emotions? Bullshit! That's how you want to play this?"

"I'm only stating facts."

"Facts? I'll tell you facts." He scowls as he slumps onto the couch. "My relationship with that woman fell apart once I found out she slept with older rich men for money. I thought she had a regular desk job. She also slept her way through my so-called friends. Except Jax, he clued me in on her *'job'* and *'side activities'*. But I was a dumb young man and shoved everyone away, believing in her lies. Ultimately, I got what I deserved. She ended everything we had for a super-rich old guy who promised to provide for her, when I couldn't. I struggled to upkeep the bills let alone buy her fancy shit." He huffs. "Happy now?"

I slice my head to the left.

He chuckles. "Imitating me?"

With a sly smile, I jut my head to the right.

"Funny one, aren't you? What else do you want from me?"

"How did you two end it?"

"One night, when I was drunk and miserable, she dropped a

bomb on me. We got into a huge fight, one thing led to another, and I never saw her again. She made her choice to walked out on… on me. The end."

"Not the end. What happened to you afterward? And don't you dare say *'a story for another day'*."

"Fine. One of those odd jobs was working for Jax's dad at the restaurant he owned. And here we are, years later, I'm all better."

All better my ass.

"Why don't I believe that's the whole story? The way you carry yourself isn't the way a man acts when he has all his ducks in order."

"Maybe it took a while for them to find order, but none of it matters in the here and now."

"I wish I had that kind of attitude toward my past. Some days it runs my life and others it's like nothing ever happened, but that's usually when I drink or I'm fully medicated."

"It's not easy for me either. I still have those days, lass."

"Yeah, it's noticeable. I didn't mention the stink on you earlier, but liquor brims from your breath. What'd you do, dip yourself into the entire bottle?"

"Close to it."

"The whole Molly and Jax situation upset you that much?" I scrunch my brow.

"Sure did. Is it so unbelievable a man has emotions and shows them? Can I not be affected by the people around me?"

"You can, but that's not what I meant."

"Part of you did, and you know it."

I've offended his inner beast. Don't force him any further.

"Not at all. I'm the last person to judge. Obviously, your emotional side is a touchy subject and the alcohol running through your veins isn't helping, so let's drop it."

"Oh, you can get touchy and prickly over the shit I say, but I can't, is that it?" He flails his arms in the air as he stomps to the windows.

What the hell is wrong with him? His body's trembling. How can I help when I don't know the root of his problems?

"Damn it. That's not what I am saying at all. Calm down."

"I'm trying."

"What has you so riled up?"

"Everything. My life was alright for a while, Ruby. I played along for everyone's sake. Made sure I appeared to be fine, but I never truly was."

Shit. He sounds just like me. He's lied to himself for far too long, and shit's hitting the fan.

"Why pretend?"

He places his hands leans his head against the window. "I couldn't cope with their pity anymore."

"That's the worst part, isn't it?"

"Aye. The worst." With a heartbreaking sigh, bangs his head on the glass.

Why are we so alike, yet utterly opposite? Our similarity draws me to him like no one before which is why I want to run as far away as possible from this man. *'Be there for him'*, my heart screams, but can I do that without destroying myself in the process?

Yes. I can and will. I'm stronger than Ray and my foster father thought.

I walk over to him and place a finger on his shoulder. When he doesn't shove me away, I lay both of my hands on his body, massaging his arms. "Just breathe. It'll be okay. You'll never see pity in my eyes because I couldn't pity the strongest man I've ever met." I whisper.

He sighs and the muscles in his back relax beneath my palms.

"I don't know the extent of what you've gone through, but your pain is visible." I lay my head on him and wrap my arms around his waist. "One day, Maeson, you'll trust me —*like I've trusted you* —and you'll tell me about it. On that special day, you'll see the true emotions I hide from you."

5

MAESON

Did I hear her right? All along, she's been bullshitting about her nonexistent feelings.

Air rushes from my lungs and my shoulders sag. Ruby isn't the only one, is she? I'm a class-A coward.

She doesn't know the half of it.

I expected her to run from the nonsense spilling from my mouth, but she's still wrapped around me. How can I explain it to her? Will I? Not today, I've said enough for now. It's time I turn this conversation around and soothe her worries. She has enough on her plate as is it. "Lass?" I whisper.

"Yes?"

"It's not you I don't trust. I'm the issue."

"Okay." She places a soft kiss on my back before unraveling her arms from my body.

"What no argument?" I face Ruby, instantly freezing.

Tears cascade down her face, and she bows her head.

"Princess, why are you crying?" I reach for her, but she places a hand on my chest.

"We have too many problems. I wanted this to be easy, carefree, and emotionless, but it's not possible for people like us.

Your past is as raw as mine. How can a relationship flourish when we're worried about who will take care of who?"

"That's not true. I'm fine, and you'll be soon, lass. I'll help you. I'll fix everything to make sure you move on."

"People can't be *fixed* that easy. You're proof of that. The longer we deny it, the worse it'll be for us. I meant what I said before—when we're ready for the fluffy stuff, I'll let you know. Until then, our emotions can't be involved. We run a business together and the less we feel, the better off we'll be." Her beautiful amber eyes meet mine.

An ache surfaces in my chest.

She's leaving me before we even started. My runner is making lame excuses to dig the knife further into my heart.

Where's my beast when I need him? He's hiding in a fucking corner like the weaklings we are. Instinct tells me to pull her into me, kiss her, and show her she's so fucking wrong, but the pussy in me stays put.

Coward.

"Does that mean we can't open up to each other, spend time together, or have sex again? You want to go back to a strictly professional level?"

She shakes her head. "I… I don't… know. My head is a mess right now. I enjoy our time together, but it seems useless…"

"I see." With a stiff nod, I brush past her, stomping to the kitchen counter where my keys await. "For the record, I don't see what we could have as *useless*, and that coming from a man like me, speaks volumes. Get some rest. Call me when you grow up."

"Wait." Ruby grips my arm.

"I'd wait forever, but you won't let me."

"Don't say that kind of shit! How can I believe simplistic words? Actions, Maeson, actions."

"That's what I'm trying to show you! Bloody fucking hell, woman! Why do you think I'm here?"

"I don't know. I'm confused. I'm lost."

"Me too." With a sigh, I reach for her hand, entwining her fingers with mine.

"Didn't expect to meet someone like you." A single tear slides down her cheek and she quickly wipes it away with her free hand.

"You took me by surprise as well, Princess."

"So, what now?"

"The ball's in your court, sweetheart."

"Then, can you stay? Please?"

I place a kiss on her hand. "Your wish, my command."

She tugs at my arm with a smile. "We need sleep."

"That we do." I deepen my smile to its fullest extent.

"You're so bad." She giggles as she dashes to her bedroom.

I follow her step for step and lift her in my arms.

"Oh, my God! Put me down! I'm too heavy!"

"Are you insane? Have you seen my muscles?" I chuckle and toss her onto the mattress.

"Sure have. I wouldn't mind seeing them again."

"Not happening. Sleep remember?"

"You suck. But you're right." Ruby slides under the covers and pats the empty space beside her.

I'm tempted to sleep in my usual attire—butt ass naked—but that's too much temptation. The adorable pout on Ruby's face isn't helping either, but I hold steady and join her fully dressed—jeans and all.

She scoots closer, laying her head on my chest and sighs. "I'm sorry I'm such a mess."

I kiss the top of her head. "I'm sorry I'm not any better, lass." I wrap my arm around her, listening to her breathing slow and deepen as she drifts into sleep.

Once I'm sure she's in dreamland, I'm ready to say the words I've been holding back. "Please don't leave me. I need you more than I'll ever admit."

The only way she'll believe me is if I prove it, but how can I do that? Make promises?

I despise promises. They're too easy to break. Maybe for her I can keep them? The thought of shattered promises breaks me into a sweat, and I struggle to breathe.

Just breathe. Take a deep breath. Just … breathe …

"Ruby?"

She stirs but doesn't respond.

Keep your mouth shut damn it.

"I promise to stand by you for as long as you'll have me, to protect you like no one ever has, and to show you what it's like to be cherished by a real man."

"Hmmm?"

I don't move a muscle and hold my breath.

Did she hear me? Fuck.

Ruby shifts, turning on her side.

Panic sets in, and I have an urge to wake her to find out for sure, but I stop myself. Even if she did hear me it doesn't matter. I'm a man of my word.

Just breathe. I can and will keep these promises.

I'M ONE LUCKY SON of a bitch. Ruby shows no sign of hearing what I divulged yesterday.

Are you sure you don't want her to know how you really feel?

Right now, it's best if she doesn't, especially when a shattered woman's heart is involved.

"Old man." Ruby appears in the doorway of her bedroom with her hands on her voluptuous hips. "Quit staring in the mirror and get dressed already. Molly and Jax are almost here."

I cross my arms against my naked chest, flexing and smile as Ruby exaggerates an eye roll. "You don't like what you see, Princess? That's not what you said this morning, but I'll cover up if that's what you want." I grab my crumpled t-shirt from the corner of the room and slowly lift it over my head, stalling before I slide it down.

"Hmmm. Maybe you should keep it off for a little longer. We have a few minutes…" She glides a warm hand across my abs, inching south.

"Oh, no you don't!" I grab her wandering fingers, stopping her insistent fondling before Maeson Junior gets too excited to stop.

Ruby pouts. "Fun killer."

I laugh and kiss the top of her head. "Later, love. We've been at it for a day and a half, you should be tired of me by now."

"Not tired at all, but then again, I'm wayyyy younger than you."

"We're going back to the old man shit? After Mo and Jax leave, I'll prove how very wrong you are."

"Bring it on, but if you break any bones, it's your fault." She giggles and dashes for the kitchen.

With her gone, I finish dressing and take one last look in the mirror.

I'm not that old, am I?

No bloody fucking way. I'm in my prime at almost thirty-eight years old. And with Ruby by my side, I feel young. She makes me smile again. She reminds me there's still a chance for some sort of happiness.

Is her affect on me the difference between her and the other women I've been with? It has to be. And unlike everyone else, including Ashlie, Ruby isn't using me.

Shit, I thought Ashlie loved me only to realize she'd expertly weaved a facade to get what she wanted.

But what did she want? Money? I didn't have any at the time.

No, she needed a pathetic foreign man to depend on her so she could shove it in his face later. *'Get a better fucking job. You're a loser. You'll never amount to anything,'* she'd say.

"Maeson. Help me set the table, please." Ruby's sweet voice flows from the kitchen.

I inhale and exhale, removing myself from the past and push my unruly hair back before I face Ruby.

I'm not sure what she's making, but the onion and garlic smell amazing. "What's for dinner, lass?"

"Meatloaf." She giggles.

"What's so funny about a classic American dish?"

"I was thinking of my dad's expression the first time my mom made it for him. It was hilarious." She hands me four plates and the utensils to go with.

I grab them, setting them around the table. "Tell me about it? It sounds like a happy memory."

"It sure is." A huge smile graces her lips as she drops a wooden spoon on the counter and leans against the granite. "My mom's mission in life was to make traditional Greek dishes for my dad so he wouldn't miss being home as much. She literally printed every possible recipe she found. Sometimes I wished we'd just have a cheese pizza, but nooo, everything was Greek. She didn't concede to something else, until one day, I begged for her mom's special meatloaf. When my dad came home from work, he knew something was off right away. He didn't even get to the kitchen before he goes *'What's that smell, Natasha? It's no Greek'*. What was even funnier, was when he saw it. The way his face contorted, he looked like he was dying just from looking at the meal. Watching him take his first bite, made me and mom laugh so hard, we almost peed in our pants. But once he got over the initial shock, he devoured the entire plate." She laughs.

"Sounds like something my Da would do with an American dish too." I chuckle along with her. "Those are memories you should never let go of."

"I'll never forget that night. We'd tease him about it all the time, and before he passed away, he actually admitted meatloaf became one of his favorites." Ruby closes her eyes and a tear slides down her face. "I miss them every day…"

"How can you not? They were taken away from you at such a young age. I miss my mom too, but reminiscing about the good times helps ease the pain. You'll have to tell me more about your parents, and I'll do the same. That's how we'll help each other."

"You're right. It'll be a good place for us to start. The other day, I pushed too much too soon."

"No, you didn't. How could I expect you to bare your soul, yet I don't reciprocate? It's my fault. I was too drunk and what came out of my mouth didn't make any sense. Next time it will." I set the last place setting on the table and fold the fancy napkins Ruby bought for my apology to my best friends.

"We both had a lot on our minds…"

"Aye, lass."

The elevator chimes, ending our conversation. Ruby leaves to welcome our guests as I stay put, too embarrassed to face them.

Can we say, weakling? Aye, perfect word for a dick head like me.

"Mae Mae." My southern belle, Molly enters the kitchen.

"Mo …" I lower my eyes.

She pounces on me, hugging me with all her might. "Mae Mae. It's okay. I'm not mad. Don't look so sad."

"I fucked up. I let you down. I …"

"Shut your pretty face. Everything is fine. I love you. Your reaction was shit, but you're my big brother, and I forgive you." Molly's blue eyes bore into me. "Show me those dimples."

I can't help the smile from forming on my face. "Love you too, Mo Money. I'm so sorry." I pull her into my arms and kiss her cheek. "I'll never let you down again. I promise."

"Shush. I said it's fine. Ya'll worried for nothin'. I surprised everyone, and I shouldn't have lied to you. I'm sorry, too." She plants a kiss on my cheek before dashing to Jax's side.

"Feeling better now?" Jax shakes my hand as he smirks from ear to ear.

"Aye. Much. How are you doing?"

"Excited as fuck. Me, a dad? Can you believe that shit?"

"Sure can. It's about time, gramps."

Jax shakes his head, and we both laugh.

"Dinner's ready." Ruby calls out. "Take your seats."

Poor Ruby's been nervous about this dinner for two days. Tonight isn't just an apology dinner, it's her first official get together since she moved here.

Ruby places three glass filled with a familiar red liquid next to each of our place settings and winks at Molly as she hands her a glass of water. "Sorry, mommy to be, no liquor for you."

"That's alright," Molly drawls. "This mama's gonna to do right by her baby."

"I got a good woman here, don't I?" Jax grins.

"Sure do." Ruby smiles and takes her seat at the table. "I'd like to make a toast." She raises her drink. "To Molly and Jax, congrats on starting the family you both deserve. You'll be amazing parents to that little pumpkin. Cheers!"

We clink our glasses together.

"I second that." I sip on the Ruby Apple before setting it down. "Also, I need to add an apology to both of you. My reaction was terrible and undeserved. I'm truly sorry." I focus on the empty plate in front of me.

"We both forgive ya, so please quit worryin' so much." Molly pats my hand. "And once our baby is born, you can really make it up to us by babysittin'."

"I'd love to see that." Ruby snorts. "Maeson taking care of a baby? That'd be a sight or more like a disaster."

My gut clenches from the verbal punch she landed. I peer at Jax who's frowning—he felt it too.

Don't make a scene. She doesn't kn—

"Right? But he's gonna be an amazing uncle." Molly squeals.

I force myself to smile. "Aye, I'll be the best. The wee one will like me better than his or her Da."

Pretend… Just breathe…

Jax clears his throat. "You wish."

Molly leans into her man. "Don't worry, babe, we'll make sure you're always number one."

Jax pouts like a fucking lost puppy as Molly plants kisses on his face.

"You two are so pathetically in love, it makes me sick." I deepen my smile as I tilt toward Ruby, whispering in her ear. "We could be like them, if you'd let it happen."

She frowns and elbows me. "You guys ready for dinner? It's getting cold." When everyone nods, she literally runs into the kitchen.

So easily spooked, little lassie.

Imagine how spooked she'd be if she heard my promises a few nights ago.

6

Ruby

Maeson. That bastard. It's been over a week since I held the *'apology dinner,'* and I've avoided the man since. Why does he have to say things involving so much emotion? I know we could be as happy and in lo—Gah!

It's too soon for that kind of crap. After the messy conversations we had last weekend, I can confidently confirm, it's too freaking soon. He's disorder, and I'm chaos. The combination certainly doesn't equal lo—

Deep breath. Don't think about it. Just breathe.

There are plenty of other things to worry about, so why I am stressing over him?

Focus.

Molly's thirtieth birthday is right around the corner, and I should be frying my brain on ideas for her party. Her special day needs to be perfect. I failed as a friend once, and I'm not doing it again.

What kind of bash does one throw a pregnant thirty-year-old? I can call Sam, she might have some ideas.

After three rings, she picks up. "Ruby, to what do I owe this honor?"

"Well, I'm planning Molly's special b-day and need help with it."

"It's simple. Have it at Crossroads. I'll shutdown for the night."

"Can't. Molly's uhh…. Pregnant."

Sam clears her throat. "Mo is—"

"Prego."

"Seriously? This isn't like an April fool's joke in November?"

"Dead serious. Maeson and I recently found out."

"Wow. That's amazing, but who's the father? Didn't know she had a boyfriend."

I laugh. "You ready for this?"

"No, but go ahead."

"Jax."

Sam shrieks, and I jerk the phone away from my ear. "Jax as in Maeson's best friend?"

"That's the one."

"Holy shit. That must've been a scene when ya'll found out."

"Sure was, but things calmed down since, and everyone is beyond excited. That's why I want to make this day super special for Mo. She deserves it."

"Agreed. Having it at the bar isn't the best idea. What about Maeson's place? I heard he has a paradise on his rooftop."

He does? How come I've never seen it? Probably because we spend most of our time in his bed versus taking a tour of his place. I guess I've been so self-involved, nothing else mattered. But that's changing, from now on, I'll be more attentive.

"That might work, but I'll have to discuss it with Maeson. He's particular about his belongings."

"Oh I know. He warned me to stay away from you on the first night we met at my bar."

"What?"

"Guess the gigs up." Sam giggles. "Maeson sees me as competition, but as I've explained to him many times before, I'm taken by Bekka."

My mouth drops, and I scramble to gather my thoughts.

"Holy shit, woman! I didn't see that coming. Everyone is full of surprises these days, damn it!"

"You're okay with that? You're not… disgusted?"

"No way! Why would I be? As long as you're happy who cares what anyone else thinks?"

"Im so glad! I was scared to tell you. Bekka and I have lost too many friends over it. We didn't want you to be one of them."

"Not at all! I'd never unfriend someone because of who they love."

"Thank you. That means a lot to both of us."

"Don't thank me. Are you crazy?"

"A little."

"I figured that out the night you danced on the bar with me." The mention of our dance reminds me of what Sam said before. "Wait a sec, you said Maeson warned you off? Like he was jealous?"

"Big time. But it wasn't just me he did it too. Every man in the room got Maeson's death stare when they came near you. Only Dave, the dumb ass, had big enough balls to ignore him and approach you."

"I had no idea. Even then he—"

"Wanted you and was jealous when you gave others your attention. Can I tell you something?"

"Yeah."

"Maeson's… different. We all know he has an on and off again drinking affair, and he's rigid as hell on the outside, but I know things I shouldn't. He thinks buttoning his shirts to the top keeps his secrets—*his pain*—safe. A lot of women say he's an asshole because he fucks them and leaves them, but what if it's all he can manage? What if anything more terrifies him? What if meeting a certain someone with the similar fears attracts and confuses the shattered man hiding beneath those pristine suits? Could you handle that?"

"Uhhh."

"Everyone has a story to tell. For some, it's not always easy to face. You know what I'm talking about?"

"No. I mean. I don't…" I hold my breath.

She can't know. Just breathe, you're panicking for no reason.

"I saw the scar on your back when you bent down."

Sweat beads on my forehead as I pace by the windows in my living room. "You did?"

"Yes."

"His scars aren't less painful than yours and keeping him at arm's length isn't the answer to the healing you seek."

What is she a fortune teller? There's no way she knows anything about me other than the basics. "Did Maeson tell you?"

Deep breath. She knows. I can't bear her pity.

"I haven't spoken to Maeson in a few months. He's been sticking to his club ever since I kicked him out. No one had to tell me anything because I have eyes and what they saw was enough."

"Oh…" A rush of air leaves my lungs as I lean against the wall, closing my eyes.

She doesn't know everything. It's better this way.

"I used to work with foster kids and juvenile delinquents, so I've seen a few things. That's how I figured out you haven't had it easy in life."

It was a far cry from easy.

"I see. Now it's my turn to ask. Are you disgusted?"

"And it's my turn to say, no way. You're an amazing friend who accepted me for me. I'm returning the favor by telling you I know you're in pain, and I'm here for you. It's also why I'm telling you you're not the only one. Everyone depends on him, but who does he have?"

"I thought Jax or Molly, but you seem to think that's not the case?"

"He's alone, Ruby. No matter how many women or friends he surrounds himself with, Maeson's always alone."

"How do you know this?"

"I…" Sam coughs. "I unknowingly dated his ex."

My mind short circuits. "No, you didn't!"

"It was before I met Maeson. When I saw him for the first time, I almost passed out. She had a picture of him, but at the time he was just a random guy. Please don't say anything to him. Neither of them know they have me in common. I never had the guts to tell them."

"I'm not sure I can keep this from him. We talked about her once and it didn't go well. He's still affected by her."

"I know. She's a fucking bitch and the biggest liar I have ever met. Her name is truly fitting. Look, don't say anything. I don't want you dealing with his wrath. I'll tell him myself."

How can I face Maeson now? Like him, I despise lies.

"By you telling me, I'm already involved, so you better tell him before I see him again. I won't lie to anyone, especially Maeson."

"I promise, I will. When we hang up, I'll call him. I'm so sorry to put this on you. I thought the information would help, but it was selfish of me. I guess I just wanted to talk to someone about it." She sighs. "He's going to hate me."

"Maybe not hate, but definitely mad. I recently experienced how much he detests dishonesty. The sooner you tell him, the better."

"Fuck," Sam mutters. "I'm not sure how it's gonna go when I tell him, but please remember what I said. Be that person for him."

"I don't know how."

"Based on what I saw on your back, I'd say you've been the shoulder for the wrong people, yet you don't know how to for him? That's bull, and you know it. Face your fears together."

"I can't…"

"You can. The girl I met a few months ago and danced my ass off with wouldn't have said she can't. She would tell me to fuck off because she could do anything. Be that woman, Ruby." For a second it seems as if Sam hung up, but then, there's shuffling in the background. "I gotta go, sweetie. Don't forget to text me the deets on Mo's party."

The line goes dead, and I slump onto the couch.

Where do I go from here? I can't talk to Maeson about this until Sam does, so what should I do?

Plan Molly's party, and hopefully, everything else will fall into place.

He'll stop soon, won't *he*?

I wish he wouldn't hurt them anymore. They can't handle pain like I can. This is my fifth time begging him to leave them alone.

Where is my foster mother when we need her? Maybe she can stop him?

"I'll take their beating," *I say.*

The evil man doesn't look my way, he simply grunts and continues with the whipping.

I'm older than them, and I only have another year left here, why shouldn't I take their place until I can actually save them?

The onslaught sickens me. Fury ignites within me. "I said, I want to take their place." *I ball my fist and shake it in the air.* "Fuck face, didn't you hear me?"

One of the little boys cries out as the end of the leather whip lands on his leg. My rage takes control. I grab the whip from the devil's grip and crack it against his flesh. "How's that feel, you sick bastard?"

He howls.

In a panic, I wrench the thing back, but he's too quick. He yanks me toward him, and I land in a heap at his feet.

I fight to lift myself. Breathe. I have his attention. Now's the time. "Run, guys. Call the police. Run!" *Those are my last words before my foster father's big rough hand clutches my neck.*

He twists my ponytail between his fingers, jerking my head back to face him. "You've made a grave mistake, Princess."

"NO!" I jolt upright, searching my surroundings.

I'm home. In my bed, alone. Thank God.

That night, I received the worst beating of my life. It was worth every lash knowing I saved those kids — even it if it was only one time. When he was finished with me, I crawled up the stairs and into my room to find three of them waiting for me with towels and a bowl of water. They cleaned the blood dripping down my body and spent the entire night with me while I cried myself into a deep and dark oblivion.

Those children were the reason I did what I did in the end. It was never about me. Everything I ever did was for someone else, but after all is said and done, I don't regret any of it.

Even catering to my crappy ex.

Speaking of crappy, I need to call Maeson and ask about Molly's party.

Wait.

What if Sam's in the middle of her confession? That's not something I want to interrupt, so I'll keep my distance on that front for now.

What else am I supposed to do then?

Shop for the party goods. That'll soothe my soul, and give Sam enough time to royally piss off Maeson. Either way, those two need to kiss and make up before next Saturday. The show must go on because Molly had no fault in their drama.

November nineteenth will be the most memorable day of my best friend's life.

7

MAESON

It hasn't gone unnoticed Ruby's been avoiding me, but what the fuck am I supposed to do? Force her to see me? That's not the answer. Especially, not after all the shit we bared to each other last weekend.

Maybe she's right—we're too fucked up and a relationship is impossible. But for how long can we do the sex-without-emotion rigmarole? I need a tall and stiff drink. That's how I'll forget this confusing bullshit.

Why am I feeling so much lately? What's changed?

Ruby and I had this love-hate game going on for a while, but my icy heart cracked at the edges and released the fire I was holding back.

When did it happen, though?

I close my eyes, envisioning the woman who bombards my dreams.

'Please don't hurt me. Everyone hurts me. Always alone.' My eyes pop open. Ruby was so vulnerable that night, yet she fought to appear strong. I'll never forget the glimpse of pain I witnessed in her eyes. But that wasn't when I started to change, was it?

No, her admission caused a small tremor, nothing significant.

I shut my eyes again, letting the images flicker behind my eyelids.

THEY MAR HER PERFECT *olive skin.*

S. C. A. R. S.

Terrifying scars. I can't look away.

They're everywhere.

Who the fuck did this to her?

She's so beautiful and doesn't even realize it. How do I fucking tell her? I have to show, not tell her. It's the only way.

Crack.

The ache in my chest worsens as I kiss each purplish pink mark.

MY EYES FLUTTER AS another vision pushes to be relived.

Were her scars what broke down my defenses?

I struggle against it, but the memory streams through my mind too quickly.

"MAE MAE, SHE NEEDS *you. We're at the hospital," Molly's high pitched voice pierces my foggy mind.*

Ruby needs me. I'm needed again. What if I can't save her? I've failed before.

"Let me see her. I'm her fiancé. She needs me. She's all I have." I plead with the woman at the front desk.

They better fucking let me in. They have to.

Crack, goes my heart. Pieces of me are changing. It's happening. Again.

Princess… She's so still… "Is she…" I ask one of the nurses before he shuts the door.

He pats my shoulder and smiles. "No, sir. She's sleeping. Go on in, they can help you further." The man widens the door as I step into Ruby's hospital room.

Today, I see her for who she is… Strength.

A smile graces her lips, and I almost kneel at her bedside in front of all these people.

Crack.

I'm not the only one with a shattered soul, am I?

Tʜɪs ʟᴀsᴛ ᴍᴇᴍᴏʀʏ ᴘʀᴏᴠᴇs it wasn't one specific day which changed me. It was multiple occasions.

Lass, I wish I could tell you.

Ruby's nothing like my ex-girlfriend. She actually gives a shit about people. When Molly embraced her into our *'family'*, I knew she was different.

Fuck. I'm turning into Jax. I'm turning in to the pussy I used to be when I catered to Ashlie's every whim.

If I tell Ruby what's going through my head, will she turn on me? Or worse will she change, turning into the gold-digging women before her?

She has money, though.

When did that ever matter? A man is always expected to provide and maintain unrealistic standards.

Fuck it. I'm better off not trying. There's no need to exert this much effort into someone who doesn't give a damn.

Even though Ruby didn't ask for it, her silence speaks loud and clear—she wants space from me. So, space is exactly what she's getting.

I pull my phone from the back pocket of my jeans and search the contact list for someone who'll help me forget … everything.

No. I'm not that guy anymore.

As I'm shutting down my search, the screen changes. A call is coming through.

"Sam, to what do I owe this pleasure?"

"Can you meet me? We need to talk." Her tone is harsh, tinged with a bit of sadness.

"Aye. When?" Sam's morbid tone aside, I smile as my accent slips from my lips with ease. Not hiding who I am, and where I'm from is utterly freeing.

"Now?"

"Sure. Where?"

"Crossroads."

"Be there in five."

"Okay."

An eerie feeling buzzes through me. Sammie sounded terrible, almost remorseful.

What could that little southern doll be regretful about?

WHEN I ARRIVE AT Sam's precious bar, part of me doesn't want to step foot in the place.

Grow a set, damn it. The girl probably just needs a loan to keep her business afloat.

I straighten my shoulders and trudge through the door. I'm met with Sam sitting in the corner with a drink in her hand.

"Drinking already?"

"Yeah. Join me?" She slinks behind the bar and grabs a bottle of Jack Daniels. She pours it into a tumbler over ice and slides the glass to me.

I take a sip of the amber liquid, reveling in the burn. "What's going on, lass?"

"Is that a Scottish burr I hear?" She smiles sadly.

I slice my head to the right and grin.

"You hid it well."

"Tried to."

Sam raises her eyebrow and frowns. "Why?"

"Because of simple minded dick wads."

"I get that. Met a few myself." She shakes her head.

People shunned her for being herself. For showing her true nature.

"Yeah," I say and peer at my black sneakers. "So, tell me why you urgently needed to speak to me?"

She lifts her drink to her lips, downing it in one gulp. "Right. Back to business."

I pat her thigh. "Don't be scared. If you need money, I'll help you."

"No. It's not about money. Shit. How do I tell you without pissing you off?"

"Simple, just say it."

"Promise me you won't flip?"

"Sorry, no can do. I only make promises I can keep. But I'll try not to flip, how's that?"

"It'll have to do." She refills our glasses, but doesn't return to her seat.

"Sit. You're shaking, woman."

She flicks her eyes to the floor. "Better to stand."

How bad is this news?

"As you wish." I cross my arms against my chest.

Her deep brown eyes meet mine. "I dated your ex... Ashlie."

"Not possible." I shake my head. There is no way those two could've met.

Just breathe. Maybe it's a different Ashlie.

"Your full name is Maeson Lachlan Alexander. You started dating her at 19. She is a cheater by nature. You had—"

"Stop." I leap to my feet. "How?" My fingers tremble and sweat beads on my forehead. I couldn't let her finish her sentence. I knew what she was planning to bring up right away. The memories from that part of my life are hard enough to keep at bay and hearing someone else bring it up would be a disaster in the making.

She has to be lying. But how does she know so much?

"We met a few years ago at a night club opening."

As my head wraps around what Sam is saying, I pace. "Then you knew who I was when we first met?"

Sam squeezes her eyes shut and sighs. "Yes."

"So, you've been lying to me this whole time? You acted like you didn't know me for the last four fucking years?"

"Yes."

"How could you? I thought we were friends. This makes you no different from her." I slam my fist against one of the wooden tables. "Liars. You're all liars." I grab the bottle of Jack from the counter of the bar, lifting it to my lips.

"I'm not like that. Please hear me out."

"What's to hear? You and my ex conspired against me. Why would you lie to me?"

"I didn't lie. I just kept it from you so this"—she points back and forth between us—"didn't happen."

"I would've found out at some point. She still calls me, damn it." I drop on to a stool, and stare at the woman who's watched me crawl out of this bar countless times, yet it never once occurred to her this was information I needed to be informed of. "I had a right to know. Fuck. That means she talked about …"

"Yeah, she did."

"Are you fucking kidding me? She had no bloody fucking right. It's no one's business. She didn't go through it, I did. All the fuck alone." I scrub a hand over my face, attempting to ward off my past as it flashes before my eyes.

Don't think about it. Just breathe. You've found your own kind of acceptance with it. Do not go back to that time of your life.

Sam leaves her shelter behind the bar to sit on the stool next to mine. "I know. After she cheated and left me, I noticed how much she did lie about. But I also know what she didn't lie about." She lays a hand on my thigh, but when I flinch, she pulls it away.

I glare at her. "You betrayed our friendship. You fucking lied to me this entire time." I guzzle a sizable shot.

This isn't the progress you committed to, asshole. You made promises you won't be able to keep if you travel this dark road again.

"Fuck you, Maeson. I didn't betray you. I don't owe you an explanation. No one does. I could've kept my mouth shut and that would've been just fine too. The only reason we're discussing this is because of Ruby. I came out to her, and accidentally, slipped about dating your ex. But you know what she said?" Sam raises her eyebrow until I acknowledge her question with a nod. "That I better tell you because she doesn't want to keep things from you. What did you do? Scare her into telling you everything? You want to be Mr. Almighty while everyone follows your no lies-no secrets bullshit rules, yet you lie and hide your secrets from them? Fuck that, my friend. This girl isn't willing to follow your narcissistic guidelines."

"Ruby knows everything too?" My heart pounds as I hold my breath.

"Seriously, that's what you got out of my rant? And no, she doesn't know anything other than I dated your ex."

"Good." I release a heavy sigh. It's not the way I want Ruby to find out. If anyone tells her it will be me.

"Wow. Did you even hear anything I said?"

"Aye, I did."

"Okay, and?"

"And… nothing."

Or more like you're a dumbass, and this woman just put you in your place, but you don't want to admit it.

"You've got to be kidding me! You flip out on me, but when I return the favor, you shut up?"

"Aye. That's how a dick head like me rolls." How does she not notice how affected I really am by her words? Because women only see and hear what they want to—when they want to.

"I see that."

Time to turn on pompous ass mode. It's who everyone thinks I am anyway. And whose fault is that? Mine. I had no other choice.

"Your commentary has been noted. I understand why you didn't tell me. All I ask in return is you keep your mouth shut. My life is no one's business but mine. Does this answer suffice?"

"Yeah. Got it. Loud and clear."

"Good. Time for me to go, and I'm taking this bottle with me. Any objections? If so, charge my tab. Have a good day, Sam." My legs are heavy as I make my way to the exit, but a scary thought hits me, and I stop in my tracks. "Oh, and Sam? Make it a point not to date any more of my ex's. Sloppy seconds don't suit a classy lass like you." I wink, then force a smile. "Or worse, the current woman I am seeing. Don't take her away from me. *Please.*"

"I wouldn't dare. Remember, I didn't know you when I met Ashlie." She shrugs. "Besides, I'm with someone already."

"Oh, and who might that be?"

"Bekka."

"No shit." A smile graces my lips as an image of sweet

innocent Bekka and the closeted badass Sam appears in my head.

"Don't look surprised, your woman radar blows just like your taste in them. Well, except for Ruby, of course." Sam licks her lips. "She's delectable."

"Fuck off and quit jerkin' me around when it comes to her."

"Why? Does the big bad beast have feelings for her? Is he actually admitting it?"

"Seeing how you know more about me than most people, yeah, I'll admit I do. But keep your lips sealed because I'm doing this my way. I don't need another Ashlie to deal with."

"Totally get it."

With a nod, I open the door, and I'm met by blinding sunshine. I shield my eyes with the bottle of whiskey as I stumble to my car, processing what Sam revealed.

I wish she'd asked me for a loan instead. That would've been cake.

"Maeson."

"Yeah?" I open the car door.

"If you ever need to talk." She smiles sadly.

My frustration with her dissipates. "Thanks." I wave the alcohol in my hand at her with a smirk. "But I got this for that."

She flashes her middle finger as she strides closer. "No, you don't." She laughs as she simultaneously grabs my keys and the bottle from me. "Have Stavros pick you up. Ruby would kill me if I let you drive drunk."

There's the Sammie I know.

As INSTRUCTED, STAVROS CONTINUES to drive aimlessly around the neighborhood. I need time to work through the hundreds of questions bombarding my mind.

I can't think straight. My irrational side is pissed off. The realistic side is confused, surprised, worried, and hurt.

Sam might be right, but that doesn't mean her lies bother me any less.

People assume if they were on the other end bombshells wouldn't affect them at all. Which is total bullshit.

Whatever. I'll continue to look like the sensitive asshole since no one understands where I'm coming from. Nothing fucking new there.

How will I ever explain my pain to Ruby?

Do I have to? Maybe I can avoid this like I've done for so many years. If Ash-fucking-lie would've kept her big fat mouth shut with Sam none of this would be an issue.

Why is the damn woman even discussing our past with others? Oh, I know why. She loves pretending to be the victim. I bet she milked the shit out of what happened. Yet, it was my … I went through it alone. Not her.

Before I derail further, I'm frozen in place by the ringtone playing on my phone. The one I set up just for her — *'Imagine Dragons, Believer'*. I clear my throat and tap the green button on the screen. "Well, well. It's about time I hear from you."

"Uh… Hey."

"Hey, to you too. What's up?" I balance my phone against my shoulder as Stavros turns into the Rose Garden's parking lot, pulling over in front of Ruby's building.

"So. How are you?"

"Fine, and you?"

Stavros turns off the engine and peers back at me.

I lift a two fingers up, and he nods.

"Good," Ruby whispers.

Why is this woman being so damn weird? Did Sam tell her more than she let on?

"Are you okay?"

"Just dandy. I wanted to ask you for a favor."

"Shame on you, lass. I haven't heard from you in a week. But when you need me, I'm good enough to call on?" My lip twitches as I tease her with ease.

"No, it's not that. Sorry, I—"

"You don't have to explain. I'm kidding. Tell me, what is it you need?"

She releases a soft sigh and laughs. "You know how Molly's birthday is next week? I wanted to know if we can host it at your place."

"Of course, anything for my favorite assistant. Actually, that's a perfect idea because I have a major surprise for her, and I'll have everything I need there."

"Thank you. I was hoping you'd be alright with it since mine isn't fancy enough, and I want it to be special for her. She deserves it, especially with how hard she's been working."

"I agree." I sigh. "Can I see you?"

She breathes deeply. "Sure. When?"

"Now?"

Ruby mutters something undecipherable, then, "Okay, Maeson."

"See you very soon, Princess." Before she can reply, I hang up.

"My boy, you should tell her already. She need to understand you. Stop hiding. Seek love." Stavros frowns.

"I will, one day, just not today. I want her to love me for me. Not pity me. Once she knows, our relationship will change."

"I don't believe that, but you're smart man. Do what's best for you. I love you, son. Go see your girl." He smiles and waves me out of the car.

He's right. I need to open up and sooner than later. But like I told him, not today.

As I hit the elevator button for the tenth floor, I realize hearing Ruby's voice, even if it was only for a few minutes, halted the war brewing within me.

I said halted not ended.

Deep inside my body, there's a warning telling me my journey has only hit its mid point, and I'm far from the end.

Very far.

8

Ruby

To my surprise, Maeson wasn't pissed off. Unless, Sam didn't say anything yet? If that's the case, how do I face him?

I've never been a good liar, and my poker face is shit. So, that means, I'm not even going to try. Honesty is best.

I throw my hair into a messy bun, splash water on my face, and apply a bit of makeup. I'm tempted to change my outfit, but what woman likes to leave the comfort of her yoga pants?

Definitely not this woman.

At the sound of the elevator, butterflies flutter in my belly and little electric sparks flicker through my body. With tentative steps, I approach the foyer.

He's standing there in his sexy, knee crippling glory with his hands stuffed in his pockets, his hair slicked back, and his dimples displayed in full force.

I must be the biggest fool for pushing this man away so many times. Yet, does that make him an even bigger one for coming back? Or maybe, that's why we deserve each other? When one pushes, the other doesn't let go?

"Ruby, lass." He lowers his head, placing a soft kiss on my cheek.

"Maeson."

He seems as calm as ever. But I assume the liquor infused on his breath is masking his true emotional state.

He clasps his hand with mine. "Stop watching me like that. I know what you're worried about, and I'm not mad. Relax."

I exhale. "Thank God! After your reaction to Molly's revelation, I wasn't sure how you'd handle this."

He shrugs. "Don't get me wrong, I was livid when she told me. But when she tore me a new one, I had no choice but to see the light."

I study him again. Something is off. I've been around him long enough to spot the signs. "You're lying. Someone who's fine doesn't reek of alcohol. Why the act?"

Maeson drops onto the couch, leans his head against the cushion, and groans. "It's not an act. Aye, I drank, and I'm still mad, but not at you. There's no reason to blame the innocent party."

"I'm shocked. You're actually going against the genetic make up of most men?"

"Aye. Because I'm not most men. How many times do I have to prove it?" He peers at me with distress in his green eyes.

"If you plan on sticking around? Probably, all the time. Not sure I'll believe in fairytale crap ever again."

"I'm with you there. When I was a young lad, my mother would tell me happy ever after stories, and the dumbass I was, believed in them. But we know what happens when you rely on nonexistent shit, right?"

"Yeah, we're knocked down to our knees and forced to crawl from the darkness." I plop next to him, frowning. "Although, I have no clue what you've been through, other than a cheating ex which doesn't constitute as a soul-shattering heartbreak. Unless there's more you're not telling me."

"If there was, would you try to force it out of me?"

"Never."

"Thank you. In time, Princess, I'll tell you the whole story."

"Fine, but drinking like a fish won't solve your problems." I shake a finger in his face.

"Oh, you're one to talk? What about those pills you take? In a very unsafe manner, might I add." His lips form a perfect semicircle, and he creases his forehead.

"If you must know, I finished them and don't plan on refilling the prescription." I give him a cocky smirk and puff up my chest.

His eyes widen. "Is this some kind of revelation?"

"In a way, yeah. Witnessing Aria's withdrawal from the crap she took scared me. I refuse to experience it personally. Instead, I'm choosing to be an adult and use the strength within myself to deal with my past."

Maeson's perfect, sparkling teeth make an appearance. "I'm proud of you. You'll be an inspiration to the women and children you plan to help." He lays a big hand on my thigh, caressing it.

Fiery heat flows through me. "Thank you. I'm proud of me too, and I really do hope we make a difference in their lives."

"We will. The three of us make a great team. There's no way we can fail. Speaking of, I have some good news."

"Oh?"

"The property we purchased has finally transferred to our names. And the permits are approved. Now, are you ready for even better news?"

I bob my head, grinning from ear to ear.

"Since there's a building on the land, we will begin renovations immediately. As long as no problems arise, it should be ready for occupation within six months. This way the hard work is done before our Godson arrives in the spring."

I pounce on him, wrapping my arms around his body and squeeze. "How amazing! I can't believe this is really happening."

Maeson flips me on my back, towering over me. "Believe it, babe. Your dream is coming true, and I'll do everything in my power to make sure everything runs smoothly." He plants a hot kiss on my lips.

I melt into him. The fire between us ignites, but before I'm a complete goner, I pull away. "I have a few more questions. How will one building work when we planned multiple?"

"I figured we'd use the top three floors as the foster care sector, the middle two for the women's shelter, and the main one for offices and a top-notch security desk with metal detectors. How's that sound?"

"It sounds like I'm glad Axel suggested you as a business partner."

"As am I. Then again, knowing how nosey I can be, I would've invited myself into your venture." His devilish grin reappears.

"I wouldn't doubt it. But is there anything else we need to do?"

"Yes. Meet with Nate and Axel to finalize the minor details. Is next week okay?"

"Sure. I'm ready whenever."

Maeson laughs. "Whenever, you say?" He licks my bottom lip. "Like, now?"

"No, no. I have one more question."

He nuzzles his face against my neck, nibbling on my tender skin. "And that is?"

"Ahhh… What is... ahhh... Molly's... birthday surprise?" I pull his hair.

"Och, Princess, that doesn't hurt. In fact, quite the opposite. And it's a promotion."

I shiver beneath him as his soft touches travel across my scar. The caress eases my internal pain. His lips feed my hunger for him. The spicy aroma of his cologne livens my dulled senses. My body pleads for more, but my mind intervenes. "Promotion?"

He rubs his beard on my tender flesh. "VP. It's time."

My mouth drops. "That's amazing!" I plant my hands on his chest.

Maeson peers down and laughs. "These wee fingers don't have enough power to keep me away from you."

I shrug. "I had to try. Anyway, why the change in Mo's position?"

He straightens and leans against the couch. "I figured after all the years she's dedicated to me, she deserves the title."

"I agree. Friends like her are rare and should be cherished."

"Aye. Now, are you finished with the interrogation?" There's a glimpse of his to die for dimples before he closes in on me.

"For... now."

For now, but not forever. Someday and someday soon, I'll question him further on the secrets he's hiding. It's only fair since he knows my dreadful past.

He grabs a fist full of my hair, wrenching my head back and seals our lips together. His liquor infused tongue flicks against mine as he rips my shirt down the middle, exposing my breasts. "I need you."

"And I you." I purr against his ear.

SWEAT DRIPS DOWN MY back as I force myself toward the bathroom on shaky legs. I wipe the smudged mascara from my face and meet the fiery gaze of the woman staring back at me in the mirror.

What's one more time in the grand scheme of things? Show him who you truly are. Give into your deepest desires.

From the bathroom door, I peer at Maeson who's hanging partially off the bed, tangled between the rumpled sheets and grinning from ear to ear.

Take control. Let loose for once. Plus, he's so drunk, he's bound to forget anything happened.

My well-concealed lioness is more alive than ever. She demands to be sated by her beast. I stride to the edge of the mattress. "Spread your legs."

He lift his head and licks his lips. "Och, Princess, it takes a powerful woman to confidently command a man, and it seems, you've found your rightful place."

"Shut up and do as you're told." I place my hands on his thighs, thrusting them apart.

"What are your plans for me, lass?"

"No questions." I clutch his cock. "Do you want this in my mouth?" I grin, flashing my teeth.

"More than anything I've ever wanted in my life."

After one final stroke, I replace my hold with my lips, licking, sucking, and nibbling every sweet-salty inch of him.

His body shakes and he groans, spreading his legs farther apart.

"Don't!" I squeeze his dick. "Lean against the headboard."

With a shit-eating smirk, he lifts his legs onto the mattress, pushing himself backward.

"So cocky for a man eager to cum two minutes into a blow job."

His smirk falters.

My ego roars.

Our faces are mere inches apart and the strong musky and spicy notes of his cologne penetrate my senses, amping my craving for control.

"Arms at your side." I straddle him, placing his dick right where it belongs.

His eyes roll to the back of his head, and he jerks his hips, entering me deeper.

I forcefully clench my thighs. "Don't fucking move."

He closes his eyes and moans. "But you're so fucking wet."

"For you? Always," I whisper.

"Hhhmmm?"

"I'm going to fuck you like you've never been fucked before."

I'm going to show you a side of me you've never seen.

9

MAESON

Sex, sex, and some more sex. Some parts of those glorious moments, my foggy hungover mind remembers, but others seem like a made up dream.

My body aches as if I was pummeled by a bull at full speed *or* what I think was a hallucination, actually did happen. I wrack my brain for the full details, but all I manage to do is worsen my headache.

Realistically, the minor shit doesn't matter. By the way I feel, I know we had an amazing night, and with Ruby nestled in my arms, all is right in my world.

I twirl a few dark curls between my fingers, enjoying the softness of them as I contemplate something more important—how to tell her she's *'the one'*? Better yet, how do I show her?

Before I do, the constant back and forth needs to end. The first step on her end? Let go completely and put her faith in me. My first step? Explain everything. Once she understands... Maybe it's better she doesn't.

I fight to convince those around me—*including myself*—I'm a good man, but it's a lie. Years ago, I wasn't very kind.

But I made those mistakes out of sheer anger and fear. Loss...

I peer at her beautiful face, memorizing every feature. Her

delectable full lips, her almond shaped eyes surrounded by thick black lashes, and the rosiness to her cheeks.

There's a chance I may never see her again after she knows. The closer we get, it's bound to happen, and she'll hate me. My heart pounds at the thought of her leaving me.

Will she understand?

I'll find out soon enough.

I close my eyes, freeing my mind of the memories I've held at bay for too many years.

HER BIG STUNNING GREEN *eyes wreck havoc on my soul. She's everything.*

Heart condition they said…

How could this happen? What will I do without her? There's no family here to help. How can I fix this?

Too many questions hit me at once, and I struggle to breathe.

I need money and a lot of it. I can't afford what she needs on a busboy's paycheck.

The realization rips me apart, inside and out. I slide down the wall and allow the tears I've been holding in fall.

Stop! You're a fucking man. Stop crying.

I can't. There's too much pain. At twenty-two, I am not supposed to go through any of this alone. I prepared the best I could and stood by my word to be there every step of the fucking way. She wasn't. She lied. She broke her promise. She packed her shit the second she found an escape.

Why would she leave?

She didn't even look back. No one mattered to her but herself. How could I not be pissed off?

After a few minutes of releasing my unmanly emotions, I pick myself up and kiss her sweet face before heading straight for the whiskey in the kitchen cabinet.

I need this drink. It's not a good idea because I haven't had one in a while, but I don't know how else to make the agony disappear.

What if you go overboard again and get into another fight?

No way. I'd never harm anyone I care about, no matter how drunk I get or upset I am. I'm better than those loser men who get blooter'd and brawl like fools.

I OPEN MY EYES and shake my head in the darkness as shame envelops me.

Will the memories of my pathetic past ever leave me be?

No, they won't. This is the punishment I deserve. I lied to myself that night. If I could go back in time, I'd tell that young and stupid lad to put the fucking bottle down.

What's done is done, there's no going back. The path I took was my choice and mine alone. I could've stayed home where I belonged. I was needed there, not at the forsaken strip club she worked at.

Because of her, I changed and lost the good within me. She was the one who awoke the sleeping beast.

After what Sam told me, the bitch hasn't changed in the last ten years. As long as Ashlie received what she felt she deserved, she was willing to use anyone at any cost.

There were times she didn't get enough at home, and she'd seek it elsewhere. Even went as far to give me some bullshit of an excuse claiming she had a sex addiction.

Right...

The woman acted like I never fucked her. Between school and work, I catered to her every whim, including daily sex. I managed just fine until it became twice a day, then three, and toward the end of our relationship it was four or more times. Don't get me wrong, like most men, I love sex, but I needed a bloody break.

Our troubles were on my shoulders, not hers.

She didn't cook, clean, do laundry, or work much, yet I never said a word. Not once did I bitch at her when I had to come home from working all day to make dinner for us, wash the dishes, throw a load in the washer, then dry and fold the clothes. I kept my mouth shut like a pussy whipped twenty some-year-old lad so she'd stay with me.

And look how that turned out.

"Fuck my life." I slowly release my arm from beneath Ruby's body and pad across the bedroom into the bathroom.

The soft night light shines against the walls, and I gape at who's staring back at me in the mirror. Disheveled strands of hair stick straight up and my sexy scruff has turned into a full very unsexy beard overnight.

I feel as shitty as I look.

There's rustling in the bedroom, and I spin around to find Ruby standing in the doorway completely naked. She's sporting the most sensual grin I've ever seen, and her hair is as wild as mine.

"Come back to bed. It's too early to be checking yourself out." Ruby shoves me aside to mock me by brushing her hair away from her face and flexing her muscles in the mirror.

"I do *not* do that." I crease my forehead and frown.

"Yes, you do." She struts in a circle around me with her head held high. "Your wanna be insulted expression doesn't work on me one bit, Gramps. Besides, you look like you're about to have an aneurysm. And given your advanced age, you might want to stop." The little devil winks before she dashes out of the bathroom.

Her high-pitched evil laugh fills my ears, and I give chase.

The woman thinks she can escape me? Never. I scan the bedroom, but she's nowhere in sight. "Come out where ever you are. You can't hide for long." I lower myself to the floor next to the bed and lift the material blocking my view to find… nothing.

I rise to my hunches only to have Ruby pounce on me, laying me out flat. "Fffuuuuccckkk," I release a muffled groan.

"Got ya." Ruby snickers and proceeds to assault me with tickles.

When her fingers land on my ribs, I flinch, but force myself not to laugh.

She notices my meager attempt to remain still and baggers me at full force. If she keeps this up, I'm bound to burst.

Must. Stop. Her.

"Quit fighting it. Your face is so damn red." She digs her fingers further. "Let go, Maeson. Let go."

"Nnnooo." My defenses fail me, air rushes from my lungs, and I erupt with laughter. "You suck!" I growl between her ceaseless attack.

She wraps her legs around my waist and squeezes. "You wish."

I grab her arms and look up at her smiling face. "Do I? Or is it you who wishes?"

Ruby licks her lips as she gyrates against me. "I'd say a bit of both."

"Me too," I whisper.

Heat ignites between our bodies, and I'm tempted to take her on this floor, but there're a few things I need to clear up first.

I've made a grave mistake closing my heart off to everyone, and Jax was smart for ignoring my idiot pep talk. I was a fool thinking that big hearted teddy bear would listen to me anyway.

It's time I nix my ego and accept the facts I didn't want to believe months ago. On the surface, I knew Ruby had the power to change me. But deep inside, I didn't want to admit what she'd really be capable of—healing my broken heart.

I have to go about this discussion the right way so she doesn't think her traumatic past is the reason I care, it only intensified my admiration for her. As a fath—

"Maeson? Where'd you go?" Ruby's soft voice cuts into my thoughts.

"Nowhere, was just thinking."

She frowns. "About?"

"Us."

"What about us?" Ruby slides off of me to lay on the rug.

"I'm tired of the back and forth. The entire rigmarole is exhausting. And it's not because I'm used to getting what I want when I want, either. Your *no emotions* rule is too difficult to keep." I shake my head. "I can't believe I said that out loud," I say more to myself than to Ruby.

Cue the runner. One… Two… Three…

"I… I don't know what to say." She places a hand on my beard. "They're so beautiful, you know?"

"What?" I wrinkle my forehead, glaring at her.

"Your eyes." She smiles sadly. "When I look into them, I see what you're hiding. On the first night we met, I avoided the intensity in them because I knew I'd lose myself in what I saw.

It scares me. And in the last five months, my fear hasn't changed. You shield yourself externally, but those green orbs of fire give your true emotional state away."

"Then why do you run from me at every chance you get?"

"I'm afraid." She closes her eyes and a tear glides down her cheek.

I brush it away. "Of me, lass?" My heart ceases to pound. *Please don't say yes.*

"No. I fear letting go and what happens after you see the real me. I fear the pain of being hurt or worse, being left once I completely give myself to you." She whimpers and releases the floodgates.

I reach for her hand, but she pulls away.

She wipes her eyes. "I wish I was different, someone less complicated. I wish I was as carefree as Molly, as strong as you, and as willing to start over as Jax. But I'm not, I'm a fake. I act shocked by how Aria stays with her boyfriend, yet if my ex hadn't killed himself, I'd still be with him too. How could anyone want to be with me? Especially, someone like you. You're sex on a damn stick who can have anyone you desire. Women would crawl on their hands and knees to have you. Your every desire would be fulfilled because they aren't lost within their past like I am."

My gut clenches. "You're not the only one who worries about those things." I pull Ruby's shaking body into my arms. When she rests her head on my chest, I murmur in her ear, "As hard as it is to believe, I wish I was different too. We're all complicated in some way, but what you fail to acknowledge is you're all of those things. For example, the strength you claim I have, you have ten times that from starting over too many times to count. Carefree? Who was that woman tickling me just before? She's been carefree around me more than once, but only in glimpses because you keep her hidden."

Ruby continues to cry, but manages a nod.

I stroke her back and kiss the top of her head. "I believe at some point, you would've had enough and left your ex on your own like you did at your foster home. And for the record, Aria isn't you, you're a survivor."

Ruby rubs her eyes, smudging black mascara down her cheeks. "Survival is all I know."

"Which is exactly why someone like me—*as you said*—wants to be with you. Thin mints are meant to pass time with. They provide a needed service, nothing more. That's why they're called *'thin mints'*, *'linchpins'*, and a *'means to an end'* for lonely pathetic men like me." I snort. "Lass, having a past, thinking for yourself, and rising above the ridiculous standards women live by makes you the amazing girl I know you are. To go further, if those women had fulfilled even an ounce of my desire, I'd be with them longer than one night. You've awakened something in me I've been missing for a long time. Something I didn't think existed in my soul anymore. You and I are the shattered pieces to a beautiful puzzle only we can put back together."

Ruby she sighs and peers up at me with gleaming wide eyes. "Really?"

"Aye. I believe it with my entire being." I lower my head, lingering near her lips. When she doesn't push me away, I strike. Our mouths connect, fitting perfectly against each other and pure bliss flows through my veins. How can one person calm me to my core so easily?

Because she's your soulmate, you bloody fool. Accept it, your beast has.

"Maeson show me. Make me believe too." She wraps her arms around my neck, tugging me flush against her. Her tongue glides in and out of my mouth as she sears my back with her nails.

The tattoos beneath her touch tingle, and I push against her fingers, digging them deeper into my skin. Pain and desire blend together, creating the perfect cocktail for a bastard like me.

My dick hardens and the need for sex dominates my brain. The beast wants out, but first, I need a true answer from her on our non-professional relationship.

Surprise, surprise. I'm as willing as every other bloody chump to settle down.

The choice is Ruby's. Either I stick by her side or we go our separate ways, and I continue with the meaningless day to day sex.

Slowly—*fucking begrudgingly*—I detach from Ruby's warm body to peer down at her flushed face. My dick twitches. Fuck it, I don't need an answer, do I? "Bloody hell. Just looking at you makes me want to tear your clothes off."

Ruby bites down on her swollen bottom lip "Same here. So, why don't you?"

I shake my head fiercely. "I can't. Won't. Not yet."

"Why?" She raises an eyebrow.

"Because. I. Fuck! I never thought I'd give a shit again, but you need to decide where we stand. I heard you out, and I gave you nothing but honest answers in return, yet where are mine?"

"Honest answers? Really? If my memory serves me right, I've told you about my life. You even know my favorite color is red, and what do I know? Shit! That's what. You've given me crumbs and not once did I push. So, don't talk to me about unanswered questions." She exhales and quirks her top lip. "Would you like to rephrase your question?"

I laugh at her assault and place a hand over my heart. "After that ass whooping, I think I should." I clear my throat. "Lass, even though I put myself out there, and you violently shot me down, I'd like to explain what I meant."

With a curt nod, she folds her arms across her chest.

"I ask you to have patience when it comes to my past. Give me time, and I'll answer all of your questions. If you're willing to accept that, then I'd like to voice a concern."

She nods again.

"Will we commit to each other as more than sex partners? Shit, I don't even know if you're seeing other people or if you want to. I never asked because until recently, it wasn't my business." I raise a hand in the air when Ruby growls. "Correction, it's still none of my business. But I'd like it to be. If after five months we can't clear up our relationship status, then when will we?"

She curls her lip and rolls her eyes. "You're basically asking me if you can fuck other women."

"What?" I jump to my feet. "Are you fucking kidding me? Bloody fucking typical! Women love taking what men say out of context. It's like a damn game between the two genders."

She shrugs. "I simply repeated what I heard."

"You heard wrong." Why is it every time I bring up something more than just fuck buddies, she finds a way to push me away? Be it by running, evading, or fucking spinning it against me.

I stomp to the wall of windows facing the city I've come to love, regardless of the bad shit handed to me ever since I moved here.

Just breathe. She's been hurt worse than you can imagine. Deep breath. She doesn't know how to handle more than what she's given you. Just fucking breathe. Calm down. You know she's not like Ashlie. The poor girl is as terrified as you.

"Maeson." Her voice cracks as she whispers my name.

"Aye?" I don't move to face her, regardless of how sad she sounds. I'm too bloody drained to argue over it because she'll never be ready.

Which leaves me at a crossroad. One I'd prefer not to be at since my life is too complicated as it is.

Thanks, Molly the rude awakening you wished upon me has arrived at my doorstep.

"I commit to stand by your side. I pledge to never lie to you. I promise to be faithful to you. I, Ruby Bennett, will oblige by giving you all I have, only if in return you do the same."

Silence fills the room as her words brand themselves into my brain, and I attempt to speak. But when she places her hands on my bare skin, my thoughts vanish into thin air.

She traces the wings tattooed on my back. "Never use flourished words filled with fancy sayings on me, they mean nothing. Candy, cards, flowers, and shiny things won't buy my affection nor my commitment. I have enough money to acquire anything I desire without the help of a man. And one last thing, you don't own me, you never will, and don't ever act like you do. Like our business venture, we're equal partners. Step over those lines, and I'm gone." Her soft caress shifts to the words inscribed between the wings. "That's what I can offer you. As worthless as it might seem, this is my sacrifice for you." She lifts her hands, and I immediately miss the heat of her gentle touch.

Her words along with what she caressed as she spoke struck a chord deep within my soul. A tear slips down my cheek. My first instinct is to wipe the intruder away and man the fuck up, but the move would only prove I'm not giving her all that I am.

Just breathe. She won't laugh in your face. She won't laugh at your pain because she'll understand it.

I turn ever so slowly to face the most beautiful women I've ever laid eyes on. "I, Maeson Lachlan Alexander, commit to everything you asked of me and more. I pledge to prove my worth and show you not all men are made the same." I know my words aren't enough for a woman who's heard lies most of her life, but I'll *show* her my truth.

I've fought the emotions for too long. My chest constricts and it's difficult to breathe as fresh tears cascade down my face. I close my eyes, inhaling as deeply as I can. The sound of our synced breathing helps me focus.

"You shed tears for me?" Ruby sighs as she wipes the wetness from my cheeks.

I slice my head to the right.

"For a man like you, that's a sacrifice." She leans into me.

I cover her naked body with my arms. "Showing you is my only proof that I feel, I hurt, and I care as much as you. I've paid the ultimate sacrifice once before, and I'm not sure there's anything left for me to give up. I can only gain as long as you're by my side."

You've given me something worth caring about.

10

Ruby

I did it. I took a step forward and committed to him. I should be scared, but I'm not because Maeson's nothing like the men in my past. He's the calm to my storm.

Plus, I can't live in a sealed box forever. If I'm preaching to Aria, then I need to follow my own advice. It's mind over matter. Always is.

I've endured beatings requiring more strength than devoting myself to a relationship. What's the worst that can happen? Maeson leaves me? Nothing new there. I'm a survivor. If I've learned anything from my past, it's I can continue living with or without someone by my side.

The thought makes me smile, and I peer at Maeson's sleeping body. "You hear that? I'm fine with or without you, old man." I pounce off of the bed.

Maeson pulls the blanket over his face. "Not old."

"Yeah, yeah." I pull Maeson's long t-shirt over my head before patting his leg, which dangles off of the edge of the bed. "Time for coffee."

He groans, but doesn't move.

With a shrug, I dash down the hallway into the kitchen.

"Today will be a good day." I say to myself as I turn on the Nespresso.

Before Maeson leaves, we need to finalize Molly's party details so I can shop for the decorations. We have less than a week to get everything together in between our meetings with the lawyers and my visits with Aria. Luckily, I'm free today to get most of it done.

While the coffee brews, I grab a pen and a notepad from my office. The first item on my list is hundreds of balloons in every shade of the rainbow. Very fitting for Molly, the light bringer to those surrounded in darkness—including me.

The machine stops, and I top off my mug with a teaspoon of raw sugar and fluffy foamed milk. A moan escapes me as I take a generous sip. "Perfection."

Now to get my muse flowing, I need music. I hook up my iPhone to the Bluetooth speakers and tap on my playlist. The smooth rhythm of Dean Martin's *'Sway'* fills the room.

While the song continues, I settle onto a chair with my coffee and focus on my list.

Balloons, candles, cake, present, streamers, birthday hats, special music playlist, catering, drinks (alcohol and non—for prego lady), send e-vites.

Guest list: Me (of course), Maeson, Jax, Axel (ask if he has a plus one?), Sammie, Bekka, and Aria (Maybe?).

"Why does your name say, *'of course'* next to it, yet mine doesn't?"

Gasping, I fly out of my chair. "Are you crazy? Never sneak up on someone like that. I could've had a heart attack!" I slap Maeson.

He snorts. "Oh, really? What about when you snuck up on me last night? That was okay?"

"It's not the same. You knew I was hiding. I freaking thought you were sleeping."

"Semantics." He graces me with a sexy smirk as he leans in to kiss my cheek. "More coffee for you?" He points to my empty mug.

"Thanks, but I'm good." While he fixes a cup for himself, my cellphone vibrates. Tiny spikes crawl down my spine. "Aria?"

"I can't stay here anymore. I need to go back to him."

"Why, honey? What happened?"

"I'm clean now. I can manage without the drugs. I promise."

"Aria, it's too soon. You've only been off the drugs for two weeks. Let me pick you up. We can talk it out."

"No, Ruby. I've made my decision. This is just a curtesy call."

"I see…"

"Sorry. Not tryin' to be a bitch. It's my life and this is what I want to do."

Maeson was right, Aria and I couldn't be more different if we tried. Our similar situations don't make us the same person at all. I wanted to be saved—begged for it—but she's pleading to return to an abusive relationship. Regardless, I'm not giving up on her. I'll fight for her well-being like no one ever did for me.

"Can we at least meet up before you go home? I'm going shopping today. Maybe you can help me?"

Give me a chance to convince you life is better without that kind of man.

Maeson smiles and gives me a thumbs up. As I wait for Aria's answer, he scribbles on my note pad *'Good idea. Proud of you.'* My heart soars at his encouragement.

"Shopping? Like at a mall?" Surprise laces her tone.

"Yeah, and a few other places too. What do ya say?"

"I guess okay." Aria sighs. "But, I don't have any nice clothes. People will laugh at me."

My stomach plummets and tears brim at the corners of my eyes. "Oh, sweetie. Don't worry about that, I'll bring you clothes. Give me half an hour."

"Okay."

"Wait for me. Don't go home."

"Okay."

"Thirty minutes. Please."

"I'll be here. I promise."

After we hang up, I toss my phone on the ottoman and face Maeson. "She said she'll wait. You think she will?"

He shrugs. "Hard to say. Neither of us know her well enough. I hope she does, though."

"Me too."

Maeson pulls me into his embrace. "What will you do if she's not there?"

"I'm not sure. I haven't thought that far." I press myself against him, inhaling his sexy spicy cologne.

"Call if you need me."

"Will do." Reluctantly, I pull away from him.

He grabs my arm and stares at me. The yellow flecks in his eyes darken. "Be careful. Please." His words are rough and ragged.

"Always am." I smile.

With a brisk nod, he seals my lips with his.

As his tongue circles mine, my body ignites. Heat. Hot. Aroused. Sex.

NO! Snap out of it. You have somewhere to be.

Damn it. My inner monologue is right. "Got." I murmur against Maeson's mouth. "To. Go."

"Okay, lass." He gives me one more peck. "See you later."

With my purse and keys in hand, I rush into the elevator. As the doors slide across the tracks, Maeson's gaze meets mine and something I've never seen before flashes behind his eyes. It appears to be…

Fear.

WHEN I PULL INTO a parking spot behind the Women's Shelter, I spot Aria on the porch. I grab the bag of goodies I bought and hop out of the car.

"Hey," Aria says.

"Hi, hun." I smile and cloak her small frame with a tight hug. "Try these on."

Aria takes the bag from me with a frown. "This… This is a lot of stuff. They look new, I can't take these." She shoves the bag toward me.

"No, please take it. These are my gifts to you for being so brave and committing to a sober life."

"I'm not that brave." She hangs her head.

"Yes, you are. You've proven it, and you'll continue to do so every single day. I won't give up on you, and you shouldn't either. You have to believe in you, sweetie." I pat her hand. "Come on, you've got so many outfits to try on."

"I LOOK LIKE UTTER shit." Aria huffs as she flings her arms in the air.

"No, you don't." I laugh. "You look amazing. Those jeans hug all of your lady curves. Which, by the way, are fabulous."

She doesn't respond but, her lip quirks as she fights a full smile.

As far as I'm concerned, that's progress.

She's tried on five outfits and most of them fit her perfectly. Fortunately, there was a petite woman in the store, and she helped me choose the clothes.But the shoe size I picked was pure luck.

"Okay, pretty lady, let's get out of here. Ready for some good ole fashioned shopping?"

She bobs her head. "It'll be my first time."

I raise an eyebrow. "Seriously?"

"Mmhmm. Always had hand me downs or found stuff on garbage days." She looks down at her new white and black sneakers. "These are nice, you know? People wear these on TV."

"Good, I'm glad you like them. I wanted to get you something comfortable. I actually have the same pair of Nike's, but they're all black. Next time we hangout we should both wear them to match and pretend to be sisters."

Her face lights up as she giggles. She's so beautiful when she smiles, yet she has no clue. I wish she could be this way every day, but that won't happen because she's reuniting with the dick head.

An image of Aria's bloody body flashes in my mind, and a prickly shiver creeps up my spine. Her condition was worse than the first time her fucking boyfriend had his way with her. Dread invades my mind, body, and soul, but I force it away and focus on the sweet girl before me.

I won't have our day ruined because of that bastard.

For both of our sakes, I fake a smile. "Let's get out of here and have some fun." I wrap my arm with hers as we walk to the car.

Aria squeezes my hand. "Lead the way, my friend."

With a deep inhale, I look up at the sky. This is the first time Aria called me a friend. I might have a chance at saving her after all.

Time. I'm in dire need of it to persuade and show her she can be this happy without a shitty man by her side.

WITH PLEADING, TEAR FILLED eyes, I watch Aria step out of my car. The extra time I wished for has reached its end.

A few more steps, and she'll enter that horrendous house, back to a hideous piece of crap boyfriend.

My insides quiver for her safety, my heart pleads me to rush after her, and my mind screams to save her.

But how?

I made a few attempts to change her mind, but Aria was silent the entire drive home. She refused to listen when I practically begged, 'Stay with me for a while. I'll help you. You'll be safe, I promise. He won't find you there. I'll make sure of it.'

Now we find ourselves silently waiting for the inevitable by her broken-down front door.

Aria stares at me with dark tears staining her face. She wipes them away, smearing her mascara further.

She seems to be seeking some sort of validation, waiting for me to tell her it's okay, but I won't.

"Don't go in there. Please."

"I have to. Please don't make me choose." She looks down at the cracked pavement and digs her sneaker in the gap.

"That's not what I'm not asking. I want you to choose... yourself. A few weeks of healing and staying clean isn't enough."

"But that's what I'm doin'. I'm choosin' me, and what I want." She sniffles. "I need him. He loves and takes care of me."

I sigh and shake my head. "He's not the only one, you know? The women at the shelter and I care for you. More than you realize. But you need to let us in. How else can we prove it to you?"

"It's too late. I made my decision." She turns away from me. Without a fleeting glance back, she murmurs, "Goodbye, Ruby."

She's found a way to break another piece of my already shattered soul. Tears invade my eyes, and I struggle to blink them back.

Don't let her walk away.

DO SOMETHING.

Chase after her, but how can I when she's made up her mind? I must accept it and hope she'll change her mind. "Aria."

She rubs her face. "Yeah?"

I invade her personal space and give her the tightest hug I can. "This isn't goodbye. It's I'll see ya later, you pain in my ass." I kiss her cheek and squeeze her one last time. "I'll always be here for you. Don't you dare forget that."

Aria sobs as lays her head against my shoulder. "I won't forget. I can't. You're the sister and the best friend I never had. You saved my life and you made me laugh again. I will never forget your kindness." She straightens. "This time will be different."

The impracticality of her words shock me, but I maintain my composure by simply nodding as she waves from the doorway.

Please let her be right. She deserves a better life. One I can't help her find until she wants it.

MY DRIVE HOME WAS a somber one. The ascent to my condo was worse. My derailment there after—expected.

Note to self, too much alcohol lands you on the cold floor of a living room with a muddled brain. Why do I blame myself for decisions others make?

Because she needed salvation, and I couldn't give it to her. I pleaded for it, but no one came for me.

Maeson's words find the perfect moment to intrude my thoughts, *'As much as you think it, Aria isn't you. You're a survivor.'* But that doesn't mean Aria isn't, does it? She's dealt with so much, wouldn't that make her as much of one as I am?

You. Wanted. Out.

"So?" I slam my fist against the floor. "Fear still controls her. She has no other choice." My insides clench, threatening to expel my liquid dinner.

Doesn't she?

I may be foolish for caring this much and letting it affect my well-being, but how can someone like me not? If you've suffered in life, you simply cannot look, walk, or crawl away. It's your duty to help those in need.

But for how long?

That's the million-dollar question I don't have an answer to.

Maybe Molly does?

Yes. She's the perfect person to ask. I grab my phone from the ottoman. It rings a few times before I'm transferred to voicemail.

Damn.

My next instinct is to call Aria to check on her, but I'm blocked by an incoming call.

Maeson. Just breathe and fake it to make it.

I clear my throat. "Hey, old man."

Shit, that's too cheery. Tone it down.

"Ruby."

I laugh. "Maeson."

"Are you drunk?" No matter what tone he uses, his voice is delicious.

"No. I'm relaxing."

Maeson doesn't respond.

"Are you there?" I'm met with silence. "Hello?" Still nothing. I peer at my phone through the hazy film covering my eyes.

He hung up on me. Damn it. I shouldn't have answered the phone. Guaranteed he's on his way here.

Mr. Always Protective can't stay away for long, can he?

I toss the phone aside to make an attempt at sitting up but fail. Maeson can't find me this way, he'll freak and panic like a little old lady.

With a second try, I succeed to rise to my hunches. After a bit more effort, I'm standing. The room spins and my stomach heaves. "Shit. Need water," I grumble as I trudge to the fridge and grab a cold bottle, lifting it to my lips. The refreshing liquid slides down my throat, and I swallow gratefully. "Ahh. Just what I needed."

When the elevator chimes, I jump into action.

Put on your game face. Make him believe everything is okay. Just breathe.

11

MAESON

The further I move into Ruby's condo, my nose is flooded by the stench of distilled spirits and smoke. "Och, my little liar. Relaxing, are you? With what? That bottle of booze on your counter?"

Ruby shrugs and rolls her eyes. "Yeah. Got a problem with that?"

My lip twitches as I take in her current state. She's a complete mess with smudged makeup, wild curly hair, and the only material covering her luscious ass is a gray oversized t-shirt. "No problem at all." I kiss her cheek. "Wish I could've joined the party is all."

She pushes past me to grab the opened bottle. "Sorry, Gramps, this is a party for one. No guests allowed, not even you."

Tempting the beast, are we?

I grin, flashing my teeth. "You're very wrong. This guest will always be present in anything involving you."

She huffs and struts away, flopping on to the couch. "Put those dimples away."

"I will once you tell me what's made you drink."

"Do I have to?" Ruby pouts.

"Aye, you do." I wrap my fingers around the neck of the vodka bottle she's cradling and place it on the side table.

How times have changed. I'd be the first to join a party, but this time, I want to be sober for Ruby. As Sam says, *I'm in it to win it'*.

I'm in to prove my worthiness.

"Fine. Aria chose *him* over her own safety. I couldn't convince her. I failed." She looks up at me with pleading eyes.

"You did no such thing." I tuck her under my arm and twist a fallen silky curl around my finger. "She can't be controlled, only advised. And that's what you've done. Anything more would be overstepping the boundaries of your friendship. Would you want someone telling you how to live your life?"

She shakes her head.

"Exactly. Just keep in mind, if and when she needs you again, you'll get the call. Until then, don't force her hand. Believe me, pushing someone against their free will only makes them want the opposite more."

"Ugh. When I don't want it, the all-knowing crap spews from your mouth."

A laugh escapes me, and I tug on her hair. "You know you like hearing my wisdom, so don't act like you don't. Be the big girl you're supposed to be and buck up. Focus on what you can control, like our business and Molly's party."

Ruby smirks. "I won't admit you're right, but fine, I'll move on. For the moment."

I shake my head. "I guess that's all I can ask for." I rise to my feet, extending a hand toward her. "It's time for you to sleep the booze off."

Sex, then sleep.

She needs to release the tension she's harboring.

Does she, now? Or is it you who craves? Both, damn it.

She grumbles and slices her head to the left.

Could this woman be any sexier?

"Princess, don't make me drag you to bed."

Another slice of her head to the left.

My inner beast claws at my chest. *Want her.* "Och, now you've done it." With one swift and fluid motion, I lift her on to my shoulder.

"No. I don't want to sleep. I wan—"

I slap her ass, then squeeze it. "You want what?"

Ruby releases a moan and grinds against my shoulder. "Sssllleeeppp," she says between giggles.

"That's more like it." Without warning, I toss her on to the bed.

She yelps. "Someone's hungry."

I want to tell her so many things. Like how her laughter makes my heart soar, but instead, I slice my head upward and to the right as I tug her t-shirt off.

I watch in fascination as her nipples harden. "Fuck!" I grasp the puckered peak between my lips and suck—hard.

Ruby moans. "Naked. You. Now."

"Aye." I wrench off my shirt, losing a few buttons along the way, and toss my remaining clothes on the floor. My dick is rock hard without her touching me.

If only Ruby knew how much something so trivial means to a man… to this man. With my previous escapades, I needed a blow job or a handy to start.

"Whatcha you doing over there? Pondering your future?" Ruby's soft voice pulls me from my thoughts.

"No, lass. I'm contemplating the many ways I'll fuck you."

FUCK WE DID. THROUGH the night and into the morning. Now, it's mid-afternoon, and Ruby's lounging on the couch watching TV while I prep brunch. "Lass?"

She twists to face me. "Yes?"

"Bacon or ham with your eggs?"

A saucy grin surfaces on her swollen lips. "Got any sausage?"

"Nope. You devoured the last of it this morning."

"Aw, shucks." She scrunches her brow and waves a hand in the air. "Bacon will do."

"Okay." I toss four slices on the sizzling pan. "Oh, do me a favor and flip to the weather channel. We need to check what it'll be like for Molly's party."

"Good idea." Ruby pulls up the TV guide and scrolls until she finds it.

'Unseasonably warm this weekend.' The reporter's voice comes through.

"Seems we're a go to have the party on the roof and we can use the pool. I'll have a crew sent over to rearrange the furniture." I cover the bacon slices with a paper towel to soak up the extra oil, then add the beaten eggs into the leftover grease. "By the way, how many people are coming?"

"So far, I have Molly, Jax, Sam, Bekka, Axel, me, and you. But I'm a little unsure about a few things."

As I'm stirring the eggs and onions together, I look up at Ruby with a raised eyebrow. "Like what?"

"Is Axel brining a date?"

"He's coming solo."

"Okay. Next is Aria. Do I invite her?"

"Hmmm. Tough question. Honestly? You're the only one who can answer it."

"I don't know what to do."

Neither do I.

I keep that tidbit to myself, it'll only make it harder for Ruby to decide. Instead, I hand her a plate piled with eggs, bacon, and buttered toast. "I have an idea." I grab her makeshift list. "Everything on here is finished except one questionable guest, right?"

Ruby nods as she digs into her breakfast.

"Alright then, give yourself the day to think about it before making a decision. It might be last minute, but I'm sure she wouldn't mind the late notice."

"You're right," she says between mouthfuls.

"I know." I smirk and raise my arms in the air, flexing my biceps.

Ruby snorts. "Ssseee. You never miss an opportunity to show off your goods. This time it's a double banger, dimples and muscles."

"Not true. I'm a bloody modest fucking man." I can't help myself as I join in on her infectious laughter.

"Modest, my ass." She hops onto my lap. "You're a typical Class A, my-shit-don't-stink kind of guy."

"Aye, and I'm damn proud of it. Haven't you realized I'm the greatest thing since mint chocolate chip ice cream was created?" I nuzzle my face into the crook of her neck, exhaling against her bare skin.

She shivers and nudges me away. "Ha-ha. I didn't, but I sure do now."

"And you better never forget it."

"You got it, old ma—"

"What?" I rest my hands on her sides and squeeze.

She bursts into a fit of giggles as I assault her tickle spot. "Noth… ing."

I thought it would be impossible after the night we had, but the joyous sound makes me hard for her again. She'll be the death of me. Death by sex.

I'm not sure I'd mind that.

Ruby notices my aroused state and grinds against it.

Between her laughter and the friction on my dick, I'm tempted to tear her clothes off.

Meeting. You have one in an hour.

I groan and release my hold on her. "We have somewhere to be, remember?"

"Grrr. No! I'll have blue pussy!"

"You're not the only one, lass." I hoist her onto my shoulder.

This is the second time you've done that. What are you a fucking caveman?

We need to get out of here before I take her right now, and man handling is the only option.

The damned woman woke a sexual aggression I didn't know I had. I've always believed fucking was simple. Pound into them until they screamed—in pleasure, of course. I got my rocks off and so did they, end of story.

But with Ruby it's complicated. The combination of her dark

past and the hazy glimpses I have of the fierce lioness within her require more than an easy fuck. She deserves more.

I'd never thought this beautiful and innocent looking woman was as wild, untamed, and feral as her hair.

Fuck.

The images of our sweaty tangled bodies blast into my mind. *Maybe we do have enough time for a quickie.*

An idea strikes me, and I enter the first door to my right.

"What are you doing?" Ruby wriggles in my arms.

I don't answer as I set her onto her feet and turn on the water in the shower.

She wrinkles her forehead. "Forcing me to wash up? Do I smell *that* bad?"

"No, lass." I pull the thin white shirt covering her body above her head, dropping it to the ground. My heart pounds furiously against my chest from the sheer perfection standing before me.

Her waist tapers in, blossoming out at the hips. Further south, are her voluptuous thighs, protecting what I desire most. She isn't sporting the typical landing strip I despise. She's completely bare.

I lower my head and suckle on her neck. "Princess, you're" — I nibble harder — "beauty in its most humble form."

"No." She moans. "I'm not."

I suck deeper and feel her pulse beating against my tongue. "Yes… you fucking… are." I pick her up and walk into the shower.

The hot water scalds my back, as I slam her against the tiled wall and continue kissing her skin down to her nipples.

Ruby shoves her breast further into my mouth and drops a hand between her legs. She slides two fingers between the pink folds, moving them in circular motions. "Yesss. Harder."

I oblige. Only for her. Anything for this woman.

The sight of her pleasuring herself has my body trembling with excitement.

"Grab my arm. Hold it above my head. Tight."

The command shocks and exhilarates me, yet also, sounds

familiar. I want to dig deeper into my subconscious, but I refuse to falter and do as I'm told.

She rubs her clit with uninhabited passion. Her eyes meet mine, and our gazes collide. Fire blazes between us.

"Cum for me, Princess," I whisper in her ear.

"Your wish… my command." She explodes with a shout.

Her legs shake as the orgasm hits. Once the last tremor subsides, she grins evilly and turns, facing the wall.

When I don't move, she peers back. "What are you waiting for? Fuck me!"

I'm floored, absolutely fucking floored. People say I'm the devil in disguise? Then they haven't met Ruby Bennett. She's pure evil in the form of an angel—exactly who my beast's been searching for. His other half—the missing piece.

'Fuck me,' she said. How can I not when she asked so nicely?

"Your command, I wish to please." With my knee, I spread her legs, entering her.

She's so damn wet.

I grab her hips, moving in and out of her at a leisurely pace. Screw a quickie. I want to enjoy every minute.

"Faster! Harder!" Ruby urges. "Old… Man… Wrinkle… Can't… Handle…"

Hell to the fucking no.

"Can!" To prove it, I pound, thump, bang, thrash, pummel, and hammer into to her. My legs slap against hers as our bodies collide.

The noises emitting from us are as indescribable as are the feelings piercing my heart.

She's too close.

Parts of me quiver at the idea, yet the others revel in the idea of letting go and being one hundred percent real with someone. It'd be freeing not to keep my secrets to myself all the time.

She'll judge you.

Where is this shit coming from?

Focus asshole. Don't let doubts cloud your mind. Everything is fine.

I close my eyes, shoving the nonsense aside. The here and now is what matters.

Ruby Bennett is different. She has to be.

"Princess." I pick up speed, thrusting with all my might. "I'm falling in —" My orgasm hits before I can complete my sentence.

For. The. Best.

A frenzied groan erupts from deep within, and I thrash against her as I release.

"Mmmaaaeee!" Ruby's pussy pulses around my dick as she joins me for her second go around.

Gradually, we detach from each other, and she faces me with an enormous smile. "I guess your ancient bones *can* handle it." She giggles as she wraps her arms around my waist.

"Never doubt my abilities, lassie." I step aside and water splashes her face.

Ruby sputters and swats at my arms. "You ass-hat!"

I laugh. "Be still my heart. She's also adorable with her insults."

"Hardy-har. Funny guy, aren't you? Never underestimate *my* abilities, Mr.-stick-up-your-ass."

"I wouldn't dare." I wink and show off my dimples.

As expected, she melts into me, or is it me who's melting into her? I dismiss the ridiculous thought. I certainly do *not* melt for anyone.

Lasses do that kind of shit. Not men.

Drops of water fall from my hair onto her face and she moves to rub them away, but I beat her to it with my tongue. Once they're all gone, I capture her mouth with mine, suckling on the bottom lip.

We stand in the shower kissing for what seems like an eternity and by the time we actually bathe, our skin is as wrinkled as a shriveled prune.

"Okay, out you go. We've somewhere to be, remember?"

"Yeah, yeah." Half-heartedly, she wraps a towel around her body before leaving the bathroom.

For the first time, I'm not reluctant to partake in a meticulous meeting. Ruby's vision is truly inspiring, and my ultimate goal is to make this dream come true for her.

After the pain she's suffered, she deserves it — bloody earned it.

JUST WHEN I THINK three hours of discussing every possible question and creative idea regarding our venture is over—it's not.

"One last thing. Who's handling the interviews for the staff?" Axel says.

I roll my eyes and shrug. "Not me. I'm the enforcer kinda guy. You know I detest the whole bullshit hiring process. Everyone's amazing on paper until they start the actual job."

Ruby shakes her head, but I don't miss the twitch of her upper lip. "Since Maeson is out, and I'm a terrible judge of character, would you mind doing it, Axel?"

"Not at all. I could use a change of pace."

He's so full of shit.

I smirk and narrow my eyes. "A change or an opportunity to find a new wife?"

Nate spits out his drink and Ruby gasps, but I don't give two shits because I know this man better than anyone else.

Whether Axel wants to admit it or not, his failed marriage plagues him. He'll be that guy who searches for the next *'forever'* women until the end of his days.

And Jax may be fooled by his one night stands—I'm not. Axel's using them as a cover. His *'I'm single and love it'* act.

Axel shoves his middle finger in my face. "Change, asswipe. This isn't America's Next Top Wife."

"You sure about that?" Why am I instigating when his love life is a touchy subject?

Because I'm exactly what he said—an asswipe.

He curls his lip. "Yeah. What's it to you?"

Ruby faces me with a frown. "Yes, Maeson, what's it to you?"

"Nothing. I'm just making conversation." I laugh. "See what happens when you keep me in a meeting for too long?"

"You turn into a pompous bastard." Axel curls his lip.

"Prom Queens. Relax. It's been a long and draining meeting, but let's finalize this so we can all go home."

"Fine. Go ahead, Ax." I grumble.

"As I was saying, I can gather a list of the final potentials before we pick the top contenders. That way we all have a vote. How's that?"

"Sounds good." Ruby smiles.

"Any more questions?" I peer around the table.

Next time, I'll stay home. They can handle it without me, like they did in this meeting.

Ruby giggling at Axel's pathetic jokes was enough to drive me up a wall, then add those two practically ignoring me the entire time—how can I not want to jab a few of Ax's nerves?

Ruby smiles *again* before rising from her seat. "That's it, for now." She walks around the table to shake Nate's hand. "Thank you so much for meeting with us. As always, it was a pleasure."

As always, my ass.

"You're welcome, Ruby. And since everything is in place, all of you should be set. Just call me if you need anything further." Nate returns the smile, but doesn't meet her eyes.

Smart man.

After Nate leaves, the room fills with an awkward silence.

As I open my mouth to speak, my cell phone vibrates.

Incoming Message: *Apologize to him. You were beyond rude for no reason. I'm going to the bathroom, so take care of it.*

I peer up at her with a raised eyebrow.

She grins as she approaches me. "I'll be right back." Ruby points to Axel and I. "You boys better be good while I'm gone."

The moment Ruby is out of sight, Axel explodes. "What the fuck is your problem?"

"Nothing."

"Bullshit. What did I do to you?"

"Noth—"

"Say nothing again, and I *will* deck you."

He can try, but he wouldn't succeeded.

Not in this lifetime.

But for Ruby's sake, I give in. "You flirted with Ruby the entire meeting."

"WHAT? I'd never."

"Yeah, you bloody fucking did. You two acted like long lost lovers—all smiles and jokes."

"No, that's what friends look like when they're on the same page. Besides, you know me better than that. So, stop acting like a bullheaded bozo when I'm around her." He stares at me for a second, then his eyes widen. "You think I'm this pathetic single guy who'd try and take your woman?"

"No."

"Then why treat me like shit?"

How can I explain my feelings when I don't even know the reason?

Yes, you do. You just don't want to admit it.

The man codes are pretty clear—don't ever show weakness, always be on top of your game, and take care of what belongs to you.

If I open up to Axel, it'll be like breaking one of the rules.

"Seriously?" Axel huffs. "Now you're tight lipped? You had no problem embarrassing me in front of your woman and Nate."

"It's not you I'd be embarrassing … it'd be me."

"All hail, King Maeson. God forbid you were taken down a notch or two."

"That's not what I mean."

"Then what?" He leans into his chair, bending one leg across the other.

I close my eyes, unable to face him as I admit to weaknesses. "I'm worried she'll leave me for a better man. A spiffy clean cut one like you."

Axel bursts into a fit of laughter. "Like that'd ever happen. Ruby's all about you and then some. If only you could see through my eyes, you'd notice it too. Don't be a dumbass barbarian—especially with a friend."

"But what if—"

"No, man. She's not like Ashlie. Not for a second does she remind me of her. This girl cares about everyone else but herself, she finds happiness helping others, she lives off of her own money, and she is very independent. Want more examples? Cause I can keep going."

"When you put it like that, no, I don't." Shame fills me as I stare at the floor. "I'm sorry, Ax. I shouldn't have — "

"No, but you did. Grow up and soon because another man might not take so kindly to your insults."

"I can protect myself, don't worry."

"That I know. I've seen you in action when things went downhill. But is that the man you want to become again? I'm sure Ruby wouldn't like you very much if you did."

A slice of my head to the left is my only answer.

"Then learn to trust. More importantly, learn to trust *her*. Move forward, forget the past."

I snort. "You're one to talk."

"Yeah, I am. I, unlike you, know where I fucked up and am dealing with it."

Raising an eyebrow, I smirk. "Are you?"

He gives me a sheepish grin. "In my own way."

"You're such a lawyer. You always have the right answer, don't you?"

"I wouldn't be a good one if I didn't." He pats my leg and stands, extending his hand to me. "Never pull that shit with me again, okay? I'm not your enemy."

I grasp his hand, giving it a firm shake. "Yeah. Just being stupid, I guess."

"Not stupid — you're afraid and there is no shame in that. Being a man doesn't mean pretending to feel nothing."

"I wish someone taught me that when I was an impressionable kid. Now it seems to be a moot point. Changing my views isn't something I foresee in my future."

"Maybe not change per se, but adaptation?"

"Aye, buddy. I can try."

"Holy shit. I forgot to congratulate the Scotsman on his return. Wasn't sure how many years it'd be before I heard that burr again." He slaps my shoulder. "Ruby's done a number on you, my friend. Can't say I'm upset about it."

"Shut your face, Ax. I have a reputation to uphold."

"Don't worry, the entire world realizes that." He grins from ear to ear. "Anyway, it's been fun, but I should go, you know, find me that new wife." He laughs.

Luckily, Axel isn't the kind of man to hold a grudge. If he was, he'd never speak to me again after the shit I make him deal with daily.

As we make our way to the door of the conference room, Axel stops mid stride. "Maes, kidding aside, find a way to believe in her. She's suffered enough and keeping parts of your life a secret won't help either of you. Just tell her... everything."

"Everything..."

"If you don't, you're bound to relapse and that'll cause Ruby more damage than you think. She's connected to you in a special way. Don't be stupid and break a bond with someone as fragile as her."

"But she's not fragile." I sneer at the filthy word. "She's the strongest person I know."

"She sure is strong, but not in every aspect. Like you, she's hurting. Her soul begs for someone to piece her broken heart back together. But how do you think she deals with it? Have you taken notice?"

"Aye, I did. What can I say to stop her? We both drink and lose ourselves in sex, so it's not just her. I'd only be a hypocrite."

"Then you need to show her you can live without those things as a means of running away from facing the facts. Your pasts were shit, but make your future better before it's too late." He steps into the hallway toward the elevator, leaving me behind with my mouth wide open.

He slips past Ruby who hops to me with a massive smile spread across her lips.

As she gets closer, a shiver runs down my spine.

What the hell did he mean by before it's too late? Like anything will happen to either of us. Unless... No. I'll make sure nothing does. I will protect her from any harm, even if it's from me.

12

Ruby

How is it that I haven't seen this luxurious rooftop before? A massive gray sectional is placed on the left hand corner next to a top-notch built in kitchen and grill. The pool on the other end seems to be the same size as mine, but his has the initials MA engraved at the bottom and black lounge chairs around the perimeter.

Holy shish kabobs. This is the best place to host any party. Molly will be so surprised.

Thinking of the birthday girl reminds me there's no time for dilly dallying. I set down the bags filled with party goodies and dig into them.

An hour later, I'm admiring my work. Birthday decorations hang off of the glass railings, the walls, and the palm trees. I can't help but laugh at the stark difference of the before and after. It looks like pink and purple threw up all over the place.

"Fuck." Maeson groans as he strides onto the roof. "This is the girliest shit I've ever seen." He slides his aviators over his eyes and scrunches his nose.

I slap his shoulder. "Oh, shut up. It's beautiful."

"Ummm. No." Maeson steps forward. "You are beautiful.

This"—he waves an arm around—"is Molly to a tee, over the top and annoying." He curls his lip.

I grin. "Yet you love her to pieces."

"I do, but I don't have to love the colorful crap defacing my personal space."

"Whatever. You're full of it."

He peers over his sunglasses as he crosses his arms, flexing his muscles in the process. "Am not."

My lips twitch. "Are too."

"Am." He shows off his sexy dimples. "Not."

Moments like these remind me the fun things I missed out on as a kid. Sparring and teasing with friends is one of them.

When he acts this way it's truly entertaining and no matter how hard I fight it, laughter bubbles from deep within. "You're such a child."

"Aye, but aren't we all? Each and every one of us has a juvenile side we release from time to time."

Not me…

I frown, wishing his words didn't sting.

Maeson clears his throat. "I mean—"

"It's okay. There's no need for you to censor your words. Reality is I had a shitty life—simple as that." I assure him with a smile. "Anyway, people should be arriving soon, and we have more work to do."

Maeson nods, yet his eyes are filled with regret.

"Stop. You can't change what happened." I grab a bag filled with ice. "Take care of this and get the drinks ready. Please."

He straightens his shoulders and stares at me with a deadpan expression. "Alright." His voice is rough and heavily accented as he takes the bag from me. "Just so you know, the bedrooms are set up for our guests in case they decide to stay the night." With that, he brushes past me and slams the ice on the counter.

Could my pain bother him that much? Or is it something more?

Move on. Don't dwell on it. Your guests will be here any minute.

True.

Before I leave, I observe him as his back is turned to me. He shoves ice into a small bin and shakes his head multiple times before mumbling something incoherent.

I strain my ears to hear, but only make out a few fragments — 'I can't go through that again… Change… Too late…'

I should talk to him. Ask him what's wrong. No, wait until after the party.

Part of me wishes to stick around to listen further, but I force my feet to take me further away from his troubled voice. Snooping on someone isn't the best idea, I've learned that valuable lesson a long time ago.

AN HOUR LATER, EVERYONE but Molly and Jax have arrived. Sammie, Bekka, Maeson, and Axel are mingling and Aria's alone in a corner by the grill.

To my shock, she agreed to come. But I knew something was off right after I picked her up. She was considerably reserved, and my attempts to make her laugh failed. When we arrived at Maeson's condo, she retreated further.

I was hoping she'd warm up to the group before our honored guest makes an appearance, but it seems I'll have to break through the thick layer of ice surrounding her. I grab a mixed drink — my peace offering.

Mid-way to her, Maeson — who appears to be in a better mood — stops me in my tracks.

I smile.

He frowns.

Ugh. What's with him constantly giving me the sad and lost look today?

He leans in and whispers in my ear, "Is she okay?"

"I'm not sure. Why?"

"Don't make a big deal of it right now, but I think she's back on the drugs. Her makeup isn't hiding her bruises as well as she thinks."

My gaze travels toward her as shock radiates through me. "How did you —"

"I see everything. The smallest of twitches don't go unnoticed."

"Oh…"

"She's watching us, so don't make a scene. Smile, kiss me, and even add a sexy hip shake when you walk away. You know, to seal the deal."

I smile, but not because he told me to. "You sure it's to '*seal the deal*', or is it to please that beast of yours?"

"Both." He smirks before planting a hot kiss on my lips.

My knees buckle and my insides melt. If people weren't around I'd lay him out flat right here right now, riding him until he begs me to stop.

Whoa. Where did that come from? The past. That's where.

Forget those days and focus on the task at hand.

Smile, completed. Kiss, done. Sashay my ass in Maeson's face, active my entire walk to Aria.

I approach with a smile and extend the cocktail to her. "Why don't you join the crew?"

Aria shrugs. "I'm nervous." She brings the glass to her lips and sniffs it. "This might help loosen me up, though."

I nod. "I bet it will. Axel tends to mix drinks on the stronger side."

Aria peers over at Axel and smirks. "He's cute."

Her statement doesn't surprise me. The man *is* good looking. "Yeah, but he's not my type. My kind of man is next to him." I laugh.

Aria joins me, seeming more like herself. "Yup, big, bad, and scary." She watches them for a moment, then turns to me. "Why does he hide them?"

I furrow my brow. "What?"

"His tattoos," she whispers. "When I was… hurt… you brought me to your house, and I saw him helping. There were tattoos all over his arms, but today he's in a suit that literally covers everything—including the huge tat by his neck."

"Oh… I didn't realize you were awake. Please don't say anything. He prefers to keep his privacy… private."

"I won't. I'm good at keeping secrets."

"You've proven your abilities on that front very well." I raise an eyebrow at her.

"Not today, Ruby." She grins. "You shouldn't worry about me when it's your best friend's birthday."

"Doesn't matter what day it is, I'll always worry about you. If you haven't noticed, you're my friend too."

"Birthday girls trump everything on their special day." There's a flash of sadness in her eyes before it's replaced with what appears to be excitement.

"You're right. And if that's the case, then you need to socialize. After I introduced you to everyone, you didn't try to get to know them. Maybe you can now?"

Aria looks down at her shoes. She's wearing the sandals I bought her. "Okay… but will you stay with me?"

"Of course."

She squeezes my hand. "Do you think I'll ever be as happy and free as them?"

The question stabs me in the gut. "Yeah, but you have to want it."

She nods slowly. "I do… I really do."

"Happy birthday!" The five of us shout at the top of our lungs as Molly and Jax arrive.

"Wow! You guys." A teary-eyed Molly places a hand over her mouth. "This is…" She looks around and her smile widens. "Beautiful. Thank you everyone. Ya'll are…" She chokes up. "The best of friends a girl can ever ask for."

"You're welcome, chicky." I embrace her, squeezing lightly. "You look amazing for a four-month prego." I rub a hand over the tiny bump. "Not just stress fat, was it?"

She giggles. "Nope."

I hug her once more. "Happy birthday, sweetie."

"Thank you, love." Tears fill her eyes again, threatening to fall. "Ugh. Pregnancy hormones, I hate them."

"I heard they get worse as you get further along, so be ready." Sam says.

Jax groans. "Don't scare her."

"Such pussies." Maeson scoffs. "We getting this party started or what?"

Jax slaps Maeson's shoulder—hard. "Bout time we do, Mae Mae."

Maeson narrows his eyes at Jax, practically throwing daggers at him with the intensity of his glare. "Say that name again, and I'll deck you."

Jax grins from ear to ear. "Noted, brother."

"Enough bullshitting. Let's celebrate our mama-to-be already." Axel squeezes between the two men and hangs his arms over their shoulders.

"Here, here!" Bekka and Sam raise their glasses.

Everyone settles on the couch except Molly and Aria.

Time for a proper introduction between these two.

"Mo this is Aria. She's the friend I told you about who I met at the women's shelter."

Molly being Molly, tugs the fragile girl into her arms and embraces her.

Aria's jaw drops and her eyes almost pop out of her head, but she doesn't reciprocate. She remains with her arms flat at her sides for a few seconds until she seems to comprehend what's happening, then she hugs Molly back.

If there is one thing a person can't resist it's Molly's mama bear hugs. They're filled with so much love it's overwhelming.

Mo pulls back slightly and smiles. "Aria, I'm so glad to finally get to meet ya. Ruby's told me such great things."

"Oh, I'm sure she did." Aria peers at me with worry in her eyes.

"Yup! She told me how kind you are, and how you've welcomed her at the shelter. I think because of you, Ruby's more optimistic and found the courage to help others in similar situations." Molly winks at me. "And I think she'll do great things once the new place is up and running."

I shrug. "One can only hope."

"Don't say that." Aria frowns. "With the amount of passion and motivation you have, I know you'll save so many women and children," She says with a confidence I've never witnessed before.

Molly nods. "What she said."

Pride fills me. "How can I not believe in myself with two besties like you?"

Molly lightly elbows Aria. "See, this is why we gals are as awesome as hot sauce."

As the girls laughter fills my ears, I find myself wishing our lives could always be this lighthearted and joyful.

"Quit stealing the birthday girl." Sam pokes me in the arm.

Molly widens her eyes as she notices Bekka and Sam holding hands. She curls her lip. "You lying, bitches. I knew something was up with ya'll, but ya'll acted like I was a dumbass for wonderin'."

Oh shit. She didn't know either?

Sam rolls her eyes. "F you, woman! We weren't ready."

"Bullshit! Ready for what? To clue your friends in on your new carpet eatin' diet? Like I'd ever judge. And it's, Fuck you, not F you, you fucking prude." Molly erupts into a fit of laughter.

While those two banter back and forth, I take a peek at Aria who has shock written all over her face. I'd probably look the same if I hadn't been around these women before.

Molly and Sam are loud and proud, while Bekka is the shy one, and I somehow, fit in the middle of the crowd.

"That term, my friend, isn't politically correct." Sam pretends to be offended as she laughs "And I'm not a prude. I'm classy."

"Politically correct, my ass. How long have we known each other? Long damn enough for you to know I'm not political about shit, so shove your correctness up your… where ever you like it nowadays." Molly scrunches her eyebrows. "And classy? L to the fucking O to the fucking L." She gawks at the rest of us. "Can you believe this woman? She had the gonads to say it with a straight face."

"Hey, quit picking on my girl." Bekka giggles.

Molly's gaze whips to Bekka. "Oh, the mouse has spoken ya'll. Bekka, sweetie, want me to start on you?"

Bekka swipes her head from side to side. "Nope." She shifts away from Sam. "Sorry, babe, I think you got this on your own."

"Do none of you bitches have my back?" She grunts.

There's a chorus of no's.

"Fine, then I'll go party on my own. F you!" She pouts and struts away.

Bekka sighs. "Well, looks like I gotta join my ball and chain."

"Bek!" Molly calls after her and Bekka turns back. "Seriously, though, congrats to ya'll. She needed someone like you by her side."

"Thanks, Mo. I needed her too."

When Bekka reaches her lady, Sam faces us and sticks out her tongue, then flips us off.

"Looks like we're almost all set for life. Now if only you two would get your shit together, we'd be the perfect set of friends."

"In time. We're working on it. Just need to pick the right person."

"And, Mae Mae, isn't?"

"Not sure about that. He's still a mystery to me, so I refuse to fall to my knees for him."

"I get ya. In time, it is." Molly grasps Aria's hand. "Let's go girl, we've a party to join."

Molly's affection towards Aria warms my heart and a tear slides down my cheek.

These are my friends. My new family. They're the reason I have a chance to live a normal life, and maybe, Aria's too.

"I THINK IT'S A girl." Jax says.

Molly smiles proudly. "Me too."

Maeson shakes his head. "Who cares? First and foremost, what really matters is a healthy baby. And secondly, the selfish side of me is looking forward to have a little one in the family who'll inherit my fortune. Especially, since I don't plan on having any of my own."

He doesn't? For such a conceited specimen, you'd think he'd be first in line to reproduce.

Jax scowls in Maeson's direction, and Maeson quickly shifts his gaze to the floor.

Hmmm… What could their interaction be about?

No one else seems to notice, instead they're commenting on how they wouldn't mind being adopted by Maeson and what gender they think the baby is.

Molly's excited high-pitched voice over powers the rest. "We'll know for sure on Tuesday, so just a few more days!"

I smile at my best friend. "I better be the first phone call you make."

"You know it." The song playing on my iPod changes, and Molly jumps to her feet. "I love this song!" She grabs Jax's hand and dances around him.

I don't recognize the song, so I check the screen—Luis Fonsi's *'Despacito ft. Daddy Yankee'*, scrolls across it. Maeson must've put it on my playlist. He knows my appreciation for cultural music so well. Even the title speaks to me. I recognize the word from the little knowledge I can recall from my high school Spanish classes.

Despacito… Slowly…

Thick muscular arms cloak me from behind. "Slowly, I want to kiss your naked body…" Maeson's warm breath strokes my skin. "Slowly, I want to enter you…" He sings, harmonizing to the beat with expertise.

My heart flutters. "As beautiful as they are, your lyrics are wro—"

"Slowly, my feelings grow for you…" He nibbles on my ear. "Slowly, my future becomes clearer…"

His future might be, but mine isn't.

When he said he wouldn't have kids it resonated with me. Regardless of how bad my past was, I've never stopped envisioning myself as a mother. I pray daily for the possibility to show a child what true love is and cherish them like my parents did.

When the time was right, of course.

"Stop for a sec, please." I face him, only to be met by his hungry gaze. "I… umm…"

How do I say it? How do I tell him no children is a deal breaker?

"What's wrong, lass? You're ashen."

"When you said..." I swallow hard and take a few deep breaths. "You really don't want kids?"

"I—No, I don't." His eyes turn into a stoney dark green. Happy singing Maeson's gone. "Does that change things between us?" His tone matches the harshness of his glare.

Lie. Say no. Things are good right now. Maybe, in time, he'll change his mind? No. I won't succumb to another man's wants and needs. Mine matter too, and it's time mine matter more.

I stare at the ground, scrambling for the right answer. "Yes, it does change things on my end." I glance up at him as tears form at the edges of my eyes.

He knits his brow and frowns. "How so?"

"I want a family one day, and you don't. How'd such a drastic difference in opinion work in our favor?"

He stares at me blankly.

"Exactly, it wouldn't. I'm glad you told me now versus later when it'd hurt more." In the distance, someone calls my name. "I'm sorry. I have to go." The intensity of Maeson's scowl is unbearable, and I almost look away, but I stand my ground.

I matter. I matter more.

He opens his mouth, but snaps it shut and nods toward our guests.

Ignore the pain he's projecting. Turn around. Walk away.

"Ruby!" Molly shakes a fist at me.

I raise two fingers in the air. "She needs me," I say to Maeson before walking away.

When I reach Molly, she squeezes my hand. "You okay?"

"Yeah. Great." I force a smile to my face.

"Don't bullshit me. I'm pregnant, not stupid."

"I'm trying not to lie to you, so can we talk later? Please?"

"Sure, doll."

"Thanks. I'll be right back. You continue enjoying your party."

"Where ya goin'?"

I point the far corner of the rooftop where Axel and Aria

seem to be deep in conversation. "The make shift smoking section's calling my name."

Molly laughs. "Smokers. Can't live with 'em, and you sure as shit can't live without 'em."

"Real world problems, I tell ya." I don't fight the grin surfacing on my lips.

"Uhhh… Where's he going?" She points to Maeson's retreating body.

I shrug. "Who knows?"

"Jax might." Molly shakes her head. "Mae Mae and his temper tantrums."

"We're ruining your party. I'm so sorry."

"No way! Look at everyone dancing without a care in the world. I'm the borefest who's ready for bed. Honestly, hanging out with drunk people is exhausting."

"Yeah." I close my eyes, fighting off the tears threatening to spill.

I should've kept my mouth shut. Maeson would still be here having fun, and I wouldn't be apologizing to Molly for my actions.

"Stop. Open those pretty eyes. I promise I'm not mad. I told you, I'm tired, so no big deal."

"But—"

"No buts. Maeson set up the extra bedrooms for whoever want to stay. And if anyone wants to leave, Jax can take them home since he's the only sober one. Don't worry about us. Go get your man." She winks at me and gives me a soft shove.

"Not yet. We both need some space. But are you sure you're okay with me leaving the party?"

"If it was me, wouldn't you be?"

"Of course."

"Then shut up and enjoy your cigarette."

I nod and smile sadly. "I'm sorry."

"What did I just tell you? Listen to me, lady. Take a few minutes to yourself, then get out of here." She tugs me into her arms. "Love you, sweetie."

"Love you too."

"Remember to breathe. Just breathe, love," she whispers.

Just breathe is what I've been trying to do.

I back away, slithering to the smoker's corner. The closer I get to Axel and Aria, the better I can make out what they're saying.

Don't snoop.

I'm not.

I light my cigarette, inhaling then release a big white puff of smoke. As it swirls around my face a portion of the tension knotted in my shoulders dissipates.

I force myself to tune out Axel's conversation with Aria and focus on Maeson, who's returned sporting a deep frown.

As our gazes lock, the usual fire between us is missing. Ice. Freezing cold ice streams through our connection. I want to look away, yet I can't.

He's livid. Or is it hurt I see? Whichever emotion it is it's intense as hell.

"I'm sorry… I'm too old for you, honey. Believe me, if I was closer to your age, I'd be for it all the way." Axel's voice intrudes my glacial battle with Maeson.

"Okay." Aria voice breaks.

Even with my back turned to them, I sense a serious *'crush gone badly'* vibe.

Maybe I should interject? Make the situation less awkward.

"Don't be upset, please. To be completely real with you, I recently went through a divorce, and I'm not ready for another relationship. Then again, I don't think you are either. But if you're serious about getting better and living a sober life, you have to leave your current situation behind for good. You deserve more than a loser guy who treats you shitty for his pleasure."

"I'm trying, honest, I am. It's hard, though. I don't know how to walk away."

"I get it. My mom was like you, you know? And not to scare you, but do you know what happened to her because she wouldn't leave her scum bag boyfriend?"

"By the tone of your voice, I'm not sure I want to."

Me either…

"Then you can tell it didn't end well. Don't be like her. Be stronger. Fight for happiness. Take the help Ruby is offering you, because other people wouldn't give two shits about you after you dismissed their generosity."

Shit. He does know the pain… but from the other side of the spectrum.

"I don't… I don't want to be like your mom. To end up—"

"Then take the help you're given, sweetie. Stay with Ruby. Don't return to that place."

Yes. Convince her, Axel.

"I… can't… not yet. But soon."

Axel clears his throat. "Okay. The choice is yours."

At the sound of rustling, I stub my cigarette and pull out my phone, pretending to take a call. As they pass me, I smile and point to my phone.

Phew. They didn't even notice I was nearby the entire time.

I'm glad because hearing Axel persuade Aria to seek a better life proved to me he'll be an amazing asset to our business. He didn't have to say a word to Aria, but he did and was kind about it.

Perhaps some of what Axel said to her will stick, and she'll seek the help she needs. At least, I hope she does.

I shove my cell into my pocket and scan the rooftop for Mr. Grumpy. After what was said, we should at least talk about it— have some sort of closure. But he's nowhere in sight.

Find him.

My cell vibrates. One unread text message.

Incoming Message: *Is this the end for us?*

I want to respond, I really do, but I just don't have the right answer.

"Ruby."

Jax's voice makes me jump. "Hey." I force a smile to my face.

"Do you know where he went?"

"No. Do you?"

He nods. "It's the only place I can think of since he wouldn't go to our place or Crossroads. Too many people know him there."

"Where would that be?"

"The hotel down the street."

"Oh. I've been there once."

That's where we first met. That's when we first…

"I can drive you there."

"That's okay. I'll walk down." I shut my eyes, breathing deeply. "I could use the fresh air."

He observes me for a moment before he nods. "Be careful."

"I will. Thanks, Jax."

"Molly and I are here for you if you need anything, just call us. And don't worry about the rest of the gang, they'll be fine."

"Okay."

"Save him, Ruby. Save him from whatever mistake he's about to make."

"What? How do you know he'll make a mistake?"

"He always does when he's wrapped up in the past."

I frown. "But his past has nothing to do with what pissed him off."

"His past has everything to do with it. His past, like yours, controls his future." Jax peers down at me with glassy eyes. "Get him. Bring my brother back to me. Bring him back from the demons haunting him."

My mouth drops. I have so many questions, but all I manage is a small nod before walking away.

As my feet take me further away from Maeson's building, Jax's words replay in my mind like a broken record.

Bring my brother back to me. Bring him back from the demons haunting him.

I might not know what plagues Maeson, but my shattered soul cracks further for him.

For a man I barely know, yet understand better than anyone else.

13

MAESON

After sending Ruby a text, I also sent one to Jax, letting him know I left. He's the only one who'd understand my disappearance. With my anger above normal levels, I couldn't stay there any longer. If people noticed, Molly's party would've been ruined.

If only she'd asked the right questions.

But she didn't, and that's why I'm sitting in my car waiting for an answer from her. The outcome of my night and the path I'll take from now on depends on her response.

You have a business with her.

So? If nothing else, I'm always professional. Plus, I'm a grown ass man who can handle himself in awkward situations. Shit, I wouldn't ever have to see her again if that's what I wanted. My part in the business is simple—I'm the enforcer, the fixer, and the one who'll make her dream come true.

My phone chimes.

Incoming Message: *Please answer my call.*

Not fucking happening.
Ring… Ring… Rin—"What?"

"Hey." Her voice is as irritating as ever.

"Speak your demands." I clench and unclench my jaw.

"I don't have—"

"Bullshit. You only call when you need something. And you must really need it if you're willing to overstep Axel's warning. So, fucking speak already." Gripping the steering wheel with one hand, I'm tempted to fling my already cracked phone out of the window. Finally be rid of it. Be rid of her.

"Meet me. Please."

She must be on drugs again.

"Never."

"Please. We don't have to be this way forever. I love you. I always have."

Her pleading angers me further. Buried memories rush forward. My beast awakes with a feral roar. "Do you? Well, you've bloody demonstrated that very well over the years, haven't you? Remember the time you had the ultimate chance to prove your loyalty? Cause I do. I'll never forget. And what was it you did? You fucking—"

"I didn't know what else to do. I panicked."

"You bloody panicked? That's what you have to say for your actions?"

"It's the truth," she whines.

I snort. "Nothing you've ever said was the truth, Ash—lie. Why would I ever believe you?"

"I made mistakes, okay? Let me explain. Meet me. "

"What happened? Did your current plaything leave you high and dry?"

"No."

"Another lie. Your bullshit stopped working on me the day you walked out. Find some other fool to use."

"I'm not lying, damn it. Give me a chance."

"Give *me* a valid reason as to why I'd even want to be in the same space as you."

I'm met with a husky laugh, and I envision a nasty smirk spreading across her face. The smug looks she used to give me are forever engraved in my brain.

Too bad I don't give a shit. I'm not the weak man I used to be.

"Was that supposed to be my answer?"

She laughs again. "Oh, Maeson, baby. You haven't learned, have you? The terms haven't changed. Meet me or deal with the consequences."

"You, bit—"

"Shhh. Be a good boy and do as you're told. You DON'T own me, Pookie—I OWN you. Hilton. Ten minutes."

"Fuck you!" I hang up and chuck the phone on to the passenger seat. There's no way I'm going there. She's forced my hand long enough. It's time she learns ultimatums don't work on me anymore.

But if she follows through with those threats, they'll ruin my future. Destroy everything I've worked for and continue to build. The woman is disturbed. She won't hesitate to crush the people blocking her path— including Ruby.

If she capsizes my life, she'll in turn be eradicating Ruby's chance at accomplishing her dreams and goals. There's no fucking way I'll let that happen. I'd rather be cut off at the knees by a psychopath than hurt Ruby.

The decision—finalized. Ashlie wins again. Follow her commands like the pathetic man I am.

THE HOTEL DOORS SLIDE open, and I drag my feet to the entrance of the bar. Dread fills me.

Don't let her get the best of you. Control. Find it.

I close my eyes, forcing my mind, body, and soul to cut the connection with my emotions. If I'm dead inside there's nothing left for her to use against me.

Fucking succubus.

This hotel should remind me of the night I met Ruby—the first time in years I've felt peace—instead, Ashlie's found a way to tarnish this memory too.

She only has the power if you give it to her. Don't give it to her.

I won't. There is no bloody way she'll ever own me. I'll just let her think she does.

Within in moments, I spot her dark curls. She's cupping a drink and sporting a murderous grin. Time hasn't been kind to her. At thirty-seven she appears to be closer to fifty.

Drugs tend to have that affect. I told her so before she left me, but obviously, she didn't listen.

Her hair lacks the shine it used to have, her face is scattered with small scars and sores, and she's lost so much weight, I wouldn't have noticed her if it wasn't for the fake permed curls. This Ashlie isn't the same women I met as a teen—not even close.

"Maeson," she purrs.

My skin crawls. "Ashlie."

"Sit. We have much to discuss."

I slice my head to the left. "Fuck the bloody formalities. How much do you need?"

"Always the business man, aren't you?"

Fury burns through me, and I grip the top of her chair. "Always the money hungry, drugged out woman, aren't you?"

She rolls her eyes. "Stop making a scene and sit the hell down. You know my theatrics are much more developed than yours. People listen to a woman's cries over a man's."

I thrust the seat outward and slump into it.

There's a sinister gleam in her eyes as she reaches across the table and strokes my hand. "The payments aren't enough, baby." She puckers her thin lips. "My lifestyle… it's expensive."

"Obviously." I wrench my hand from hers. "This is the last increase you get." I rest my elbows on the table and lean forward, staring directly into her malicious gaze. "Ever."

Ashlie laughs. "Don't be silly, darling. You know what'll happen." She huffs then frowns. "Why do you enjoy upsetting me? Just accept your lawyer's scare tactics were ineffective. You'll never win."

Just breathe. There's a way out of this. There has to be.

I casually cross my arms over my chest and roll my eyes. "Don't be so sure of yourself."

"If I didn't have proof, I wouldn't be. But I do, don't I?"

"Bullshit fabricated proof."

"Regardless, evidence is evidence." She shrugs and peers down at her nails, fiddling with them. "Pookie, let's not play this game any longer. We do every time and it's tiring."

"Then why don't you stop? I'll pay you one lump sum so we can end this."

"No. You owe me. The monthly payments stay in place." Her voice matches the ferocity blazing in her eyes.

I'll never escape her. I'll never be free.

I struggle to breathe as the thought bombards my mind.

Deep breath. Don't let her affect you. Just fucking breathe.

"Why are you so desperate about the monthly plan?"

"You still haven't realized?"

Obviously, not… you psycho.

The words I wish I had the balls to say go unsaid, instead I shake my head.

"It's the only connection we have left. I've lost so much."

"You've lost so much? Are you fucking kidding me? You have the audacity to—Nope. I'm done. Send your future requests through Axel, including this one. Goodbye, Ashlie." I storm out of the bar.

The nerve she has. I need to get out of here. I need to—

"Maeson. Please." She's right behind me. Revolting heat radiates off of her body and onto mine.

"What?" I turn to face her and our bodies touch for the first time in nine years. My insides shudder.

On her end, the connection causes her expression to soften and she melts into me.

My initial instinct is to shove her away, but it'll only be more proof for her *file*.

Before I realize what she's doing—*before I can stop her*—she kisses me. Our lips touch, and my dick literally shrivels. There's nothing left between us. Not even an ounce of pity. The kiss fuels my wrath, and I seize her shoulders, pulling her away.

"Maeson?" A shattered voice echoes in the background.

NO. NO. NO.

My stomach drops, and I straighten, searching for her. She's at the entrance of the hotel as broken as ever with tears staining her face. My whole world crumbles. "Ruby—"

"No. Don't." Ruby's voice cracks as she staggers backward and runs into the darkness.

I stare down at Ashlie's, making sure she *sees* my hate for her. "You've ruined me, yet again. Congratulations. You fucking win." With that, I leave her in the hallway to rush after Ruby.

A cool breeze hits me, but I still can't catch my breath. "Ruby! Ruby!" I need to find her. But where would she go? Usually when she wanted to escape, she'd hole herself up in her condo. Then that's the first place I'll search.

Please let me find her. Please let her give me a chance to explain. Please let her understand. Please… don't let me lose her. I, unlike Ashlie, have lost too much already.

14

Ruby

Within the shadows, I cower behind the bushes. Tears blur my sight as Maeson's car speeds down the road.

Just breathe. Relax. He's gone.

The images of what just happened aren't.

Take a deep breath. Maybe it's not what you thought.

His lips were locked with some other woman's. Can't mistake that. Inhaling and exhaling slowly, I attempt to process the last few minutes. My stomach heaves, and I gag.

The second he thought we were over, he ran away to find himself a thin mint. How could he? I thought… I thought he was different…

I should've known better. There was no way a perfect man would be faithful to an imperfect woman like me. I'm a fucking fool for trusting him. Story of my life, falling for the wrong guy.

You let yourself feel, you dumb ass.

Why did I? No—how could I allow myself to let go?

I showed weakness, that's how.

Then grow the hell up and don't allow another person to bring you down.

Strong. I, Ruby Bennett, am strong.

Right now I'm not, but I will be. With or without Maeson, I can make it in this world. Fuck him.

I wipe away my tears, straighten my shoulders, lift my head toward the sky, and laugh. He wants to play petty games? I can play them better.

Not wasting another second thinking about him, I enter the hotel, walk straight to the bar, and order three shots.

The first one burns, but I revel in the pain.

"He has the tendency to do that to women," An unrecognizable voice says behind me.

I spin around, and find myself staring into eyes of the older dark-haired woman who was kissing Maeson. "What?"

She chuckles. "Maeson. He brings out the worst in us. Drives us to drink."

"That's not why—"

"Yes, it is. He's always the why." She puckers her thin lips and reaches for one of my glasses. "May I?"

I curl my lip. "No, you may not. The barman is right there. See yourself out of my space and find your own to crowd." With dark anger brewing in my gut, I grab the drink she pointed to and empty it in one gulp.

She gapes at me.

Shocked, bitch? Good. I'm happy to return the favor.

I wave my hand in the air. "Bye, bye… whoever you are. The pleasure was *not* mine."

She pulls out the chair next to me and crashes on to it. "Who the fuck do you think you are, you little bitch? He left you and came running to me because you're too weak for a beast of a man like him. Too fucking weak. What does your pathetic ass desire? His money?" She twists her upper lip in disgust. "By the looks of you, you'll need it for some heavy-duty liposuction. Haven't you noticed he likes them thin? Why would you even try to be with him? You should've known he'd come running back to me. He always does." Pure evil drips from her as she widens her smile and dips a finger into my last shot glass. "Mmmm. Bourbon. My favorite."

Too stunned to stop her, I watch as she swallows the liquid. I want to speak—*yell*—but nothing comes out. Her attack... Her criticism crushes my heart. It hurts me more than the lashes I received as a teen.

Hell no! I won't allow some stranger to insult me. Screw her and Maeson. They deserve each other, and I deserve better.

I meet her gaze. "I'm not sure who you are, nor do I care, but you can have him."

"He hasn't told you about me? Well, that's surprising because if he would've then you'd know I don't need your permission to be with Maeson. He's always been mine and only mine. The rest of you were substitutes until I came back to him."

"Oh, I get it now. You're that ex who whored around on him." I laugh at how delusional she is. "I'm sorry to tell you this, but when he spoke of you it was with revulsion and not an ounce of admiration."

She winces. "That's how our relationship is. We have our... moments."

I raise an eyebrow and purse my lips. "If that's the case then go get him. I have no need for a man who runs back to his scrubby ex-girlfriend every time she beckons him."

"Don't you worry that chubby face of yours, I always get what belongs to me." The tall and deathly skinny woman stands. "From now on, steer clear of Maeson. We have a connection you'll never have with him."

Something about her warning makes me snap. "And if I don't?"

She reels backward. "Sassy one, aren't you? How's this... If you don't stay away from him, you and I will have problems—the kind you won't walk away from. So, fuck off." She shoves my shoulder as she storms past me and out of the bar.

Did this skanky woman just threaten my life? Over Maeson? If her words are true and those two still have a relationship going, I want nothing to do with it. What I feel for Maeson doesn't matter anymore. He made his choice. And now, I've made mine.

I don't need him or any man. I say that, yet why is my heart breaking? The idea of losing him hurts more than I imagined.

We promised to be faithful. He made other promises too. Ones he doesn't know I heard.

But he lied. I lowered my safety wall for nothing.

Tears prick my eyes.

Just breathe. Go home. Get some sleep. Tomorrow is a new day. Tomorrow will be better because you'll be stronger.

"You don't have to feel that kind of pain forever, you know?" A young dark-haired guy slides into the empty seat next to me.

I peer at him through watery eyes, cocking my head to the right.

His brown-eyed gaze is soft and oddly calming. "I've been there. The agony that comes with relationship drama is the worst."

"Yeah. It sucks." With a shrug, I stand.

He places a warm hand over mine. "I can give you something to help you deal. You won't feel as much."

Feeling less sounds perfect.

My curiosity's peaked. "What would that be?"

"Oxy. 80 mills." He grins and whips out a clear baggie filled with greenish colored pills.

"How much?"

Shit, am I really considering this? If I take these, I'm no better than Aria.

"For you? Free. My gift to a beautiful girl who's hurting." He winks. "When you need more just find me here. Ask the bartender for Guy. I'm usually around here."

I stare at the pills, contemplating what to do. The decision shouldn't be this difficult, yet it is. The opportunity to be pain free is tempting — very tempting.

Don't do this. Don't travel down that dark road.

"Okay." I lay a palm upward.

He places a smaller clear bag with four pills in my hand.

"Thank you for this." I close my fist and shove it in my pocket.

"I hope it helps."

"Me too."

With a nod, he slinks away.

I wait a few moments then follow suit.

I can't believe I accepted drugs from who knows who, and I'm cradling them like they're my damn savior. What is wrong with me?

I won't take them, though. I refuse to be dragged into a never-ending cycle that's cause by these little green pills.

It was a weak moment on my part. As soon as I get home, they're being flushed down the toilet.

Are they?

Yes. I'm better than that.

I've survived far worse than some douche bag cheating on me. I just need to gather my strength, then deal with the heartbreak head on.

But you run a business together. You'll see him every day.

So what? I'll buy him out, completely eradicating him from my life. Our tiff at Molly's party proved we aren't meant to be. He wants different things out of life, and I can't accept those differences. Promises or no promises, some things aren't worth changing for.

The further I get from the hotel, the drug in my pocket feels like a brick weighing me down. Revolted with my decision, I want to chuck them, but knowing they'd be on the ground waiting for someone to pick them up stops me.

I'll get rid of them at home.

I step into the elevator of my building, pressing my floor number and lean against the cold stainless-steel wall. The recent shots I had along with the alcohol at the party kick in and my knees give out. I collapse onto the floor, breathing in deeply and focus on my parents faces as an unexpected panic attack strikes.

Deep breath, Ruby. Breathe. Just breathe. It's okay. Don't let another man bring you down. Deep, deep breath.

The technique works, and I lift myself to my feet, gripping the metal railing as the doors open. Darkness fills my home as I wobble into the foyer.

Darkness doesn't just fill this place it fills my soul. It fills me entirely. Today was supposed to be a happy day, instead it ended up being a sad, sad day.

I leave the lights off as I discard my clothes, stumbling to the couch. My bed for the night since I lack the energy to travel to my room.

Amidst the silence, there's a soft rustling sound, and I'm immobilized.

The psycho lady followed me home.

It's pitch black and no matter how hard I scan the space around me, I can't make out a thing.

Please don't let it be her.

My lungs constrict and my heart pounds profusely as I scramble to open the flashlight app on my phone. Anxiety suffocates me. My body won't cooperate. Every part of me trembles.

The trespasser beats me to it and turns on a lamp. "Ruby."

I attempt to adjust my eyesight to the flash of light, but dizziness envelops me as I meet my intruder's dark gaze.

Words. I need words, but they won't come out. My body gives up, and I crumple to my knees.

15

MAESON

"**M**aeson!" Ruby's shriek echoes in my ears as she collapses to the floor.

Drunk beyond the legal limit, I still manage to jump to her side in an instant. "Lass, I didn't mean to scare you." I caress her arm.

Ruby snaps her head in my direction with lethal glare. "Get off." She shoves against me and something small drops out of her grasp.

I've seen those before. Ashlie's brought them home many times. Is Ruby? She wouldn't…

Even in my condition, I beat her to the damn bag of fucking pills. "Where did you—how did you get these?" My heart speeds up as fear creeps up my spine.

"None of your business, asshole." She snatches the clear sack from me, thrusting it into her pocket.

"Of course, it is. You and I are—"

"Done. You've made your bed with your lovely ex, now lay in it and get the fuck out of my house."

My vision blurs as Axel's words come back to me. I will lose her. She's traveling down the wrong path. A dark, dark one. All because of me. I should've stayed at the fucking party—where I belonged.

I should've explained…

"We are *not* done. Nothing happened, I swear it. Princess, hear me out."

"Don't you dare *Princess* me. I know what I saw, you bastard—you prick! How could you?"

"It wasn't like that."

"Oh, really? So, I didn't see you throat deep in her mouth?"

"No. Absolutely not. She kissed me and it was for less than a second."

"Right. That's what they all say. Just go. There's nothing left here for you."

"I'm not, *all*. My word is true."

She rolls her eyes.

"Why would you run to drugs? You're always finding an escape from reality. Face it for once, damn it! Have you been using them to replace the anxiety meds?"

"What? No. You're so clueless."

"Then why keep your addiction a secret?"

"That's rich. Like you don't have secrets? You might keep your friends close, but your secrets are kept even closer." Ruby stumbles to the fridge, right to the alcohol. She tips the bottle to her lips and narrows her eyes. "Your supposed ex-girlfriend made it seem like you had sooo much more than a relationship gone bad."

She spoke to… Shit.

"When did you—"

"Shut up. It's my turn to speak. You've done enough damage for the night."

Her need to vent over powers my need to explain, so I clamp my lips together and nod.

"He does listen? Big bad man *can* follow commands. The bitch was right—you'll always go back to her." Ruby eyes grow wild as she expels a bitter laugh.

"Poor Maeson, his girl left him. Poor baaabyyy, was cheated on. Like those are real problems? People get dumped all the damn time. But you didn't get dumped, did you? You two never left each other. You self-righteous liar! You acted like you're perfect only to persuade me to commit to you. And against my better judgment, I believed those bullshit promises you made me weeks ago. I'm a freaking fool." She grips the bottle so hard, her knuckles turn white. "Fool me once..." She points the bottle toward me then fills her mouth with liquid, swallowing hard. "But fool me twice..." She closes her eyes. "That's on me. Only me."

"I'm not perfect, but I never *acted* with you."

"Ha! Sure, you didn't." Ruby thrusts the Vodka against my chest. "Here, you need this more than I do."

I take the thing and set it down before reaching for her.

She shoves my hand away and staggers to the couch, sagging onto it. "Look at where we are. You crawled back to your ex who, as she said, is better for you than me. Why wouldn't she be? She knows you and your pain—I don't."

"I did not crawl or seek her out!"

"Like I'll believe that!" Ruby frowns as if she remembers something, then peers up at me with sad eyes. "Why did you make those promises? Promises to stand by me for as long as I'd have you, to protect me like no one has before, and to show me what it feels like to be cherished by a real man? I wasn't sleeping. I heard. I believed you. But you've proven to be no better than Ray or my foster father. You're lower than them. They hurt me with physical pain—you chose to make me suffer at your hands with lies. Because of your promises, I almost believed in fairy tales again." She shakes her head and a tear falls from her eye onto her rosy cheek. "I must be the dumbest bitch in this world for saying this, but you look good with her. She complements your rugged appearance and asswipe demeanor."

Her last words slice deep into my soul. She can't be serious. Doesn't she hear how ludicrous that sounds? "She'll never be anything more than an ex. NEVER!" The veins in my neck pulse at top speed as the *oh-so-familiar* piercing ache arises in my heart.

I approach her and ball up my fists so she doesn't notice the tremor in them. "You, Ruby are the *beauty* to my *beast*. Inside and out. Have been since the day I met you. You strengthen my imperfections. You've taught me to have faith in second chances. Compared to how you make me feel, she'll never touch that Richter scale. She caused the pain, but *you're* the one who put a smile on my face again. You begun my healing process."

She twists her upper lip. "Bull. Shit. She can make you happier. You two shared a life together. We just… fuck."

"Bloody hell! Aren't you listening to me? I never truly loved her. You proved that to me."

"Whatever. You made your choice when you kissed her."

Exasperated, I throw my hands into the air. "She bloody kissed me. I didn't want or ask for it. I'd be the biggest dumbass if I had."

Ruby quirks her head. "And why is that? Let me guess, another secret you won't tell me?"

Please don't make me say it.

I touch her lips with my finger and take her hand, guiding her to the bedroom.

She scrunches her eyebrows. "If you think we're having sex, you're in for a rude awakening."

"Please, sit."

"I'll stand."

"Please?"

"I don't know what the fuck you're trying to do, but get on with it already. I'm tired of the damn games, so tell me every damn truth you're hiding or get the fuck out!" She crosses her arms over her chest and taps her foot on the carpet.

I'm trying. But I'm scared.

"Don't you see? Look at me. *See* what's true. Please, see *me*." I lift my shirt above my head, baring myself. "These" — I graze a hand over the tattoos on my body — "are my story. My truths." With my arms wide open, I slowly spin in a circle, stopping once my back is facing her. I close my eyes. Breathe in and out deeply, preparing myself.

It's time.

"This one"—I extend my arm backward, touching the wing tattoo.—"tells you everything you need to know. Grasp what I'm showing you, Princess."

"Oh, I'm grasping alright. You've immortalized her with a tattoo. I've avoided looking at her name every time you're shirtless. Who wants to be face to face with that everyday?"

"You can't honestly think... She doesn't deserve such a tribute."

"And why not?"

I might not be facing her, but the sarcasm in her voice comes through loud and clear, pissing me off further. For someone who's suffered so much, you'd think she'd be more understanding and in tune with other people's pain.

"You had no reservations pulling answers from me, yet when it's your turn, you clam up? Not okay in my book. Last chance—what are you hiding?"

Just breathe. She won't run. She'll understand.

"Madison is my daughter. Was ... And because of that bitch, she's... gone." My voice cracks, and I hang my head as I turn, facing Ruby.

Silence. Time freezes.

There. It's finally out into the wind. She's heard my daily anguish. The reason I wanted to die countless times since my baby girl's passing.

Ruby sucks in a harsh breath. "Your—"

"Aye. My little girl. My only child. My shining star."

Her eyes glisten, threatening to spill tears at any second. "That's why you said you don't want children?"

I slice my head to the right. "Aye. Losing one baby is enough for a lifetime and going through it again isn't a chance I want to take."

"I'm so—"

"Sorry? Don't be. It wasn't your fault, and I'm not looking for your pity."

"Pity isn't what I feel. It's empathy, maybe even sympathy. Loss of a cherished one is devastating—heart shattering. Can I ask how?"

She can ask all she wants, but am I ready to talk about it? Relive it aloud? Ruby did with her past.

Unbearable torturous memories assault my beast and I. He cowers within me, but I stand tall and push the visions forth. Ruby needs to know. "Madison's big, beautiful, and loving heart gave up on her." A tear slides down my cheek, but I don't wipe it away. For my sweet bairn, I'll show weakness any day.

"Oh, Maeson." Ruby rushes to me, warping her arms around my waist. "I can't imagine..." A sob escapes her as she glides her fingers up and down my back. It's as if she's comforting me and my daughter at the same time.

Madi, you would've loved this woman. She would've treated you better than your own mommy. I'm sorry I couldn't save you, baby.

My lungs heave. The harder I fight to inhale, the worse the discomfort becomes. "I wouldn't want you to see the things my mind replays every day. You have enough on your plate, lass." I drop my head and let my tears fall. They've been bottled up for long enough. "Losing her will plague me for eternity."

You're not acting manly.

Fuck being a *man* when it comes to my daughter. Let the world see me cry. Let the world see my bloody fucking pain.

My true emotions don't faze Ruby as she continues to glide her hands across my hot skin.

I melt into them, enjoying the reprieve they provide.

"Maybe I can help you? Together we can embrace our unfortunate yesterdays."

I nod and a few of my tears land on her beautiful breathtaking face. She's so exquisite, it hurts to look at her. "I'd like that, Princess mine. I'd like that a lot."

RUBY SNUGGLES CLOSER TO me and pulls the covers up to her chin. "Why is Ashlie back? What is she looking for, other than causing problems between us?"

"Money. With her it's always about money. You showing up when you did was a bonus for her."

"Don't I know it. She pounced the second she had a chance.

She even had the audacity to stooped so low as to attack my lady rolls, suggesting lipo. What is it with women these days? Skinny ones insult the chunky ones, and the chunky ones insult the skinny ones. People act like weight defines a person when it sure as hell doesn't. Grrrr!"

Ruby's adorable growl makes me laugh. "You know it's not just women who act that way. Men are held up to a lot of standards that are, at times, impossible to obtain. But with Ashlie, I'd suggest ignoring her because she's alone and miserable. Lashing out at others is her way of coping."

"I noticed. And now her hold on you makes sense. You two have a connection—*a bond*—no one can break."

"A bond? Anything that connected us was destroyed the day she abandoned us."

"What do you mean?"

"Well, I told you how she left me for another man, but what I didn't know then was she was pregnant. We didn't speak for months until the day she dropped a baby in my arms. Ashlie announced, *'this thing is yours'* and walked out." I shudder at the memory and the pain I felt watching the woman I loved leave without kissing her little girl.

"How could she do that? All mothers are supposed to love their baby."

"Not this one. If she could've, she probably would've tossed her at me. It was as if our child was a sack of garbage. Although, knowing how things turned out, Madison was better off without her."

"Meeting her once was enough for me to see what you mean. Can I ask you a question?"

"Sure."

"How did you know she was yours?"

"It was instinct, I think. The first time I held her it just felt right. I never did a paternity test, especially when I saw her eyes. They were the same exact shade of green as mine and my ma. There was no mistaking the Alexander in my girl."

"Aww. I bet she was beautiful if she took after her daddy."

"Oh, she was. My baby would've broken many a hearts had she grown into womanhood."

Ruby looks up at me with a frown. "You said, Ashlie called your daughter a thing… She didn't name her?"

"No, I did. She refused to give her a name at the hospital, so I went ahead and took care of all the paperwork. Luckily, Ashlie had the sense to claim me as the father."

"Wow. That's classy." She shakes her head. "Madison is a lovely name, though. Does she have a middle name?"

"Yes. Her full name is Madison Kiva Alexander. Madison because she was strong even with a bad heart. Kiva for her beauty and purity. The original spelling is Caoimhe, but in America she'd have too much trouble with people pronouncing it. My Da was disappointed, but I didn't want Madi being teased over it."

"I get it and either way you spell it, her middle name is true to your culture and elegant."

"Thank you. I thought so too."

Ruby sighs. "I'm sorry, Maeson. I really wish things turned out differently for you and your daughter. The pain you suffered is unimaginable."

"Unimaginable isn't the word. Committable is more like it. I turned into a terrible human. Lost my bloody fucking marbles. Lost myself in the grief."

Ruby eyes widen and she parts her lips. "What did you do?"

"Too much bad shit to recount in one night."

"Did Ashlie react the same way?"

I laugh bitterly. "Fuck no. She didn't give two shits. The only thing she did was pay me a visit the day we buried Madi to demand my child support payments continue."

"No she didn't! Wait! You were paying *her* child support?"

"Aye. It was the only way she saw fit for me to keep my baby. As far as Ashlie was concerned, she could drown her and be done with the *'pesky problem'*."

"No. No way. She didn't… she couldn't have cared so little."

"Little? Try not at all." Bitterness fills me, and my beast growls internally. "When she showed up at my condo with her ultimatum, I was drunk —*really drunk*— and I flipped. She got in my face, screaming and blaming me for the death of our daughter as if she was finally concerned. That's when something in me snapped, and I shoved her. I was a devastated mess. I was... lost, and she'd pushed me too far. I shouldn't have, but I did, and I couldn't take it back." My chest constricts at the reminder.

Why am I admitting this? Ruby will hate me.

"Eight years, I raised the sweetest little girl, and after all that time, I thought we'd won. I thought the surgeries paid off, but they didn't. They fucking didn't, and she had the balls to tell me it was my fault? I paid for the top care while I slaved away building a business for Madison's future. A future which no longer matter without her in this world. And what did Ashlie do? Nothing, that's what. She got her monthly checks and lived her life worry free. I was the one who woke up every single night to check on Madi, making sure she was still breathing— making sure that wasn't the night I'd..." I sputter as the words refuse to come out. Tears flow freely from my eyes.

Ruby gently wipes them away and nods.

"So, yeah, I fucked up. I shoved a woman when I should've dismissed her nonsense. I'll pay for that mistake for the rest of my fucking life."

"By paying, you mean child support?"

"No, blackmail."

"She can blackmail you because of a shove?"

"With exaggerated lies and falsified evidence, yes. After I denied her more money, she purposely got herself beat up and took pictures. Then she threatened to go to the police, claiming I abused and raped her. I had no other choice but to send her monthly stipends. That is until a little while ago, when I was sick of having any connection left to her. I told Axel to pay her off with a lump sum. But it didn't work, obviously. I'm assuming her old hag of a man dumped her ass and she needs more to sustain her disgusting addictions."

"That's pure evil! Does this mean she still has the evidence?"

"I'm not sure, but I can't afford to take the chance. I'd go to jail for a crime I didn't commit and in turn lose everything I've built."

"That's ridiculous. Fight it. Use the lawyers galore you have at your disposal. Prove her wrong or dismantle her credibility, but at least do something. You're constantly watching your back because of the *'what if's'*. You can't let her get away with this shit anymore."

"The problem is it's her word against mine, and the favor normally goes to the woman. She'll say my abuse turned her into a drug addict. How does an innocent person compete with that?"

Ruby frowns. "Good question. One for Axel, the man you pay the mucho dinero to represent you in this kind of scenario. But it doesn't hurt to at least try."

"Right. Then when I fail and end up in jail, I'll destroy your reputation and everything you're working so hard to achieve. People will see you as a fake. A woman who harbored an abuser while pretending to care about the victims in this world. No. Thank. You."

"Are you senile? You think I'd stand by you if I have doubts? No freaking way!"

"How are you so sure I'm being honest, anyway?"

"Because you're obvious when you lie." Ruby smirks.

I raise an eyebrow. "How so?"

She grins. "Every time you're avoiding the truth or extending it, you do this funny macho man thing with your head and inhale deeply."

I laugh. "Impossible. Show me."

"Don't pretend you don't know what you're doing with your own body. But fine. Here it is." She lifts her head to the ceiling, breathes in roughly, and curls her lip slightly.

"I do not do that."

Yes, I do, but I won't admit it. I'll never get away with a white lie again.

"Yeah, you do it every time and it's like you're prepping yourself before you fib. Boy, does it look cocky as hell. Then again, I did notice you do it other times as well—like when you're presented with a challenge or showing off."

"I plead the fifth."

"Plead all you want, but I know you better than you think." Her grin widens and she winks at me.

"And I you, Princess." I wink back. "For example, I know your most private desires."

Her already pink cheeks flush to a reddish hue and she bats her lashes.

"You see? We both have insider knowledge."

"Sure seems that way, doesn't it?" She puckers her lips.

"To me it does." As I watch her, I'm reminded of something and my stomach plummets.

She fidgets under my scrutiny. "What?"

"Before we continue, there's one troublesome matter needing annihilation." Lifting the bedsheet off of my body, I hang my legs from the mattress and stand.

She quirks her head to the side. "What's the problem?"

I grab her sweatshirt, searching each pocket until I wrap my fingers around them. They feel like heavy bricks. Just the thought of what they'd do to my girlfri—*no titles. She doesn't want titles.* I shut the idea down and wave the tiny bag in the air. "These gotta go, lass. I can't sleep with 'em here."

Ruby's eyes water and she sighs. "Toss them. I'm sorry— weak moment."

"I had one too, that's why I got blooter'd. I'll be right back." I enter the bathroom and smash each pill, turning them into dust. Once the deed is complete, I drop the remains into the toilet. For good measure, I flush it three times.

There's no way I'll ever let this crap ruin Ruby. I'd rather die than stand by and watch the fire in her eyes be extinguished because of a substance.

No mother fucking way. Not on my watch.

16

I'm was so stupid for accepting the drugs. A moment of weakness, which I regret. But, of course, Maeson knew how to resolve the issue.

Speaking of the Devil in disguise, he's strutting toward me in his naked glory. At the sight of his dimples, my legs turn into jello.

Our eyes lock and an unspoken mutual admiration passes between us. I project the respect I have for his strength to keep living after losing his precious daughter, and he beams with what appears to be pride.

"Your smile is like a hot cup of coffee on a cold winter morning."

"Aye, I know. Without it, I'd get into a lot more trouble." He stretches out on the bed, propping his head up with his hand.

"I bet, but there has to be someone it doesn't work on."

"Aye. Molly. She's never fallen for it and calls me out every chance she gets."

"Ahhh, she's too blinded by her man to be caught in the web of your conniving smile."

He laughs. "That she bloody is, and I'm glad for it. Her and Jax are perfect for each other."

"Good people like them deserve a happily ever after. I hope they hold on to what they have and appreciate it day in and day out because we both know how rare everlasting love truly is." There's a stabbing pang in my heart, and I frown.

Long ago, I was ignorant enough to believe that was in the cards for me too. Eventually, I grew up and stopped wishing. Day dreaming isn't a luxury I can afford. My fate isn't meant to be a typical fairytale. It's to be content with what's given to me and live one day at a time.

"Hey,"—Maeson lifts my chin—"what's upsetting you?"

I close my eyes and give him a small smile. "Memories."

"Want to tell me about it?"

I shake my head. "Let's talk about you instead. What are you doing about Ashlie?"

"Pay her, that's what. Once we have the shelter up and running, then I'll pursue her legally. There's no sense in provoking the witch in the midst of our venture. I've dealt with her for sixteen years, what's another year or two?"

"I'm not sure I agree, but it's your life." I shrug.

"What would you do?"

"Free myself at the first opportunity."

"The repercussions aren't worth it. I'd ruin everything for you."

I pucker my lips, pondering the different ways he could go about it without affecting those around him.

Maeson smirks. "Don't over work your precious brain, lassie. Smoke's spewing from your head."

I swat his arm and pout. "Give me a minute. Ideas are a brewin'."

He raises an eyebrow and slants his head to the side, eyeing me up and down.

"Not those kinds of ideas! You're such a dirty man."

"Had to try, didn't I?"

"Only you."

Maeson leans in and captures my lips, sucking lightly. "Always me, Princess."

"C. S. I."

He reels back, scrunching his brow. "What?"

"Law and Order. Shades of Blue. FBI. SWAT. That's how we'll rectify the problem with your ex."

"Come again?"

"We'll do what they do—get her to confess as you record it on your phone."

"Ahhhh. For proof." He laughs. "Someone watches too many cop shows. It'll never work. That's TV, not real life."

"We have to try. It's our only option."

"It's so sexy to see my little detective riled up for my sake."

I pout, knowing the effect it has on him.

Maeson grins widely as he stretches his arms behind his head. "Fiiinnne. Let's try, and if it doesn't work your way, we do it like I said."

"Deal." I bounce around on the bed, and before Maeson can stop me, I lunge for the attack.

In one swift motion, he rises to his knees and captures my wrists, looming above me as he pins my hands above my head. "Not fast enough, grasshopper."

I wriggle against his tight hold, but fail at an escape. So, I do the next best thing. "Shit. Ouch, you're hurting me."

Maeson releases me instantly.

Using the opportunity at full force, I throw my head back and release a high pitched laugh as I poke at his ribs. "Gotcha, gramps!"

"Nnnooo!" His resounding laughter fills the room.

My heart swells at the sound and my movements falter.

Maeson notices my momentary weakness and shoves me backward, flattening me with his big naked body.

Hello, there…

His wicked grin makes me arch my back in anticipation. Warmth bands around me, seeping down between my legs.

My beast…

Maeson's eyes bore into mine—yellow sparks blaze within

the dark green orbs. He flashes his ridiculously white teeth and plunges them into the tender flesh of my neck.

Welcome…

I revel in his proximity to my most sensitive hot spot and elongate my neck, providing him with extra room as he swipes his tongue across my blistering skin. Images of my deepest and darkest desires squirm themselves from the locked box in my mind. My heart pounds vigorously.

Only with this man do I have the courage to let go. Because of this man, I feel alive again.

"Harder." I grab a fist full of his hair, driving him further into the delicate curve above my collar bone.

He growls as he digs deeper into my flesh. With his mouth firmly connected to my neck, he grasps my right breast and flicks the nipple.

I wither beneath him.

It's happening.

Against my better judgement, I'm falling in love with the man who's given me so much…

Pleasure. No pain. Just pleasure.

Maeson releases my breast and tangles his hand into my hair, tugging forcefully. He nips my neck once more and flashes his dimples.

He looks different. The shadows normally surrounding him are gone. Is it because he's divulged his secrets? No more demons to haunt him? No more darkness to drown in?

"Och, lassie, being near you drives me to madness. You deserve so much more than what this shitty life has dealt you. I want to be the man who brings the light back into your eyes. The one that makes you realize you're the most beautiful being in this world and worth every damn breath I take."

Don't be scared. Accept his devotion.

Tears sting my eyes, and I'm at a loss for words. A nod is all I can offer him.

He nods back as he brushes the dampness from my eyes and kisses my cheek. "You're changing me, my beauty." He winces and rubs at his chest.

The pained expression on his face saddens me, but I know it well. Disclosing truths we keep buried within require a high level of effort. Our coveted sentiments are the ones we protect the most. And *feeling* them shoots a throbbing pang to an already broken heart. All the while, we pray remembering won't rip open old wounds, but will heal instead.

I smile. "You're changing me too, my beast."

A guttural groan slips from his lips. "You make life worth living." He grabs my ass with his large rough hands, lifting me closer as he drives into me.

I wrap my shaky thighs around his waist. "So do you." I buck against his hardness, matching him thrust for thrust.

Maeson. My beast. Finally, a real man who doesn't force me to forget. Instead, he encourages me to remember, to relive, to grow, to embrace, and to… let go.

Precious Tomorrow's. I scribble the name repeatedly in the notebook laying in my lap. For the longest time, I've struggled with the perfect title for our business and charity. That is until today, when it smacked me in the face.

With a triumphant smile, I toss everything aside to grab my phone.

After a single ring, he picks up. "Princess…"

"I got it!"

"Hold on, let me put you on speaker so Axel can hear." There's a moment of silence. "Okay, go ahead."

"Precious Tomorrow's."

"Aye! Good one." Maeson says.

"I'm in agreement. It represents us all," Axel says.

"Right? Not only is there a deep meaning for us, but everyone else we're helping. Tomorrow may never be guaranteed, but its the most precious thing we have to live and fight for."

"That's exactly why the name fits," Axel says. "I'll have the final paperwork filed, while you and Maeson design the logo."

"Deal. Anything else you need me to do?"

"Nope. We're good for now." Maeson says.

"Okay, guys. Talk to you later." I chuck my phone on the couch and fist pump the air.

Our plans are working out. My dreams really are coming true, aren't they? Deep breath. Life can be good, I see that now.

"Time for some music. I need to celebrate." I grab my iPod, selecting the latest playlist. Kevin Andersson's song, *'I Follow Your Heartbeat'* streams through the speakers. I turn the volume up to the fullest and snuggle on the couch with my day planner.

I have to keep better track of my days. The last few weeks were hectic as hell between my full time work with the shelter, throwing a nice Thanksgiving dinner for the gang, dates with Maeson, and spending time with Mo to plan the baby's gender reveal. As my life evolves, the requests for my time grows with it. Up next, an unforgettable Christmas party.

I'm beyond grateful for the new life I've been given. I much prefer busy days over the ones I used to have.

One of my latest favorite songs, *'Ruleta'* by Inna thumps through the speakers, filling my ears.

I also prefer dancing over sitting.

I toss my planner aside, leaping to my feet and sway my hips to the beat, shimmying around my living room, through the kitchen, and back toward the massive covered windows. I pull the curtains aside, revealing darkness lit by beautiful city lights.

How late is it?

Nine o'clock shines above the oven. Four hours have gone by, and I didn't even realize it. I'm also surprised I haven't heard from Maeson.

Maybe I should check on him?

No way! He's a grown man. If he wants to see me, he'll find me.

So, then what should I do for the rest of the night?

Sitting around alone doesn't sound appetizing in the least, and Molly won't be up for anything at this hour with her pregnancy schedule—in bed by eight like clockwork. At this point, Crossroads is my best option.

But I look like shit.

Who cares? Messy bun, jean shorts, and a tank top never

offended anyone on a Wednesday. I giggle to myself as I grab my keys and wallet from the kitchen counter.

Crossroads it is.

"SAM. LONG TIME NO SEE." I embrace her, squeezing tightly.

"Too long." She pulls away and narrows her eyes. "Shit hit the fan at Molly's party, huh?"

"A little."

With a smile, she slides a vodka cranberry with lime my way. "Tell me all about it."

I take a refreshing sip. "Not much to say. We actually resolved our tiff the same night."

"That's not what I heard."

"What do you mean? Who did you talk to?"

She grimaces. "Maes and I only have one person in common."

I roll my eyes. "Ashlie."

Sam nods. "She came to the bar drunk and spilled her soul to anyone who'd listen. She even said some pretty harsh things about you, but what caught my attention was her declaration on getting back together with Maeson."

"Is that what she thinks?"

"Yup. She said he professed his undying love for her right before you walked in on them making out."

"Wow. She's delusional. That's not how it went down, but I couldn't care less what she's telling people. Although, I do care to know what she said regarding me."

"Oh… I'm not sure that's a good idea."

"Please, go ahead. I don't mind."

"She basically degraded you in every way possible, mainly focusing on your figure. But, one of my patrons came to your defense, claiming curvy women are as sexy as thin women. The man was so adamant in his argument, Ashlie clammed up right away."

"No way!"

"Astonishing, I know!" She laughs. "Anyway, later on, I spoke to the guy. I thought you knew each other since he was so affected by the conversation, but he was upset because his daughter's constantly bullied about her size at school."

"Poor thing. I remember those days. Kids can be as hateful as adults are. Luckily, Ashlie's words don't affect me. I've outgrown my insecure stage."

Almost outgrown…

"I'm glad. She's not worth the distress."

"No, she's not. Did you get a chance talk to her yourself?"

"Yeah, right before she left. I gave her a piece of my mind. She called me a traitor, so I told her to fuck off and to never set foot in my bar again."

"Wow. You broke a bridge for me?"

"That bridge was destroyed when she left me. No sweat off of my back. Her tossing me to the curb was for the best because shortly after, I found my soul mate."

"That's true. Fate intervened for the better."

"Exactly." Sam lips turn down and she sighs. "Did he tell you?"

I peer at her quizzically. "About?"

"His…"

"Oh, yeah."

She wraps her arms around herself. "How is he? How did it go?"

"He's okay and it went as well as expected. I'm still reeling. I can't imagine the pain he lives with."

"Me either."

For a few moments, neither of us speak. Sam seems to be lost in her thoughts, and I have nothing more to say since I don't know how much Maeson's told her.

"Ruby?" Sam touches my arm.

"Yup?"

"I'm not sure if you've noticed, but Maeson's different. When you think he's not trying to be the man you deserve, he really is."

"How do you know?"

"The night you danced on the bar, he unknowingly dropped his guard in front of me. After he put you in the Uber, he spent an hour or so drinking alone. He turned away every woman who came to his table. That was not the normal Maes we all know."

"He did?"

"I swear it. That wasn't the only occasion. We've had other private discussions about you. I won't break his confidence, but you should know, in the last couple of months you've turned his life upside down as much as he has with yours."

My jaw drops.

"A lot to process. Just take some time to think about everything. Be one hundred percent sure you're willing to commit to him. Don't be like his ex and mess with his emotions. Please."

"No... I... I won't."

Sammie smiles. "Good." Her grin falters as she peers past me.

I turn to see a man waving his glass in the air.

"Sorry, sweetie, I'll be right back."

"Don't worry, I need to go home anyway." I walk around the bar and pull Sam into a hug. "See you later."

For the rest of the week, I lived on autopilot. I kept replaying what Sam told me. Her words made me realize I'm not the only one in danger of being hurt. One slip up by either Maeson or me, and we could cause each other much more damage than a simple broken heart.

But how can I promise something bad won't happen? Until I make peace with my past, I can't guarantee anything.

Nightmares continue to plague me as does the desire to run the second I'm overwhelmed. My disconnection from reality will be our downfall not Maeson's. He's better at hiding his pain than me.

Is he really better at it? Or is Maeson's pain so embedded in him, it's part of his very being? Just like it will be with you if you don't accept what has happened and grow from it. I'm trying, though. I just need more time.

Speaking of time, I have too much to do to be sitting in this car, twiddling my thumbs. There're two people I'd like to visit today—Molly and hopefully Aria. With Maeson's demanding schedule these days, I've found myself alone too many times to count and depending on a guy for company isn't the way I want to live my life.

I did with my exs, and I refuse to do it with Maeson. I finally have the girlfriends I wished for. I can't take them for granted.

During the twenty-minute drive to Molly and Jax's house, I admire the beauty surrounding me. Their development consists of mansion sized brick homes, perfect landscaped lawns, and fancy European cars.

Every girls dream—except for me.

Personally, I prefer a small cozy home hidden away from the chaos of busy streets. Living in a city my entire life changed my opinion on the area I'd like to raise my future children in.

A cute home with a big backyard so they can run around without a care in the world.

I'm so deep in thought, I pass house number thirteen. "Great. Now I have to drive around the block." Turning left and another left, I'm back on the right road. This time, I drive slowly, paying better attention.

Two cars are in the driveway—one is Maeson's.

So, this is where you've been hiding today.

I walk up the three steps and tap the doorbell.

Within seconds, Molly appears. "Hey," she whispers. "go upstairs. Quick. I'll be right up."

With a frown, I nod, but don't question her. Instead, I wander the second floor, sneaking peeks behind each door. The rooms are massive, even the baby's room is the size of a master suite.

While I wait for Molly, I find myself mesmerized by the crib against the wall. Instinctively, I lay a hand over my belly and imagine what could've been. A tear slides down my cheek, and I brush it away as footsteps approach.

It wasn't meant to be. He wouldn't have been a proper father. Don't dwell. But I would've been a good mom. You were too young. So, what? I …

"Do you like it?"

I clear my throat before facing her. "Yeah. It's fantastic. But it's missing any sign of a gender, my friend."

"Soon. You'll all know soon enough."

I lift a shoulder and pout. "But I want to know now."

Molly laughs. "No. Everything is planned for the reveal, and I want you to be surprised."

"Ugh. Fine." I giggle as she swats my arm. "Okay, then if you won't tell me that, can you tell me why Maeson's here?"

"Oh. Shhhh. Come." She drags me down the hallway and into her bedroom, closing the door behind her. "Those two are in cahoots about something, but he doesn't want you to know he's here, and I totally forgot you were coming over. Damn baby brain I tell ya."

"That's alright. Do you know what he's planning?"

"Nope. He's been tight lipped about it with me. Can you believe it? I'm his best friend." She rolls her eyes as she bubbles with laughter.

"What a bum. How could he?" I join in on her amusement.

"How could he, is right." Molly pats the humongous king-sized bed. "Sit."

I hop on to the tall mattress and lay on my back.

"Did it hurt?" Molly asks.

"What?"

"Your loss."

"I don't know what you're talking about."

"Yes, you do. Your eyes have tears in them, and you were holding your stomach protectively like pregnant women do. You'd only do that if you're currently expecting or once were."

"Oh, no. I was just imagining what it'd be like. That's all."

"Liar. Please don't shut me out. You've talked to me about everything, yet this you want to hide?"

"I just… never talked about it."

"Then do so now. I'm here for you always and forever, honey bunches of oats."

Her preferred nickname for me makes me smile. "It was a long time ago. Doesn't matter anymore."

"To me it does."

Tell her. Just breathe. She already knows the worst of the worst.

"I was a stupid eighteen year old who, believed I'd found my one true love. Our dynamic wasn't traditional, and I didn't care about the class difference between us. I assumed he didn't either, but I was wrong. Regardless of his lies, I wanted my baby, he or she had no fault in our breakup. I would've loved and cherished my little pumpkin." A sob rips from my chest, and I cover my face with my hands.

Molly's warm arms wrap around my body and lays her head next to mine. "Slow down, honey. Who is this *he*?"

"The ex before I met Ray."

"Does mystery man have a name?" She brushes my curls back and lifts my hands, forcing me to look at her.

"Angelo."

She nods. "Okay. What happened between you and Mr. Angelo?"

Don't cry. Explain facts. Keep it simple. Be strong.

I straighten my shoulders and take a deep breath. "A lot in a short time. I met him right after I left the foster home, and we connected on a level we both needed. Our age differences didn't matter since I was eighteen. So, things quickly lead from one to another. I fell in love, and next thing you know, I was pregnant. The day I went to tell him, he broke the news he was engaged to marry a wealthy girl who met his parents approval. Someone he supposedly didn't love, but had no choice in the matter. I was so ashamed and upset, I left him and never turned back." I struggle against the tears threatening to spill and shrug.

Mo shakes her head. "First, I don't like Angelo, he seems like a little boy unworthy of anyone's affection, let alone my best friend's. Secondly, what happened after you left? What about the baby?"

My head swims with the events that lead to my miscarriage. As much as I want to forget the pain, the day I lost my child is a memory I'll forever hang on to. "I was distraught over losing my forever guy. The one who didn't cause me physical pain. The one who had the same wants and needs as me. Which in the end, our similarities didn't matter, status was his deciding factor."

"But you're wealthy, what more did he want?" Mo rolls her eyes.

"He didn't know. I never told him because I wanted a man to care for *me* not my bank account." I sigh. "The entire ordeal hit me hard, and I fell into a deep sadness I couldn't escape. My life was turned upside down and my heart was broken... again. At first, I didn't sleep or eat much, but for the baby I pushed the hurt aside, forcing myself to forget him. But I was too late. The stress took a toll on my pregnancy and at eleven weeks..." Salty wetness boils over the edges of my eyes and down my cheeks, stopping at my lips.

"Oh, Lord almighty!" Molly covers her mouth. "I can't even begin to imagine how difficult that was. And to go through it alone!" Her voice cracks as she pulls me into her embrace.

The sight of Molly's distraught expression reminds me of her current condition and how bad any kind of distress is for her. So, I buck up and detach from my sorrow. "Don't worry. It was a long time ago, I'm okay now. The experience was a difficult lesson, but I learned from it. What happened after destroyed me completely, which is why I had to move. Too many sad memories to relive in one city. When I look back at the last few years, I know I mourned my baby the best I could and will always love my angel. My miscarriage happened so quickly, the realization of a chance at motherhood never truly sunk in. One second, I was pregnant, and the next, I wasn't. Most women are lucky enough to have an ultrasound or hear the heartbeat, but I was so overwhelmed, I didn't make it to the doctor in time. I was probably better off without, since the image or sound would've made it much more real."

"You're right. And I'm a big believer in what's meant to be will be. Our lives are built on multiple destined lessons, making us stronger and better prepared for the bigger picture."

"Exactly. That's why I refused to give up hope on having a family of my own. Although, I need more growing and learning to do before then." I smile.

"Don't we all." Molly frowns as she shakes her head. "Just don't shove everythin' underneath the bed and call it a day, ya know? I tried and it doesn't work. You just sink deeper into a void of the past, and eventually, you lose sight of what's real."

Perplexed by her words, I furrow my brow. "What's hidden under your bed, Mo?"

"My fear of the past repeating itself, doubt of being a terrible mother like mine was, and losing Jax the way I lost my dad. But those are only a few of the things."

"You a bad mom? Never. There isn't a bad bone in your body. And you'll never lose that man, he's stuck to you permanently—whether you want him or not. Now, regarding your past and your father, I'm not sure what happened since you avoid discussing it." I wiggle my eyebrows at her and shake a finger in her face.

"Noticed that, did ya?" She smirks.

"Sure did. Right from the start, so spill the beans."

"Well… what can I say? When I was a kid my parents were very much in love—with me and each other, but when I turned seventeen something changed. My mom changed… she threw my dad out one random night. I didn't even know she was unhappy. I was beyond shocked when it happened. Then my mom started to treat me like I wasn't even her child. She'd say my presence was disturbing because I look too much like my dad. It broke my heart. How could she raise me and suddenly, act as if I meant nothing to her? Anyway, my dad ended up getting his own place, and I'd stay with him more often than not. He was always good to me. He showed me the love she didn't." Tears shed from Molly's eyes, and she wipes them away.

I reach out, taking her hand in mine and squeeze it lightly. "If this is too much for you, please stop. I'd never forgive myself if you go into premature labor."

She shakes her head. "No, I'm okay. Actually, this is liberating."

I pat her hand. "If you say so…"

She smiles. "Where was I? Oh, right… Over the years, dad never dated. He kept hoping mom would take him back, but it didn't happen. She dated man after man—each one worse than the next. Then once I fully developed these woman curves and breasts, her boyfriends started to notice, which caused extra problems. The hatred my mom had toward me grew and it ultimately destroyed our already faulty mother-daughter relationship."

"Why would she hate you? I mean, even if you do take after your dad appearance wise, how could she feel so strongly against her baby girl?"

"It wasn't just that…"

"Oh?"

"One night, while I was at her house—cleaning the mess she regularly left behind after a drinking binge—her man of the day showed up. I told him my mom was sleeping off last night's party, but he refused to leave and barged into her room. I continued to work because if I didn't clean the house to her standards, she'd tear me a new one. After a while, I heard something break then smashing, so I panicked and rushed to her. He was… they were… not fighting." Molly releases a long breath. "I should've never went into that room. He tossed my mom aside, and she laid there watching… completely uncaring as he touched me. No matter how hard I fought against him, I couldn't get away." A gut-wrenching sob bursts from Molly's lips. "I'll never forget how she laughed the entire time or the slurred words she muttered in my face as he pinned me to the mattress. *That's what you deserve. How's your precious daddy gonna love ya' now? Both of you can rot in hell. I wanted more. He took everything from me. My youth, my happiness, and my future. For what? For a baby he absolutely had to have. A family, he said. Well here's your fucking family. Look at us now.'* She never wanted me, Ruby. My mom never loved me."

My jaw drops. "Molly…" Holding her tight with one arm, I touch her belly with the other. "You're nothing like her. You want this baby. You already love it. Don't you dare think so little of yourself."

Molly bobs her head up and down. "That's what I tell myself every day, but part of me is terrified I'll turn out like her. Like somethin' in me will snap, and one day, I'll hate the baby."

"Never. That's not who you are, love. The difference is you want this little peanut growing inside of you. And it seems she never wanted children at all."

"That's not what my dad told me, though. He said she was excited about having a baby with him. But he also thinks she had postpartum and never said anything about it. She let the depression stew until she snapped. She didn't get help, didn't want it, and refused when he tried."

"So, you're afraid of having postpartum? Is that it?"

"Yeah…"

"Then I'll watch you like a hawk after you give birth, and if I see any signs, I'll be the first person to do something about it."

"Thank you. Please do. I don't want to be like her—ever."

"You won't. I promise."

"That's what dad said when I told him about the baby."

"Oh, he knows? I'm sorry assumed—" I immediately shut my mouth and clear my throat. My thoughts took a wrong turn and this isn't the time to express what I assumed happened to her dad. "Where is he?"

"Jail."

My head snaps upward. "Really? Why?"

"He's been there since I was twenty-four. All because of that fucked up night. When my mom's boyfriend showed up, I had texted my dad, asking him to pick me up. I didn't trust any of the men my mom hung out with, and neither did my dad." Molly sighs. "Anyway, fast forward to me being pinned down. Right before the guy has the chance to… violate me… my dad shows up." She takes a deep breath and hangs her head. "He was all reaction. Beat the guy to a pulp. There was so much blood, I thought he'd killed him. And of course, my mom was quick to call the cops. They showed up before we had get a chance to get out of the house. Everything else was a blur of screaming, hands up, you're under arrest, and next thing you know my dad's in the back of a police car."

"He's been in jail ever since? Five years is a long time for protecting his daughter from a psycho, isn't it? I mean, what do I know about the legality part, but it seems much. How's that justice?"

"It's not. My dad's fate was dealt the day the guy died in the hospital. The beating he took was more than his body could handle. They said self-defense or not, he ultimately killed a man."

"Any person who can harm another person against their will should die. He was planning to rape you. Your dad defended his baby girl when no one else would, not even her mother." Disgusted, I rush to my feet and pace. "How long will he be there? Can you fight it?"

"I'm hoping with good behavior, not too much longer. I want him to meet our little one. Axel's working on his case, and he's hoping to get him released sooner than later. The judge was kind, though. He gave my dad a lighter sentence, just not light enough to prevent prison time."

I stop pacing and peer at the tears staining Molly's cheeks. "You're having this baby in a few months…" I rub a hand over my face. "We need to join forces and find a way for your dad to be released."

"Thank you, Ruby. That means a lot to me. Until I met you, I felt so alone and lost regardless of the great people in my life. Somehow, today you made those foolish fears disappear."

"You should've told me months ago, Molly. I'd told you everything—you were my outlet, I should be yours too. Unless… you don't feel the same way about our friendship as I do?"

"Oh, my lord, woman. Of course, I do. Don't you dare think that. I was ashamed. That's all. Your parents were so kind and loving, not alcoholics or in jail."

"First of all, never be ashamed around me. I'd never ever judge you. Second, your mom's troubled, but not your father. You describe him as a caring man, so why be humiliated he ended up in jail saving you from a fate I experienced personally at fifteen? Believe me, I'd rather have had someone do the same for me than live with the pain and scars my bastard foster father left me with." I caress the harsh line marking the skin across my side and belly.

Her eyes widen. "You've never showed them to me… can I… see?"

"No. They're ugly. They're the ugliest part of me. You'll look at me differently if I show you."

"I won't, I promise. Please." Molly touches my arm, turning my palm up to reveal my tattoo. "Strength, remember? You are strength." Molly peers into my eyes, smiling sadly. "One day, I'll be as strong as you, and I'm gonna get this same tattoo." She traces a finger around the black symbol. "Please. Show me."

"Okay, Mo. But I warned you." With a long and deep breath, I turn so my back faces her and reach for the bottom of my shirt. Slowly, I lift the material above my head. At the sound of Mo's gasp, I close my eyes, holding my breath.

She's disgusted. Why did I show her? I can't face her, all I'll see is pity. I don't want pity. Please don't pity me.

"Ruby." Molly's voice is a hushed whisper.

My heart sinks. I don't want to face her. I can't face her.

"Ruby, oh, Ruby. How did you... survive these?"

"Honestly? I don't know. I just did. Sometimes, I wish I would've died."

A piercing whimper flows from her. "I'm so sorry. This is worse than I ever imagined. Can I?"

I break into a cold sweat, but I force my body to stop shaking and nod. I squeeze my eyes tighter.

Her soft fingers touch my bare skin, moving across the deep marks.

I cringe as phantom pain seers through me.

She quickly retreats. "Do they still hurt?"

"Just the memories."

"Ladies..." A familiar deep and accented voice fills the room.

I don't want to open my eyes, but I do anyway.

Before us, in the doorway, stands a brooding Maeson. His hands are stuffed in his pockets and he's sporting a massive frown.

Is he mad because I showed Molly or upset because he saw my scars? Please don't be the latter. You told me they didn't disgust you...

"Mae Mae," Molly says before I can utter a single word.

Thank God. I'm not sure I could manage speaking.

Shame fills me, and I wrench my shirt down. With one last

look at Molly, I make a poor attempt at a smile and brush past Maeson, rushing down the stairs and out of the house.

Deep breath. Just freaking breathe.

The technique doesn't work and my heart continues to hammer in my chest. I put my car into drive and speed down the road as tears brim at the edges of my eyes.

I'm so ugly. My body is damaged goods. They all feel bad for me.

I. Do. Not. Want. Their. Fucking. Pity.

See past the scars. Please see past them.

We all bear some sort of mark left over from our pasts, don't we? Maeson and Molly have had troubled lives, but I don't show them pity. Never have and never will. I respect them too much.

My physical scars. Maeson's tattoos. Molly's emotional pain.

We all have…

Broken, torn, or scarred wings.

17

MAESON

Off goes my little runner. But why? What upset her enough to zoom out of here?

"Bastard! Ya scared Ruby away. Did ya see how humiliated she was? She must think we're repulsed by her." Molly's high-pitched voice pierces my ears.

Repulsed? Is she out of her mind? Mo has no idea how much more I respected Ruby after she showed them to me. Those scars reveal Ruby's strength and make her sexier than any other woman I've ever met.

Repulsed she says. Fuck. Ruby can't think… She assumed… I shake my head. "I did no such thing. I didn't get a chance to fucking speak."

Molly's arms dart into the air. "With that damn menacing expression on your face? Of course that's what she thought, asshole."

"Then you both misunderstood. When I walked in, Ruby looked distressed, so naturally, I was concerned. The sight of her body turns me on, not the opposite! Ruby's the most beautiful woman I know. I swear it. Were you?"

"Was I what?" She raises an eyebrow.

"Revolted?"

"Never! I'm in awe of Ruby. But in the moment, I was just shocked by the amount of pain she'd endured and still manages to smile every day. If only she'd given me the chance to explain. I feel so terrible, Mae Mae." Molly conceals her face with her hands.

"Believe me, so do I. Let me call her." I slide my phone out of my pocket, holding the home button until Siri's voice sounds. "Siri, call, Princess." The screen lights up, but I'm sent right to voicemail. "Ruby, lass. Please, come back. You misinterpreted our reactions. Molly and I want to talk to you. If you won't come back, call or text us, *please*." Ending the message, I tap the red button and sigh.

Deep breath. She'll call back. Just breathe.

"What should we do? We have to do something." Molly frowns.

"Right now, she needs space. If we chase her, she'll run further away. Let's wait and see."

Wait and see? Since when? Since Molly's pregnant and any added stress is a terrible idea.

"Doing nothing feels wrong, Mae Mae. She's my best friend." She rubs a hand over her swollen belly.

"I've been through this before. She needs to process her thoughts, then she'll call us. And if she doesn't? I'll make sure to find her… I always do."

"Okay. If you say so, but if something happens to her? It's on you."

Just breathe. She's all right. I know she is…

I peer at my feet then back up at Molly. "Aye, it is."

Molly narrows her eyes. "Why are ya here, anyway?"

"Oh… that's a secret."

"What kind?" A small smile graces her lips.

I laugh. If anyone loves secrets, it's Molly Briggs.

"Is it about Ruby?"

"Aye."

"Is it a big surprise?" She taps a finger on her belly and grins. "Oh! A Christmas gift? A sparkly one?" Her blue eyes shine as her grin widens.

"Yes. Yes. And no."

"Tight lipped, mother fucker. Tell me. I won't say anything, I promise."

Knowing Molly, she'll never leave me alone until I tell her. "I found something a few weeks ago at Ruby's place and it gave me a great idea for her Christmas surprise."

"Oh, my Lord! What did ya find?" She beams.

"Come here."

She skips over to me. "Spill." Impatience laces her tone.

I laugh as I pull out a paper from my pocket, containing every single detail.

Molly seizes it from my fingertips and giggles. "Ssshhhiiittt! That's gonna be amazing. She'll love it." She slaps my shoulder. "Who knew you're such a romantic? Not me, that's for sure."

"Don't be so shocked. I do have some romance left in me."

"So when will you…"

"I'm not sure. That's what Jax and I were discussing. There's some trouble finding… you know… so that'll delay things."

"Won't you at least clue her in?"

I slice my head to the left.

"Oh, come on. You must. She'll be so thrilled. She needs some excitement in her life, especially for the holidays."

"The timing isn't falling into place. Christmas is a week away, and I need quite a few more days to make my final calls."

Molly bobs her head. "Rrriiiggghhhtttt. A week. Damn. Okay, so I'll to keep my trap shut until you're ready."

I shake a finger in her face. "You better."

"Cross my heart, boss."

"Good." As I turn to leave, our phones ring.

Molly looks up at me. "It's from Ruby."

"Mine is too."

Incoming Group Message: *I'm fine. Overwhelmed. Was worried you both were grossed out by… my body… but I'm okay. Thank you for calling. Off to bed. XoXo.*

"Maybe you should go to her?"

I nod. "I will, but I have one more thing to take care of first."

Molly grins. "Ruby's gift stuff?"

"Nope. This one's business."

"Oh… lame. Okay, then text me when you get to her place so I know she's really alright."

"Aye." I pull her into a hug before making my way downstairs.

"See ya, Maes." Jax says as I reach the bottom of the steps.

"Let me know if you…"

"You got it. And make sure you take care of that… It's time, brother." He pats my shoulder.

I nod and walk out the front door.

"**Thank you for coming.**" I force the words out between gritted teeth.

The stands before me smiling as she shoves my legs apart with hers. Her long fingernails dig into my black slacks and she purrs in the most disgusting way I've ever heard.

I clench the arms of my couch. The smell of her lifts bile to my throat. I have to do this. It's the only way.

How did I ever find her attractive? You did because back then you didn't know who she really was.

I lay a hand over her roaming ones. "Let's save the fun for later."

She sticks out her bottom lip. "But why not now? It's been too long since I've had you, Maeson."

I swallow hard, biting back the revulsion she brings forth. "First, we need to talk."

"Humph. Fine." She sits on my lap, wrapping her arms around my neck. "What's going on?"

What's going on is you ruined everything. Madison needed a mom. She passed away never knowing her own mother's touch.

It takes all the strength I have not to shove her from my knees. "Ashlie, you know how you've been blackmailing me these last few years? Accusing me of hurting and raping you?"

"Yeah…" She lifts an eyebrow and frowns. "But you know I lied. It was the only way I could keep you near."

"And take my money."

"I needed it. But I love you, always have."

"I see. So, you got yourself beat up by someone else, and took pictures in order to stay tied to me? Even knowing I could go to jail for a crime I didn't commit?"

"Yes. I was upset." She pouts again. "Please, forgive me."

"I'm trying to. That's why I asked you to see me."

"I was weak, but I'm not weak anymore. I won't do that again. Honest."

"I know you won't, Ashlie. You'll never hurt me or anyone I care for again."

"Huh?"

"You heard me. Your bullshit leverage is null and void." I stand and she topples to the floor.

"Wha—Wha—What?"

I grab my cell out of my pocket and show her the screen before hitting the end recording button. "We. Are. Done. Forever," I mutter.

"No!" She shrieks and slams a small fist onto my chest. "You fuckin' recorded me?" Ashlie continues to pound her hands against me. "You, slimy bastard. How could you?"

I narrow my eyes. "How could I? How about, how could you? Our baby died, and your first thought was money? You didn't even mourn her."

"I… I did… in my own way."

"What way was that? Blackmail Madison's father so you could bleed him dry? Oh, wait. No, you showed her how much you loved her by meeting her? Nope, not once. Hmmm… You gave her the affection she needed by dropping her on my lap and turned your back on her for good. Aye, sounds right. That's how you loved and grieved for our baby."

"Fuck you!"

"That's all you got?"

"I wasn't meant to be a mom, okay? I thought once I gave

birth, I'd feel something for her, but I didn't. I couldn't bear to see her, let alone hold her."

This is the mother's touch I wished Madison would've had? Fuck that. She was better off without.

My hands shake at my sides. "Get. Out."

Get out of my life. Give me a fighting chance to forget the damage you've caused. Just breathe. There's no sense in getting riled up only to make things worse.

A hysterical sob emits from her as she lunges past me. "You'll pay for this, Maeson. Just watch. You will regret fucking with me."

Following her rushed steps to the elevator, I release a long-ragged breath. "Your threats no longer work on me, Ashlie."

Just a few more seconds, and she'll be gone for good.

As the elevator doors close, a malicious smile spreads on her lips. "You sure about that?" Right before she disappears from my view, she winks.

An eerie prickle creeps up my spine and an involuntary shiver hits me. I squeeze my eyes shut, exhaling.

What more can this woman do? There's nothing left to lose.

The tattooed wings on my back sting and pain takes over my body as my daughter's face melds with someone else's. My eyes pop open and a terrifying thought stabs me square in the heart.

I do have one thing left to lose. Ruby...

18

Ruby

The sweet hazelnut and chocolate aroma of freshly brewed coffee fills my nostrils, bringing a smile my lips. With a long, drawn out yawn, I roll over and stretch my stiff muscles.

Woken up by the scents of my favorite beverage is a pleasant surprise and there's only one person I can think of who'd do such a thing for me.

Maeson.

I peer at the alarm clock on the night stand—six in the morning.

Damn, that's early. I was hoping to sleep in.

Maeson must be in a bad mood or maybe he's worried about my overreaction yesterday? I hope he doesn't think I'm still upset. After calling Molly to discuss what happened, I never got the chance to speak to Maeson.

I need to ease his mind right away.

As get out of bed, I notice a paper covering Maeson's iPhone.

Press play. Then join me for coffee. XoXo

I pick up his phone and tap the button on the screen. Maeson's voice comes through, then…

Hers.

What the hell is she doing with him? Better yet, what the fuck is he doing with her?

My fingers tremble while I listen, and I clench my fist.

Wait. He's talking about… Oh, my God. He's recording her admission to all the lies she's told. He's finally free of her. He did it.

I toss his phone aside and rush to the kitchen. Maeson is dressed down in his usual muscle revealing, tight as hell black t-shirt and fitted black joggers and holding a steamy mug of coffee. His smile is wide and of course, dimple filled.

"You're free?"

He slices his head to the right in that sexy way I've come to love.

"See! This is why I watch cop shows. Never doubt them again." I dash to his side and seize the red cup, setting it down so I can pull him into my arms.

"But I never doubted you, lass. You're the only thing I believe in anymore," he whispers against my ear.

"Me too, laddie." I grin, peering up at his handsome face.

He returns the smile, but it doesn't seem to be genuine.

"What's wrong?" My excitement falters.

"I think I've awoken the dragon."

"So? Not like she has fire to breathe down our necks. Only Daenerys—mother of dragons does."

He chuckles then shrugs. "Never know with her."

"Let her try something. I'll fight her tooth and nail before she gets another shot at you."

"Connecting with your inner lioness, are we?" Maeson squeezes me and drops a peck on my temple before letting go.

"Aye, old man. You have your beast, and I have my own."

"That we do." He hands me my coffee.

I take it gratefully and settle on the stool next to the kitchen island. Steam rises from the mug and against my face as I relish in my first sip. "Mmm. This is fabulous. Me thinks you should be here making coffee every morning."

"That'd be a great idea, but I don't spend enough nights here. When you become less *'Miss Independent'* and more *'Miss It's Okay to Live with A Man'*, it'll be a real possibility. Until then, it appears you'll be making your own morning brews."

"We don't have to live together for you to wake me with these glorious scents. Just get up super-duper early."

Maeson raises an eyebrow and smirks. "Ah! You expect to be spoiled?"

"Why not? I'm worth it." I giggle.

His gaze darkens. "You're worth everything I have to give."

Heat rushes to my cheeks, and I peek down at my dangling feet. "Thank you."

"Don't thank me for stating a fact."

I look up to find Maeson barely an inch from my face. "Personal space. Have you heard of it? I'm not so sure you have because you're crowding mine." My tone is as sassy as the grin spreading across my lips.

Maeson breaks out in a hysterical laugh. "I can't win with you, can I? Give the woman your heart and she dismisses it." He grips his chest with a grimace.

He's kidding, but…

"I'm not dismissing it, Maeson. I'm just not ready for it."

"Not… ready? After all these months?"

How do I explain myself without offending the man?

The classic and quick answer, *'it's not you, it's me'* is over played. Yet it's the most fitting answer. Although, knowing Maeson, saying something so lame would royally piss him off. "There are too many unresolved issues in our lives."

"So? We can settle them together." He shakes his head. "I'm not asking you to marry me, Ruby. All I want—"

"One day at a time, remember?"

With a straight face, Maeson gives me his typical response by slicing his head to the right.

"I'm not worried you'd hurt me—I'm afraid of me hurting you. If I accept your heart along with anything else you're offering me so freely, and I somehow fuck everything up… I'll never forgive myself." A long sigh leaves my lunges. "I don't trust myself yet to fully commit to you because of the fears plaguing my every thought."

Maeson's scowl deepens. "How could you possibly hurt me? You're the most caring person I know. And what kind of fears are we talking about here?" He leans against the granite counter, crosses his legs at the ankles, and stuffs his hands in his pockets.

He couldn't be sexier if tried.

I shrug. "The usual stuff…"

"Like what?"

"Internal insecurities. My mind has a way of running away with these random ideas, and as hard as I try, I can't stop them."

"Please explain."

"Trust is one. I trust you, but to a certain extent. All I need is one inkling to set off my roaming thoughts. Before I moved here is when this issue started. The smallest of lies he told caused me to turn into a woman I didn't recognize. I became a paranoid mess. There isn't a day I don't fight off that part of me in fear of history repeating itself."

"I'm not him, Ruby." Maeson pulls a hand out of his jean pocket, shoving it through his messy hair, then grips the back of his neck with a sigh. "I'd never lie to you or put myself in a position to do so. Believe me, I know what it's like when someone feeds you bullshit while they cheat on you. Which is one reason I avoid doing the same and for the second reason—I respect you too much."

My heart flutters in my chest, but my mind refuses to budge. "I get that but… what if, one day my insecurities annoy you to the point you're driven to give up on me?"

"Giving up is for idiots, and I'm not an idiot." He glares at me. "Why do you live your life by *'what ifs'*? No one can see the future—*not even you*. You're just creating extra paranoia for reason. And you most certainly don't have to add additional stress over me or over us."

I shrug. "You're asking me to explain something I can't make sense of myself. I'm not as confident as you. You must understand these fears are irrepressible parts of my makeup. The unknown terrifies me, and I try to break the constant focus on the uncontrollable things. I really do. The anxiety meds helped a lot—they made me feel normal. But like I told you before, I refuse to depend on them to live a regular life."

Maeson's grim expression softens as he glides a hand across my cheek, stopping at my chin. With one long finger, he lifts my face to him. "Princess, the unknown scares us all. Everyone has their own internal fears. Shit, even the most self-assured man out there is suffocated by them. It's just a matter of how you choose to deal with what haunts you. You think it wasn't hard for me?"

I shake my head.

"Oh, believe me, the road I traveled was difficult. I didn't have half the strength you had to continue living after my life went to shit. I tried to kill myself." He touches the thin scars hidden beneath the intricate tattoos on his right arm then trails a finger up to his neck where another scar stretches across his skin.

He lifts his eyes and pure agony emits from them. "I sank into a deep depression and drowned in liquor. I fucked every woman possible so I could forget... So I could..." He grabs his hair, tugging at it. "release the beast Ashlie created. Give the broken part of me what he craved most—to destroy, to hurt, and to... protect me when I couldn't handle the loss of my baby girl. I was weak, Ruby. Too weak to manage the pain, and before I knew what was happening, the damaged man and the angry man became one. We detached from feeling any emotion. We... *I* stopped living the life I dreamed of once Madison was gone." Maeson hangs his head and groans. "See? I'm not as confident as you seem to think."

My heart rams against my chest. I didn't think those scars were self-administered, I thought... I'm not sure what I thought. Just the idea of such a strong, vital, and cocky man wanting to permanently end his life is inconceivable.

Shock courses through me as I try to imagine the agony he was dealing with.

I admit, when I was living in the foster home ending the nightmare that was my life crossed my mind, but I never had the balls to do it. I knew if I did, it would've been like slapping my parents in the face after all the hard work they'd put in to provide me with financial security before passing away.

Instead, I dealt with the abuse by shutting myself off from the world, which in turn helped me survive. I lost parts of myself in the process, tucking everything away until it was safe to piece myself together. Now here I am... I made it...

Sort of.

I've been to hell and back, yet Maeson's story guts me. I'd rather relive my life than lose a child. The trials of my past broke me, but Maeson's shattered him completely.

He understands my constant need to escape. But instead of running, he sought the eternal way out.

At the sight of Maeson's sad smile, I sigh. "No, I guess you're not really the arrogant man you make yourself appear to be."

He laughs and lifts my hand, kissing it with his soft lips. "I wish because that would mean I had an easy life."

Dimples. I focus on them and tilt my head, watching him. "Finally, your ups and downs make sense to me. I've seen each part of you before, but I didn't understand why you're as split apart as I am. And now that I do, I have much more respect for you." I capture his long fingers, giving them a squeeze. "When you said I was hiding behind a wall like a scared little girl, you weren't just talking about me were you?"

His green eyes fall shut as he exhales. "No, lass, I wasn't. No matter how hard I pretend with everyone else, you see right through me—you see my shattered soul as I see yours."

"Is this why you've been so adamant about us healing each other? Am I the cure to your beast? The glue for the fragments left unsealed? And are you the medication I'm in dire need of to treat what's been done to me?"

Maeson lifts his head, slicing it to the right. "Something like that."

"Why me?" The question I've been asking myself for the last five and a half months slips from my mouth with ease.

Maeson purses his lips. "Remember the first night we met?"

I nod. "At the hotel before I moved into Rose Garden."

A devilish grin spreads across his face. "Aye. The moment I saw you in person, my beast shifted within me. It was as if… my soul recognized you." His sexy smile disappears. "Then we *connected*, which for you was a one-night stand, but for me it was more than that. I didn't realize exactly how much more until recently. Well, I did, but I refused to acknowledge what you made me feel." Maeson glides his hand down my cheek. "When I'm around you, my rage evaporates. You make me forget. You help me heal." His voice cracks as he leans into me. "You"—he licks my bottom lip—"are why I chose you. Everything you are, is everything I am not and wish I could be."

The beat of my heart drums in my ears. I beg the overwhelmed organ to remain within the tight walls of my rib cage. Tears sting my eyes, and I breathe in deeply then exhale, releasing every emotion I held back as Maeson bared his soul.

No man has ever made me feel like a true Princess or even tried to. Yet this one has done nothing but since we met. Why did it take me this long to see it or to accept his words as genuine truths?

I open my mouth to speak, but nothing comes out. Words are not enough. Sentences are not enough. Nothing spoken will show him how much he affects me—how much he's come to mean to me.

Deep breath. Just breathe. In and out. Tell him… tell him how you feel.

I want to, but I'm scared.

He did, why can't you? You're strong. Do it.

My second attempt is worthless. All I manage is a pathetic whimper.

"Ruby, Princess. Don't cry, please." Maeson's warm arms cloak me, drawing me into his hard chest. "You asked me for honesty, and I gave it to you, love. I didn't mean to upset you."

"You didn't." I sniffle.

Maeson kisses the top of my head. "Then why are those big brown eyes shedding tears?"

"Because what you make me feel is more than my heart can handle. You treat me like—"

"The princess you are." His deep voice strokes my ears, resonates in my mind, and takes hold of my soul.

I nod and tighten my grip on his shirt.

"You deserve nothing less from me or anyone else who crosses your path." He steps back and lifts my chin, gently wiping away the wetness from my cheeks. "Accepting my words, my precious, is the first step in overcoming part of your insecurities. Know your worth, believe in your worth, and others will too."

"I can try…"

"You will do it. Not try. Do, Ruby, do it."

"How can I force myself to see more in me than there actually is?"

Maeson stares at me through a daze. He seems oddly frozen in place until he frowns. "Madison used to be very insecure. She would beg me to tell her stories of a Princess who had wee problems with her heart and beat the odds, living long enough to find her Prince Charming. Even at her young age, she needed something to believe in—something to give her strength. At times, she'd cry so hard because she didn't think she was pretty enough for a prince and it'd take me hours to calm her down. As a man, I didn't understand why she worried about such trivial things, but as a father, I didn't give a fuck about why—as a father I needed to fix it. I knew the older she got, the worse her lack of self-assurance would get, so I scoured the internet on how to build my baby girl's confidence. A video on YouTube stuck with me." Maeson's face contorts as his eyes become glossy and a single tear trickles down his cheek. "Every morning, like that man in the video, we'd stand in front of a mirror, and I'd have Madison repeat after me—*'I, Madison, am smart. I, Madison, am strong. I, Madison, am beautiful. I, Madison, am not better than anyone, and nobody is better than me. I, Madison, am amazing. I, Madison, am fearless. I, Madison, believe in myself. I, Madison, am brave. I, Madison Kiva Alexander, am loved, and I love others.'* Then I'd ask her questions, and she'd answer them. *'What happens if you fall? I get back up, daddy. What do you do if someone upsets you? I forgive them, they don't know any better, but I do. Who loves you? You do, silly. How much? To the moon and back.'* To the moon and back, baby. To the moon and back, I'll love her." Maeson's voice cracks again and his shoulders shake. The green in his eyes brightens as full tears shed from them and his breaths turn into shallow rapid puffs of air, fighting to escape his lungs.

I watch horrified as he tries to regain control and find myself struggling to breathe along with him. "Maes—"

He drops to his knees and covers his face as sobs wrack him.

My stomach clenches at his suffering, and I fall to the floor beside him, cloaking him with my body as we rock back and forth. "She knows you love her. You showed her repeatedly. You were a great father to her, Maeson. Don't ever doubt that."

"I didn't save her, though."

"But you did do everything in your power to give her a fighting chance and that's what matters. Losing her was inevitable based on her condition. It wasn't your fault."

He shakes his head as he continues to sob.

"Maeson, please, she wouldn't want you to destroy yourself like this."

Maeson shakes his head again. "You don't get it. I can't lose someone else I care for, Ruby. I need you to look in the mirror. I need you to say those things to yourself. I need to know you'll be okay. I need to know you won't buy fucking pills that can kill you. I beg of you. Promise me, like I made promises to you. Promises I will keep for the rest of my life."

The words I'll never forget.

I hear his soft accented voice in my head. *'I promise to stand by you for as long as you'll have me, to protect you like no one has before, and to show you what it feels like to be cherished by a real man.'* My insides practically melt as I remember what he said.

A sense of power flourishes within me, and I smile. "Maeson, I promise you won't lose me. I promise to believe in me and remind myself every day of each thing that makes me great. I promise I won't take any more pills and to take care of myself. I'll promise you anything you want, just please stop crying. Your devastation breaks my heart."

Maeson peers up at me with a small smile. "You better keep

your word because for once, I'm putting my full trust in a woman."

"I will, old man." With a grin, I brush away the hair covering his beautiful green eyes.

He laughs and scrubs a hand over his face. "Here we go again. Do I have to remind you what happens when you call me that?"

Bobbing my head, I rise to my feet and extend a hand to him.

Maeson looks at my offer oddly before accepting it. "Never needed a wee woman's help to get up before."

I playfully jab his ribs. "Never seen such a big burly man cry like a baby before, so we're even." Tugging his hand, I beckon him toward the bedroom.

With each step we take closer to our sanctuary, the painful ache in my heart subsides.

Today was a blessing in disguise. Today we've moved on to a new phase in our relationship. Our connection is deeper—now it contains…

Emotions.

While I wait for Aria to answer the doorbell, I clutch my travel mug filled with hot and steamy coffee. My teeth clank together as a shiver passes through me, and I groan.

For the first time, I'm experiencing one of those rare cold ass December days Molly told me about. I must've converted to a sun loving Texan because anything less than seventy degrees feels like brutal winter weather.

My bones literally ache from this arctic wind and a light sweater, long black tights, and knee-high leather boots aren't cutting it.

I reach to ring the bell again, but Aria pushes through the wobbly door. "Hey!" She grins. "Get inside. You look like an icicle."

"At this point, I am a damn icicle." We both laugh, and I pull her in for a hug.

Aria steps back, eyeing me up and down. "What's going on?"

"Nothing much. It's been a while, and I wanted to see you before the holiday madness takes over. How are you?" I check out her living room, noticing there's no sign of any decorations—not a tree, a bow, or tinsel in sight.

"I'm okay. Livin', you know?" Aria shrugs and peers down at the stained carpet.

"Sure do. So, speaking of festivities… Would you like to celebrate with the crew at Molly's place?"

Aria opens her mouth, then snaps it shut as her eyes dart toward the hallway.

He's here, hiding like a wuss. Face me. I know he won't, but I wish he would.

She rubs a hand up and down her arm, and I notice new dark purple blotches covering her pale skin.

"Aria," I whisper. "My offer still stands. Stay with me please. Those"—I point to the bruises—"are not acceptable. You said things are different. It doesn't look that way."

She shakes her head. "You don't understand. Everything is good with us. I just… bumped into the wall." There's panic in her voice as her frail body trembles.

I drop my voice an octave, "If you say so." My only option is to accept her lie. The garbage in this house doesn't need another reason to hurt my friend. "Will you come to the party, please? Molly has a big surprise for us all, and everyone would love to see you."

"I'm not sure." Her gaze travels to the darkness again. "Can we let you know later?"

Oh. She wants me to act like he's invited as well? No way. He's not welcome—ever.

"Well, Christmas is next week, honey. Tight notice already."

"Okay. Give me one second." She points to the hallway leading to her bedroom.

I do what Maeson taught me and slice my head to the right. As Aria disappears from sight, I release a harsh breath. I want to cry. I want to pound my fist into the wall. I want to scream. I want to fucking drag her out of this hell hole, but no, that's not a possibility with him home. I'm strong, but not enough to fight a man.

There must be another way to free her.

He's changed her back to her old self. My friend is withering away before my eyes, and I don't know how to stop it. The small amount of weight she did gain, she's seemed to have lost and then some. Which tells me she's on the hardcore drugs again, using them as her sustenance.

"Ruby… umm…" Aria reappears with tears in her eyes. "We can't come, but thank you for the invite. Maybe after the holidays we can do coffee?" She bows her head.

Why is it the victims carry all the guilt? Why is it the abusers get away with everything? Why? Because the world is unfair.

An idea pops into my head for a way to get her outside, away from him even if it's for a minute, and I almost smile.

Thanks detective shows.

A ray of hope fills me as I embrace Aria with a tight squeeze. Aria needs to feel my support, my love, and my understanding. "Sure, sweetie." I kiss her cheek and murmur against her ear, "Soon…"

Aria's shoulders quake. "Soon, what?"

"I will save you."

She nods and places her head in the crook of my neck as she cries in silence.

"Walk me out?" I say loud enough for *him* to hear and extend a hand to Aria.

She takes it and we step into the chilly air.

"After the new year." Aria says.

I raise an eyebrow.

"Do it then. I want to be with him till then."

My initial reaction is to demand why, but it'd make her feel cornered and that's the last thing I want to do. "You got it."

Her smile is bright and optimistic as I drive away. As much as I want to return the excitement, I can't. I've been in her position before and know the woman standing there is putting on a show only to appease me. But not for long if I have anything to do with it.

She has what I didn't. She has people who care for her—who love her. Aria has a family made of friends who'd go to the ends of the earth to save her.

19

MAESON

Christmas day. What was once my favorite holiday of the year has arrived.

I haven't had a reason to celebrate in so long…

"Ready?" Ruby wraps the last present for our friends and peers up at me with a breathtaking smile.

She's the light to my darkness.

"Aye. Let's get out of here before we're late, and hormonal Molly has a fit."

Ruby jumps to her feet and places each shiny silver wrapped gift in bright red bags that have *'Merry Christmas'* and *'Happy Holidays'* written across them.

I grab a few and we head to the ground floor.

"I can't wait to find out what they're having," Ruby says as we drive down the ramp and onto the highway.

"Me too. Soon enough, Princess."

When we arrive, the entire crew is already in celebration mode. Drinks are in everyone's hand and music streams through out the living room as they gather around a colorful tree. Molly outdid herself this year. The multi-colored decorations are placed to perfection as are the flashing lights.

"Mo, your skills are impeccable as always." I kiss her cheek and wrap an arm around her.

She rubs her swollen belly. "Thanks, but this time it wasn't me who decorated. It was Jax. He took over as I watched."

I widen my eyes. "Holy shit! Turning into a house-husband, are we?"

"Yeah. And proud of it." Jax laughs.

"Good for you. I'm not hating at all. Shit, part of me wishes I was in your place. Family life suits you."

"It will for you too… one day." Jax flicks his gaze over to Ruby who's chatting with the girls.

"I hope so."

"Don't hope. Make it happen." The sternness in Jax's voice surprises me.

"Aye, aye, Captain."

"Guys. Get over here. We have presents to unwrap. Quit gossiping." Molly shakes a red box in the air.

I grace her with my middle finger. "When a woman calls…"

"We run." Jax finishes my thought.

I approach the ladies, and Ruby pats an empty spot on the couch. I pull her into me, kissing her cheek. "I lo—"

"Okay, people. The time has come. Boy or girl?" Molly grins.

Timing is everything. And right before Mo cut me off wasn't it. Jax is right, though. If I want something, I need to make it happen. She's my better half. She's who I want to spend the rest of my life with, and I must take the right steps to prove it to her and soon.

Everyone shouts their guesses as I was lost in my own world, but I caught most of what was said and it seems they're spilt in the middle.

Molly giggles as she hands Jax the blue and pink container. With slow movements, she tears the paper away revealing a plain brown box. Then in even slower motions, she opens the thing. Blue balloons fly out of the box.

"It's a boy," Molly and Jax say.

My heart hammers in my chest.

A boy.

My brother will finally have the son he's always wanted, and I couldn't be happier for him. If there's one man in this world who'd be a perfect father, it's Jax.

"What are you naming him?" Bekka asks.

Jax beams and puffs out his chest. "My boy's name is, Alexander Lachlan Kieran."

My jaw drops. This I didn't expect. A namesake after Jax's Da I'd anticipate, but not after me.

The father-to-be meets my eyes. "We wanted to name him after his Godfather."

My mouth drops even further. "Godfather?"

"Yeah. You, Maes are my brother. Please do us the honor to be a second parent to my son."

I bow my head. "The honor is mine, brother. The honor is" — my voice cracks — "all mine." I stand and embrace the two people who've loved me like family ever since we first met.

"Oh, and Ruby?" Molly smiles.

"Yes?" Ruby's tear-filled gaze focuses on us.

"You, my love, will be our baby's Godmother."

Ruby grins from ear to ear as she rises to her feet. "Seriously?"

Molly nods. "You betcha!"

"Wow! Thank you so much. I'm beyond honored." She joins our hug session.

"Hey, we want in." Sam and Bekka pounce, wrapping their arms around us.

"Family. This is what a real family is." Ruby's voice is so low, she probably didn't expect anyone to hear her.

But I did.

My heart aches for her and the pain she's felt in her life. All she's ever wanted was a family, and it's taken her too many years to feel like she's part of one. I want to say something — anything to make her smile, but I'm frozen in place. This is her private moment, and I won't embarrass her by bringing attention to it.

As if she's heard my inner thoughts, she peers up at me with a grin. "Godparents," she mouths.

I return the smile and nod.

Jax releases himself from the group. "I have one more present." My brother holds out his hand toward Molly.

"Oh? And what is that, sweetie?" Molly licks her lips as she laces her fingers with Jax's.

"Okay, dirty woman, not that." Jax walks her to the couch, helping her sit. "Wait here." He turns for a moment, then faces Molly again, bending on one knee.

He's finally doing it. Atta boy.

"Molly, love of my life—*pea to my pod*—will you make me the happiest man alive and marry me?"

"Oh, my God. Are you serious, Jax? Yes! Yes! I will! I will! Yes!" Molly rushes to her feet, grabs Jax by the collar, and plants a kiss on his lips.

"You're my forever, Molly."

"And you mine, Jax."

Their devotion to each other makes me envious.

One day, I'll have what they have. One day…

Ruby claps next to me, and I snap out of my pathetic wonderings, joining her and the girls in their excitement.

Tonight is a celebration, not a pity party.

It's twelve o'clock sharp, and I'm in my office working instead of relaxing at home with my girl. With three days left before the New Year, it was decided Axel, Ruby, and I should have a quick meeting on our venture. So, here I am twiddling my thumbs while I wait.

"Maes. Good to see ya. How you been?" Axel slides through the door with a wide grin.

"Not bad. You?"

He shrugs. "Same." Axel looks around my office. "Where's Ruby?"

"She's probably finalizing her makeup or some crap. You know how women are." I snicker.

"Oh, I sure do." Axel settles on one of the chairs in front of my desk. "Luckily, I don't have to deal with that anymore."

I shake my head. "I have to disagree with you because I quite enjoy the feel of a woman by my side. The extra stuff Ruby does doesn't bug me at all."

"That means you're falling in —"

"Hey, guys." Thankfully, Ruby pops in before Axel can finish his sentence.

"Hey, beautiful." I smile and wave her over to me.

She places a kiss on my temple as I wrap my arms around her plush body. I breathe in deeply, enjoying the sweet scent of her perfume.

"So, what's going on?" Ruby looks between Axel and me.

Axel leans forward. "Just a few things we want to update you on."

"Okay." Ruby bites down on her delicious full bottom lip.

It takes all of my strength not to strip her down on this desk. Instead of fulfilling the vision in my head, I smile. "Nothing bad. First thing, Axel finalized the hiring process. We now have a full staff for our opening in March."

"Wow. That's two months ahead of schedule."

"Yes, it is, and I'm glad for it. But, I have one more thing... You've been invited to speak at a group home. The children there have had very troubled pasts and could use someone to look up to."

"Really? I... ummm..."

"Nervous?" Axel asks.

"Yes. I've never done that before. What if I mess up? What if I say the wrong things?"

"You won't," I say with pride. "You're one of the strongest women I know."

"Thank you. Your belief in me means a lot." Ruby peers at the door then back to me. "Okay, I'll do it. Hopefully, I can be the voice of reason they need to better their future."

"I think you'll leave a great impression on those kids. Your story made a difference in my life, and I'm older than you." Axel chuckles.

"Awww. You two are a bunch of saps." I pretend to gag. "Let's wrap this up so we can go home."

They both roll their eyes at me.

I grin. "Also, that group home you're going to?"

"Yeah?"

"All of the children there will have a new home as of March."

Her eyes widen and tears brim at the corners. "You mean…"

"Aye, lass."

"Oh, Maeson that's amazing! But what about the employees? They'll lose their jobs because of us."

"No, they won't. We hired them. No man, woman, or child left behind." I wink at her.

"Always two steps ahead, aren't you?"

"You betcha, lass. Now let's go home. I'm tired and grumpy."

"When are you not?" Axel chuckles.

I growl at him. "When you're not around."

"Yeah, yeah. Take it easy guys. See you for our upcoming New Year's Eve festivities."

Ruby lightly shoves my shoulder once Axel's out of sight. "You're so mean to him."

"No, he's mean to me." I shrug.

"Oh, please. You're both a mess."

"Eh, don't you worry your pretty face that's simply how men act around each other. We're not like you woman who love, cry, and love some more all day."

"If you say so." She shakes her head.

"I do."

Ruby peers up at me with her big amber eyes and bats her thick black eyelashes. "Thank you for everything, Maeson."

"Don't thank me, Princess. We're a team and teams work together."

I wish you realized everything you need or want is what I'll always give you.

20

Ruby

In the darkness, Club Royale glistens with shiny mirror like glass and bright white icicle lights. The building's New Year's Eve decorations make you think you're in New York City on a cold winter night.

There are days I miss the wind blowing my hair everywhere while I rushed down the busy streets of Manhattan. Then I remember how much I hated to be so cold, I couldn't warm up and the yearning for true winter weather disappears.

I smile at Maeson as I reach for his hand and squeeze. "I wish the whole crew could be here tonight."

"Me too, but you know Molly's too damn pregnant to go anywhere, and Sam needed to keep her bar open, so that leaves us with Axel who should be showing up soon. Any news from Aria? Is she coming?"

I frown. "Nope. She won't answer my calls, voicemails, or texts. I was tempted to check on her before we left, but I didn't want to cause problems."

"We should've. It would've given me a chance to meet the guy face to face, and probably, end the bullshit he gives Aria." Maeson laughs.

"Oh, I'm sure you're right. But I'll visit her tomorrow night instead."

He nods. "You're the boss, lass. And if you need me to join you, I'll gladly do so."

"I should be good, but thank you for being so protective." I wink and tug him closer toward the entrance.

Lights flash and smoke billows around us. Loud music pumps into my ears. I close my eyes as I inhale every scent, zone into every sound, and allow my muscles to relax.

This place has a special therapeutic vibe that makes you want to let go. If it wasn't for Maeson and Jax's passion to turn their vision into reality, people like me wouldn't have a place to escape and release our dance demons.

As we reach our private table, Maeson nods at the bartender Isaac.

The man raises two fingers in the air.

Maeson frowns. Not a surprise since we all know Mr. Mae Mae isn't a fan of waiting at his own club.

I slap Maeson's shoulder. "Don't rush the man. It's crazy packed tonight, so just give him time. Tonight is a *be happy* holiday not a *throw around your sour puss face* holiday."

"Aye, but I'm the boss, not a regular patron. I deserve to be served first." He scowls.

"That's not the case tonight. Suck it up, buttercup."

He shrugs and scoots closer to me. "Yes, my Princess. Your wish—"

"My command, which means listen to me more often." My giggle is lost amid the thumping beat.

Maeson's smile deepens. "No, it means less talking and more dancing." He captures my hand, lifting me to my feet.

The moment we hit the dance floor our bodies take control for what feels like hours. Sweat drips down my neck. I'm ready to sit, but the upbeat rhythm slows down, and Maeson wraps his arms around my waist, holding me still.

The DJ taps his mic. "Let's bring in the New Year right with a special song. Where all my couples at?"

Everyone cheers, and more people join us on the dance floor

as the DJ transitions the music. Special song is right. The melody is as smooth and silky soft as the man singing.

Ed Sheeran, we meet again and this time, it's a true love song.

My hips sway against Maeson's warm body, and I lay my head against his chest.

"Baby… you're perfection every fucking single night." Maeson sings into my ear, adding his own spin to the lyrics.

I flush at the glorious sound and my smile couldn't be wider if I tried. A beautiful man—*inside and out*—singing to me from the depths of his soul is exactly what I dreamt of as a kid.

Fairy tales. Happily ever afters. Too good to be true? Probably, but enjoy it for now.

"Move in with me." Maeson's vibrant green eyes bore into mine.

"What?" I couldn't have heard him right…

"Move. In. With. Me." He kisses my temple. "Please, Princess."

My heart pounds. Those are words I never thought I'd hear from a man. Wetness brims at the edges of my eyes, but I fight it off. I can't show him how much this means to me. He can't know how much I'd love to live with him like a real couple. "No." I shake my head. "Too soon."

"Don't turn me down so quickly. Think about it, lass. Please."

A tear slips from my eye, and I nod. "Okay."

Maeson captures my lips with his. "Happy tears?"

I bob my head.

"Good." There's tightness in his voice that wasn't there before.

When I peer up at him, I notice why and dab at the moisture pooling on his cheek.

Maeson closes his eyes and pulls me flush against him. Body against body, lips against lips, and tears against tears we continue our dance without another word.

The song ends and Maeson whispers, "Happy New Year, love."

"Happy New Year, babe," I whisper back with a wink.

When our mouths touch this time, the sensation feels

different. The kiss is as intense as usual, yet something *extra* accompanies it… Something more powerful… Something I'm not ready to dig deeper into…

Something I'm not willing to admit…

THIS WAS MY BEST New Year's ever. I've finally celebrated with someone who truly cares for me. I might be slightly intoxicated, but this day will forever remain with me.

"You're probably tired, but can I show you something?" Maeson's husky voice cuts into my thoughts.

"Sure, is it far away?"

"Nope. Just beyond the complex." He grips the steering wheel and sighs.

"Are you okay?" I touch his arm.

He flinches. "Aye. I'm fine."

"You don't seem so."

"Memories, Princess. Memories plague me, but I'm just dandy, don't you worry." He gives me his usual sly grin, hiding what I saw mere seconds ago.

It doesn't fool me, but I won't push. Instead, I peer out of the window as he drives past my building and down a hidden dirt road.

I've seen this before… months ago… But I never ventured far enough to find out what's hiding behind the tall trees and bushes. Now that we're past them, a small yet beautiful cottage comes into view. It takes my breath away. Like Maeson's apartment complex, bright red roses surround this home.

"Is this yours?"

"Aye, lass."

"Do you live here too?"

"Not anymore… Not since…"

"You built this for your daughter?"

"For us to be a…" —he clears his throat— "family… To live here happily. To make her dreams come true."

My heart breaks at his admission and tears sting my eyes. Losing a child is hard enough, but then add reliving the loss every time you see the home you shared? Unimaginable. "Maes—"

"No. Pity is for those who need it, and I don't."

I shake my head. "Respect, admiration, and understanding are what I offer you, not a pity party."

A small smile appears. "Come." He slides out of the car and walks around to my side, helping me out. "I want you to meet two special people."

"Okay. Do they know we're coming? It's super late."

"Nope. They like the element of surprise." This time, he beams from ear to ear.

When we reach the red door, he peers back at me and puts one finger up to his lips.

With a bob of my head, I take hold of his hand.

He guides me through a dimly lit foyer adorned with vibrant paintings. Such a stark contrast to his blank canvas condo. Why the drastic difference?

His little girl…

Now the pieces to the Maeson puzzle have come into place. It seems his daughter gave him color when he needed it, showed him what it meant to live brilliantly, and gave him hope for a better life. Then his happiness came crashing down on him… light turned to darkness…

Focus. Don't bring the abyss back to him.

I force a smile to my lips and continue through the long hallway leading to an open concept kitchen and living area.

The kitchen stops me in my tracks. One wall is bright yellow with red polka dots painted randomly, but that isn't what stands out. It's the red dots, each one has a hand print in it with a word scribbled across it. The name matching the hand.

Daddy. Maddi.

My heart melts at the sight.

How does he handle looking at this every time he's here? No wonder he said memories haunted him.

This wall must bear the same meaning to Maeson as does my treasured picture album to me—as hard as it is to see, it's just as difficult to let go of it.

"It's not some beautiful Michelangelo, but…" Maeson's voice cuts off my thoughts. "She was so little when we painted it…" He sucks in a deep breath.

"Are you kidding me? This is more than some fucking Michelangelo—it's priceless, it's irreplaceable. But why the hesitation? My opinion doesn't matter."

He peers down at his shiny black shoes and shrugs.

I'm at a loss of words. I don't know how to soothe his worries. This is just one of those times nothing said is best.

After what seems like an eternity, his glistening eyes meet mine. "Your opinion matters because you're special to me."

I shake my head. "When it comes to your daughter, it doesn't—*ever.*"

"Sure does when I want you to live here with me."

My eyes widen. "Here?"

"Aye, Princess. Here." He points at the marble floor we're standing on.

"Your forever home? You want to share it with me?"

"I do."

I slice my head to the left. "You should really think about this before we go any further. We're not talking about one of your regular condos."

"Believe me, lass, I ha—"

"Maeson." A shaky, yet thickly accented woman's voice interjects. "Is that you, my boy?"

I spin around to find an older white haired woman smiling in Maeson's direction.

"Yes, Mama bear." He strides over and embraces her. "Happy New Year!" Maeson's large frame towers over her.

The fragile looking woman wraps her arms around him. "Happy New Year to you too! Maybe it be a good one for us all." The woman peeks around Maeson and smiles at me. "Maeson? Is this future wife?"

What? Wife? Is she insane?

I cover my mouth, fighting the urge to laugh.

"Not yet, Maria. But she is my girlfriend. This"—he faces me—"is Ruby Bennett. Ruby, this is Maria, Stavros's wife. The batty old man who never agrees with me." Maeson grins down at Maria.

She slaps his shoulder seemingly offended, but the broad smile on her face gives her away.

I extend a hand to Maria. "It's nice to meet you. And Maeson is a sour puss when it comes to accepting the truths people make him face." I wink at him.

Maeson narrows his eyes. "That's garbage. Stavros is —"

"The best man you ever meet." The familiar older man joins us. "Kalí Chroniá!"

The image of my dad flashes through my mind and the proper response flows from me, "Epísis!"

Maeson and Maria stare at me blankly.

But sweet Stavros grins from ear to ear. "I knew you Greek girl. Told you, Maeson."

"I can't believe I remembered. It's been a long time since I've spoken my fathers language." My lips quiver as memories of my dad's Greek lessons flash before my eyes. At such a young age I was forced to shove everything away that I thought those moments with him were made up so I could cope with my foster life.

Maria rubs my arm soothingly. "You can't forget, it's in your blood, agapi mou, like it's in ours."

"I guess so." I shrug. "My dad was Greek and before he… passed, he taught me a few things. But I only recall bits and pieces. Just like now, hearing you, Stavros, reminded me of what he used to say."

Stavros nods. "Visit us often and we can teach you more. You should know where you come from. Be proud Greek woman like my Maria."

"Very proud, I am. And one day, you will be too. We show you everything." Maria laughs.

"Wait a minute." Maeson scowls in the older couple's direction. "You two planning on taking my woman away from me? Maybe find her a decent Greek man?"

Maria frowns. "No, you dummy! We love you like the boy we never have. Why give a beauty like her to somebody else?"

"What Maria said, you crazy man!" Stavros shakes his head.

Maeson glares at me, his green eyes darkening. "No Greek men for you. Just Scottish." His top lip twitches and a dimple appears on his cheek.

"Oh aye, Master Mae Mae. Your command—"

"My wish, Princess." His tone drops a few octaves.

"Okay, children, we go to bed," Stavros says. "You two go kissy kissy in private. Let's go, Maria mou."

Maria waves before taking Stavros's hand. "Goodnight, love birds." She winks.

They disappear into their room, and I'm left alone with my brooding boyfriend. "You were saying?"

He shakes his head. "Never mind that. Come with me. I want to show you something." Maeson strides toward the French doors, opening them in one fluid motion. Beyond the doors, he points to a hammock big enough to fit a soccer team. "Lay down."

I curl my lip. "No way. I tried one of those once, and I flipped over within seconds. They're a danger to all human kind."

He snorts then bites down on his bottom lip. "I'll make sure you won't do the same on this one. Just sit, and I'll help you the rest of the way."

I want to dismiss him and his scary hammock, but a part of me wants to know what it's like to lay in this contraption with a man. "Fine, but if I hurt myself, you're in big trouble!"

"Oh, no! Sounds terrifying. I'd better not fuck this up then." His dimples reappear, and I melt like butter on a hot roll.

Thanks to Maeson's expertise, we're on the hammock within a minute. One of his delicious muscular arms is wrapped around my shoulders and the other is behind his head.

Once I'm confident enough we won't flip over, I lay my head on his chest, peering up at the stars and whisper, "Tell me about her. Tell me about this home."

Silence.

"I mean… you don't have to…"

He sighs. "No, it's time."

"Only if you're ready."

"Ready or not, you should know."

I squeeze my eyes shut, praying asking this of him won't cause damage, but instead, purify his pain.

A shattered soul will always be in healing mode. A shattered soul will always be just that… shattered. Once glass is broken, repairing it is nearly impossible.

"I don't know where to start," Maeson murmurs.

"Usually people say at the beginning, but you've told me that part already, so how about the middle?"

"The middle it is," He emits a long and drawn out breath. "She had my green eyes, and every time I looked at her, I saw myself staring back. She was my little twin. When she was old enough to walk she followed me everywhere, even to the bathroom." Maeson removes his shirt, then points to his bared chest. "These words here — *Today, I realized my life is at the mercy of my own hands and no one else's. Today, I decided I'll no longer apologize for being who I am. Today, I stopped blaming others for my mistakes. Today, I've failed you. Today is the day my life continues and yours doesn't. Today, tomorrow, and for eternity, I will love you'* — were for Madison. After I lost her, I had this tattoo done for her and what she taught me. When you asked me about it before I couldn't — wouldn't discuss her." His voice cracks and he squeezes my shoulder.

"I understand, but please don't feel like you have to explain yourself. I figured when you were ready, you'd tell me."

"Thank you. People love to shove their noses where they don't belong, and at the times, I assumed you'd be the same. But you've surprised me time and time again. You're nothing like other people. You're so much more."

Running my hand across the raised words inscribed on his pec, I smile. "So much more is what I aim to be every day. I'm what most folks like to call amazing. Nothing less can describe a being like me." A giggle escapes me, and I smother my face against his warm skin.

"Amazing you sure are, just like my Maddi. That's why I try so hard with you, woman, but you took too damn long to notice it."

"Bla, bla, bla. What's this? A romance novel with those yuppy words on the inside?"

"Deflect all you want, lass, but my words ring true, and you know it."

I wrinkle my nose. "Anyway, continue. I much prefer listening to your baritone voice describe your angel of a daughter than the person you think I am. So, please keep going on that route."

"Fine. Now, where was I?"

"At the middle."

"Right. When she was a wee one it was very hard for me, maybe too hard, but I did it. Feedings every two hours, sometimes, less in between because daddy had no idea what he was doing. But somehow, we both got through it. Then the fun times began—she started to speak. Her first word was, of course, Dada. Proudest moment of my life. I swear, I think I might've cried that day. Before I knew it, speaking turned into walking, then dancing, then…" Maeson clears his throat. "She asked me to take her to school. She wanted to play with kids her age. Daddy didn't have friends with kids, but school did. Jax used to tell her about it and that's where the idea came from. Bastard should've kept his mouth shut—who was I supposed to spend my days with when she was at school?"

I nudge him. "A bit obsessive where you?"

He shrugs. "Maybe a little, but her heart… I worried about certain activities harming her and school was one of them. The idea of her running around with mangy rug rats gave me anxiety. Luckily, we got past that scary hurdle once the doctors advised me she'd be all right under those circumstances. They even went as far to say the social interaction would be good for her." He shakes his head and rolls his eyes. "Fucking doctors."

I laugh. "Oh, hell no! How could they!"

He grins. "I know, over protective much?"

"I'm glad you can admit it."

"I definitely can, especially now, since I've had many years to reflect on my choices." He sighs. "Anyway, moving on. School happened, and I survived it. Then after kindergarten, I decided we needed a real home, not a dingy apartment or Jax's parent's house. So, I built my complex alongside this home. While everyone worried about Rose Garden, I focused on this slice of heaven for us. I laid each brick and stone with my bare hands. I remember how she'd run around the yard while I worked. Sometimes, she'd beg me to take a break so we could play hide and seek—our favorite game." He laughs. "Usually she was the hider since my skills at concealing this six foot plus body were severely lacking. *Daddy, I see you, silly.*', she'd say laughing the entire time. God, her giggles. Ugh… They made my days, nights, and forever's."

"If her laugh sounded anything like yours, then I see why."

"Her's was better, by far. I have to dig out the videos of her so I can show you. You'd love her as much as I did."

"I bet I would've. And you should, I'd like to see them. Children are so precious, and they're definitely my soft spot."

Maeson nods. "Mine too." He squeezes my hand and sighs. "I'm sorry, I got off track with my ramblings."

"No, that's fine. I like hearing about this side of you since you rarely share. I'm willing to take anything you'll give."

"It's difficult replaying a past you want to forget, yet you don't want to let go of either, you know?"

"To a certain extent, I agree with you. But I do wish I could forget mine altogether." I close my eyes, fighting against the reminders.

"Rightfully so on your end. I couldn't even begin to imagine, since my memories with Madison were all amazing. No matter how bitter I became after losing her, I'd never replace the memories." Maeson exhales. "Lets end this discussion and focus on something lighter. Starting the New Year off with heavy hearts doesn't seem right for either of us." A sly grin surfaces on that devastatingly beautiful face of his.

"And what would you consider *'lighter'*?" I lean into him, releasing a puff of air as my lips linger against his.

His mouth hovers over mine, then he licks his top lip and smirks. "Staring up at the stars while I imagine what a brighter future looks like."

"Seriously?" I poke him. "Wise man prophecies over here."

"You know it, lass. We all need to momentarily relinquish our hectic schedules and reflect. Lucky for us, we have the perfect place to do it—a hammock underneath the heavenly sky on a cloudless night. Oh, and I can't forget—amazing, sexy, and fantabulous company to go with some much needed *'contemplation of life'* time."

"Why, thank you. I'll gladly accompany you anytime, as long as you keep the compliments coming." I wink, then lay my head against his broad shoulder.

"Compliment you? Silly woman, I was talking about myself. *I'm* the glorious company *you* get to enjoy while analyzing your life questions with the shiny stars above." He laughs and squeezes my arm.

Rolling my eyes, I slap his bared chest, leaving a red palm mark.

"Och, lass. That'll bruise my sensitive skin." His laughter deepens.

I can't help but join him. "Sensitive, my ass."

"Ass? Yes, please. I wouldn't mind yours cuddling my di—"

"Shut it! Quit sidetracking and focus. I think you need more life reflection than I do. Or maybe, you need an extra dose of Jesus in your life." A giggle escapes me.

"Or maybe… *just maybe*, I was purposely made this way by the man upstairs specifically for you." His delectable dimples reappear as he lifts his chin to the sky.

I curl my lip. "Conceited much?"

"Nope, just speaking truths."

"Truths, my ass."

"Back to your ass, are we? I wouldn't mind traveling back there at all."

"Of course, you wouldn't." With a shake of my head, I dismiss his nonsense and peer up at the black sky. "Maybe you're right, Maeson. Reflection seems like a good idea, especially on a night like this."

"See, I'm always filled with fabulous ideas."

As I watch the glowing specks, I slice my head to the left. "Don't get ahead of yourself, old man."

"Fine, *ego killer*, I'll reign in my amazing wit."

"Thank you. Now, follow my lead—head back, mouth shut, and stare straight ahead."

Maeson chuckles, then to my surprise, he does as I suggested.

So old dogs can learn new tricks. Good boy.

At first, it feels awkward laying together in complete silence while staring into the abyss, but then, there's a shift in the air, and I find myself relaxing like never before. In this moment, as I focus on the flicking stars, my mind's no longer at war with itself—it's at… peace.

In this moment… my past doesn't exist, only the present does.

21

MAESON

The heat of the morning sun warming my bare skin wakes me. I stretch my stiff muscles and open my eyes surprised to find we managed to sleep on the hammock all night.

A smile graces my lips. We started the New Year off right by trying something different—slumber under the sparkling night sky. For me personally, that sort of romantic activity wasn't my cup of tea until I met Ruby. But last night, snuggling that way, felt... *right*.

Speaking of Ruby, my beautiful princess is snoring lightly in my arms. I'm tempted to wake her, but doing so would be wrong since peaceful nights are rare for her.

I'll wait until she wakes on her own and bide my time planning my next discussion with her. The idea popped into my mind a few weeks ago, and when I asked her about it last night, she didn't give me a proper answer.

I need one and soon.

Once I'm plagued by *feelings*, they have to be fulfilled otherwise I won't stop wondering. And wonder is all I've done for quite some time now.

Will she or won't she?

I haven't asked a woman to live with me since I was a stupid, hormone filled teen, and now that I have, I'm actually nervous as fuck. Not just because her answer might be a big fat no, but the fear of our relationship turning out like my last one terrifies me.

I can vividly see history repeating itself and that shit isn't okay in my book. I'd like to avoid colossal heart ache at all costs.

Then stick to what's already working and slow the hell down.

Good advice, but too late.

I'm midway through this path and it's time I reach the finish line—properly.

Ruby stirs, shifting to her side and peers up at me with a wide grin. "Good morning, handsome."

I lean in, crushing my lips against hers. "Morning, hot stuff. Sleep well?"

"Mmmhhhmmm. You?"

"When I'm with you, how can I not?"

She rolls her eyes. "You're such a sweet talker, Mr. Alexander."

I nod. "Always."

She graces me with another roll of her eyes, before inspecting our surroundings. "I can't believe we slept out here."

"Me either. Nice, wasn't it?"

"Yeah. It's so peaceful. I love it."

"That's why I bought the land." My chest clenches as I realize this is the perfect opportunity to broach the subject I've been harboring.

Live with me.

My heart and mind plead. But how does a man say such crap out loud without sounding like he's begging?

He can't.

Fuck it. Beating around the bush has never been my style.

"Ruby, I want to live here together. Be the family we both yearn for. I want to fulfill the future I envisioned for this home with you and only you. We can renovate—make it *ours*. Please?" The words along with my fears heave themselves from my mouth in a cluster fucked mess.

I hope she doesn't notice.

She slices her head to the right in a cocky, yet sexy way. "Aye, Maeson Lachlan Alexander, I'll move in with you."

My jaw drops practically to the ground, and I can't widen my eyelids any further even if I try. I was prepared to validate my point of view in every way possible. I was prepared to beg on my knees if she asked me to. But I wasn't prepared for a flat out yes.

The beat of my overwhelmed heart hammers in my ears. Maybe she isn't serious? I clear my throat. "Really?"

"Yup. Let's try, but on a trial basis. If it doesn't work for either of us, I'm out. I refuse to be *trapped* again. History will *not* repeat itself. Shit, I'll fight you until we're both bloody before I allow that to happen. Get my drift?"

"Aye, my feisty lass, the drift has been gotten. You have nothing to fear with me, I'm not a monster." I caress the smooth skin on her pink cheek. "Remember, I had a daughter, so there's no fucking way I'd ever hurt you."

"People say that shit all the time. Actions prove your word. Until then, your word isn't bond, it's elastic plastic."

"Then actions are all you'll get from me."

"Good."

"Is every kind of *action* approved?" I wink.

"Argh. Your gutter brain always goes there."

"I'm a man, what do you expect?"

"My list of exceptions can go on for days, but for starters, keep your dick in its place until you give me the grand tour." She hops off of the hammock.

The damn thing twists, and I fly off of it. "Thanks, *Woman*! Just the wakeup call I needed." I grumble as she bounds to the sliding doors.

When I finally make it inside, Ruby's laying across the couch with a mischievous grin spread across her face. "Took you long enough."

"My bones aren't as quick as yours. They don't lubricate before moving. I *am* almost forty, remember?"

"Shoot, I almost forgot! Old man. Old brain. Old body."

"Watch it, Princess. You should hope to be lucky enough to look as great as I do when you're *forty*." I match her wicked smile tenfold—dimples and all—*of course*.

"I betcha all your money in the bank, I'll look B to the E, to the T, to the T, to the E, to the R."

I raise my hands above my head, clapping slowly. "Look everyone, Ms. Bennett can spell."

She curls her lip, concealing a smile. "Douche."

"Heard that one before. What else do you have?"

"Bigger balls than you, for one," she says in a serious tone.

This woman never ceases to surprise me.

No matter how hard I try to keep a straight face, it doesn't work. Laughter bursts from deep within my chest.

"Done teasing?" she says deadpan.

I raise an eyebrow and smirk. "Aye, when a woman claims to have bigger *assets* than a man, it's most certainly time to end the game."

"Smart man. Now, can we begin the tour?"

"As you wish, Princess. But first, I have something for you." I incline my head and extend an arm.

Ruby grins as she takes my hand. "Oh? What is it?"

I tug her against my body, whispering in her ear, "Happy birthday, Princess."

"My... Oh my God! I forgot my own birthday! How did you—"

"Remember? I'd never forget something so special." I kiss her temple. "Come with me."

As we walk through the kitchen to the dining room, butterflies flutter within my stomach. There's a chance she won't like my gifts, and I ruin everything with what I thought was perfect.

When we reach the long dark wooden table, I pull out a chair, motioning for her to sit. "Wait here. I'll be right back."

I hope she loves it. Please, let her love it.

I return with a medium sized black box tied with a white bow. Handing it to her, I smile. "For you, my sweet lass."

As she removes the shiny material and lifts the top, I notice a slight tremor to her hands. "It won't bite you, I promise."

"Oh, I'm not worried about that. I just never got a gift box this fancy before. I don't want to ruin it."

I laugh. "Destroy the fucking thing, if you want. All that matters is how you feel about what's inside."

She nods and peels back the tissue paper.

My breath hitches in my throat.

My heart stops beating.

My mind ceases all thoughts.

She looks up at me with a questioning expression. "A photo album?"

"Aye." I open the book, turning to the first page.

Her eyes dart to the thick black writing inscribed, and she inhales sharply.

"Today, my life belongs to me and only me. Today, I stop apologizing for who I am. Today, I promise to accept the past, live in the moment, and await precious tomorrows. Today, my sorrow ends. Today, my happiness begins. Today, tomorrow, and for eternity, I'll love myself, even if no one else will, because I deserve it." I smile as the words flow from my lips with ease. It took months of struggling to write the perfect inscription for a woman deserving the best of everything this world has to offer, but she is worth it.

"Maeson..." Her voice cracks.

"Ruby..."

Our gazes connect, green clashing with amber, ice cooling fire, and gratitude tinged with passion.

Tears cascade down Ruby's face. "It matches your tattoo — the one you wrote for your daughter."

"Aye, except these words are more meaningful for you."

"Why?"

"Because I saw how much you cherish your parents album, and I want you to have another one filled with what makes you happy in the present." I look away, staring at a painting on the wall. "If you don't like it, though, I can return it."

"No! This is the most thoughtful gift anyone has ever gotten me. It's perfect!" She tucks a hand in the crook of my arm, and leans her head against my shoulder. "You could've bought the most expensive thing in this world and it wouldn't equal in value to what you just gave me. Thank you, Maeson. Thank you from the bottom of my heart."

I bend to kiss her plush lips. "You're so very welcome. I hope this made your twenty-sixth birthday a little more special than it normally is."

She nods. "It's the best birthday I've had since I was a kid, and I can't thank you enough for remembering."

"Don't thank me. The pleasure was all mine."

"I was raised with manners, so my appreciation will be voiced every time a person does something nice."

"Then I guess you should prepare an appreciation speech for part two." I smirk wickedly.

"You can't be serious!"

"I sure am, but the downfall with this reveal is, I can't tell you any details until it's set in stone."

"That's lame! You know I hate surprises." She wiggles her eyebrows. "Maybe you can give me a itty-bitty clue?"

"No chance, lass. If I disclose any information, a very memorable present will be ruined."

"Fine. Have it your way." She huffs.

Grinning, I tap her adorable button nose. "Soon—very soon—you'll have the explanation you seek."

"Okay. Just don't keep me on edge for too long. I'll start snooping for answers, and beware, I'm a great detective." She laughs.

"I know you are, which is why I'll do my best to expedite the process." I interlink my fingers with hers. "But until then, you ready to resume the tour?"

Beaming from ear to ear, she squeezes my hand. "I thought you'd never ask."

RUBY SPENT THE LAST hour asking about the original decor decisions while skipping from room to room. She wanted to know every single gritty detail—the real reasons of why I chose the things I did ten years ago.

At first, I didn't want to tell her because knowing would affect *her* decision on what to renovate. My original intentions for this house are not the same anymore. Ruby needs to have a place she can call her own. One we customize to our tastes, not just mine or just hers.

But in the end, Ruby didn't want to change anything except for *'our future bedroom'* as she called it. She wants to redo the entire room, which I agreed to with one exception.

I'm sorry, my baby girl, but it's time.

My daughter's room. It needs to be… *changed*… for lack of a better word. The space is no longer Madison's, it's occupied by her spirit, her ghost, her everything. Madi's room was the only part of the house I flat out refused to go into for years—until more recently, that is.

The reminders are too much—they always will be.

So, we agreed to convert it into an office for both of us.

Please forgive me, love. Know I'll never forget you, I just can't… deal. I'm not sure I'll ever be able to.

WHAT'S THE SAYING PEOPLE use when it feels like months pass by before your eyes?

Time flies when you're having fun.

Well, that's been the case for Ruby and I. It's like just yesterday was New Year's Day when we decided to live together, yet here it's March already.

January and February were filled with massive changes— *good ones, luckily.*

Ruby moved in the first week of February, which was surprisingly quick because I expected her to fight me the entire time or change her mind. But I think Molly made sure Ruby didn't flake on me.

We also redid the master bedroom and it looks like a sex Goddess went wild with our favorite colors. Red and black everything.

Our. I said… our. The word is still foreign to me, even though I've been using it for a few months.

It amazes me how much my life has evolved in the last nine months — *how much I've evolved.* I went from a total miserable prick to… not so miserable, but still a prick from time to time. To my defense, when you're a business man, prick is part of the job title.

Or that's what I like to tell myself, anyway.

Speaking of business, the logo for Precious Tomorrows was finalized and not only does it represent our mission, but also us as a team.

The design incorporates Ruby's black strength tattoo as the background and the words *'Precious Tomorrows'* are intertwined into it with a beautiful red color. Similar to my tattoos, the two images are integrated seamlessly. When Axel and I saw it we couldn't believe Ruby drew it by hand.

She has more untapped talents than I imagined.

"Hey, Mae Mae? You ready?" Molly's cheery voice cuts off my thought.

I peer up from my laptop and smile at her as she stands in the doorway of my office, caressing her swollen belly. "Yeah. Sorry. I got caught up."

She nods. "You've been doing that a lot lately. Are ya okay?"

With a cocky grin, I slice my head to the right, jutting it upward. "Am I ever not okay?"

Molly laughs. "Do you really want my answer?"

"Nope. Let's go before your hormonal self goes off on a tangent."

"Good choice." She pats my shoulder as she waddles past me. "By the way, will you tell Ruby about her big surprise after we finish dinner?"

"If the time is right, yes, but only then and not sooner."

"There's no such things as perfect timing, boss." Molly points to her stomach. "Prime example." She laughs.

"True, but you know me. I tend to—"

"Chicken out?" Molly smirks.

"Umm. No." I wave my hand in the air, motioning for her to exit the building already.

"It's alright, you don't have to admit it."

I growl. "Woman…"

"Maeson… you giving my best friend a hard time?" Ruby steps out of her car.

"Not at all. She was giving me the hard time." I pout.

Molly snorts. "Bull—"

"Children! Enough battle of the siblings. We have a celebratory dinner for our upcoming grand opening to get to, so *páme* before my Godchild decides to pop out of his mommy's belly."

My lips quirk up at my serious girlfriend. "Point—"

"Made." Molly finishes.

Women. Can't live with them. Can't live without… well, maybe I can, especially when they're like these two.

22

Ruby

I'm a big believer good things come in small doses and the bad in huge chunks. Which is why I cherish, memorize, and embed every cell in my body with these special and rare moments with my newfound family. I just don't know how many more I'll get in this life. As humans, we look so far into the future we forget about today, we forget to enjoy every second, and we forget to appreciate what we do have versus what we don't.

The people I've come to love showed me it's okay to slow down, smell the damn flowers, and inhale the fresh air filled with freedom. Speaking of love, Maeson's deep and husky laughter pulls me back to reality. "What's so funny?"

Sam shakes her head. "Maeson suggested we guess when Molly will go into labor, and his guess was three weeks late as punishment for being mean to him. Like the poor girl wants to be pregnant longer than she has too."

I scrunch my forehead. "Are you insane? Have you seen Mo's swollen feet? I don't care how mean she was, she doesn't deserve your bad juju. Take it back, old man!"

"Yeah, take it back, *Mae Mae*." Molly shakes her finger at Maeson, then looks down at her stomach. "Xander, listen to mama and come out on time—not later like your Godfather said."

"Yes, for my sake, come out soon. Mama's a bit grouchy." Jax rubs Molly's belly.

At Jax's proclamation, snorts and chuckles are heard from each person at the table—except Molly. She doesn't get it, but we do. At one point or another, we've all be on the wrong end of Molly's hormonal temper and it wasn't pleasant.

Based off of the deathly glare Jax is receiving, he's in need of help. So, I attempt to lighten the mood. "April twenty-fourth. I think you'll go earlier than your due date, for sure."

"My guess is May first on the dot. I like that date," Sam says.

"What do we get if we guessed right?" I ask.

"Nothing. Ya'll givin' me agita just thinkin' about birthin'."

"I bet. I'd be freaking out about it too." I pat her hand. "But we're here for you whenever Xander decides to show."

"Thank you. That soothes my soul. Now, back to the reason we're here—the grand opening of your amazing venture." Molly raises her glass of water in the air. "To Ruby, Maeson, Axel, and Precious Tomorrows. May our tomorrows be as precious as they are today. I love you guys!" Her crystal blue eyes shine.

Glasses clink against each other. "Cheers." We all respond in union.

"And to you Molly, may you have an easy birth and healthy son." I add.

"I second that." Maeson grins from ear to ear.

I hope he stays this happy and free forever. If anyone deserves it, it's him. He's lost so much and gained so little after he lost his little girl.

Our food arrives and the conversation continues, but my last thought causes me to zone out. As usual, my mind is easily distracted and wanders into the abyss without advanced notice.

This time it's about Aria.

I miss her.

She's been MIA for a while, and I'm worried about her. We were texting daily and talking on the phone weekly, but one day she just stopped answering.

I went by the shelter many times hoping to see her, but she

hadn't gone there for some time either. My last option is to go to her boyfriend's house, but the idea scares me. The visit can go one of two ways—she tells me to fuck off and leave her alone, or she invites me in for coffee.

Fuck off will probably be more like it.

Once I told her I moved in with Maeson, everything changed. She told me I was no different from her and to *'get off of my high horse'*. Where her anger came from, I have no clue.

Could it be because I've finally found peace, and she hasn't?

But I've tried to help her every chance I got. I even attempted to persuade her to stay with me—what more can I do? It's not like I can drag her from her home. She's a grown woman who can make her own decisions.

Maybe I should take the plunge and go to the house? Whatever happens once I show up... happens.

At least I'll know what's going on. If she truly believes I'm treating her badly, then she can tell me to my face. Or if she only said those things because he told her to, I'll understand that too.

Either way, I'm better off seeing for myself instead of losing sleep over it every night.

Yes, that's exactly what I'll do. First, I'll message her to see if she's up for a visit, and then if I don't get a response in a few days, I'll drop by. I grab my cell from my purse, swiping across the locked screen and type a quick, *'Would love to see you... Meet up soon?'* text.

She's my friend, and I care about her wellbeing. I wish she'd understand that. I wish she'd realize other people in her position beg for a friend who cares enough to fight for them. Instead, she continues to disregard anything I say.

That's okay, though. I'm a fighter and giving up on someone I care about isn't part of my DNA.

Which is why I refuse to act like Aria's disappearing act means nothing. I'll pound on her door until someone answers. I'll break the thing down if I have to. I'll—

"Not to change the subject, but Ruby, what's it like living with the grouch?" Sam asks, interjecting my self-motivational speech.

Remember, you're living in the moment. Live for today. Leave the worries alone... at least for now.

I close my eyes, reviving myself, then smile at Sam. "It sucks! He's terrible!"

"Say what?" Maeson rolls his eyes.

No matter what's going on in my head, this man has a way of making the bad shit disappear and suddenly, I find myself laughing. "I'm just kidding, *grouch*." I shift in my seat. "I'll adjust my answer — he's *alright* to live with. The man is so neat, it drives me nuts."

Sam snickers and peers at Bekka, who's watching her intently. "Mine's the same way. But without my mess, she wouldn't have much to do all day, right Bek?"

"Ha. Is that what you think?" Bekka shakes her head and jabs Maeson's arm. "I swear these jokers are insane. We need to reevaluate our choices in partners, Maes."

"I couldn't agree more." Maeson's heart melting, dimple filled smile appears as his eyes meet mine. "Would you like that, Ruby? Or are you willing to pick up your socks from time to time?"

"Blah, you and my socks. You've created the routine not me." I shrug. "I slip them off while I'm relaxing on the couch before bed, and you pick them up in the morning. It's just how it goes."

"You do that too?" Bekka asks Maeson.

"Unfortunately. And if it was up to Ruby, they'd pile up between the couch cushions for months." He winks at me.

"Same with mine. Guess it comes with the perks of living with someone messy," Bekka laughs.

Sam curls her top lip. "Really?"

"Yup, but I wouldn't change a thing. You're my —"

"Ying." Sam finished for Bekka.

"Sweet Jesus, you guys are adorable." Molly's blue pools fill with tears again. "We seem so boring in comparison, Jax." She pouts.

Jax shakes his head. "Hell no, we don't. Babe, we're having a baby — they're bitching about socks. Whose more interesting at the end of the day?"

"That's true." Molly kisses Jax's cheek. "Okay, emotional roller coaster wreck averted."

"Now who's adorable?" I squeeze Mo's hand. "You and Jax are filled with cute, lovey dovey nonsense, not Sam and I. We live with clean freaks. Nothing amazing there. Right, Sam?"

"Oh, for sure."

Maeson looks over at Bekka, rolls his eyes, and mouths *'fucking women'*.

"Right?" Bekka covers her mouth, attempting to hide a very visible grin plastered to her face.

Everyone continues to bicker and laugh, and as they do so, I take a second to myself.

This moment right here, is one of those rare ones I was talking about.

Keep the glorious sounds of my happy friends forever in my heart.

Cherished. Memorized. Embedded into every cell of my body.

It's been a week since I texted Aria and no response back. At this point, I don't know what I should do—give it a few more days or go to her house?

Wait until tomorrow. What's one more day when she's been avoiding me for months?

I check my phone again, before I slide off of our massive king size bed.

The damn thing is so tall, I need a step stool to get on and off it.

As I stroll into the kitchen-living area, I spot Maeson stuffing his face with something that smells delicious. "Maria's been cooking again?"

His mouth is too full to be used for speaking, so he nods.

"I thought we told her not to work so hard anymore? When I moved here we agreed to take care of them and make their lives easier."

"You… know… how… she… gets," Maeson says between chews. "She loves making food for us."

"On top of cleaning, gardening, and making our bed every morning." I raise a newly threaded eyebrow.

"She loves that too. Up keep of the house gives her something to do. With us gone all day and some nights, she needs to stay busy."

"But she's not a maid, Maeson. She's the grandmother I never had, and I want her to feel appreciated. Even Stavros won't listen. He's still out there chauffeuring people around."

"I know, Princess, but it's part of who they are. Taking away what they enjoy doing is like cutting their legs off at the knees. No one loves those two crazy Greeks more than I do, but I've learned when to push and when not to. Maria's house stuff and Stavros's job are off limits."

"I see." I peek into the pan Maeson's digging into. At the sight of it, my eyes tear up. "My mom used to make that for us."

"Really? So, does that mean you know how to make Moose Caca?" His devilish grin appears.

I laugh. "It's Moo-saa-kaa, not the crap you just said. And yes, I do. It was the first meal Mom taught me, but we used chicken, not beef."

"Maybe you can make your version for me sometime? I'd love to see you messing around in the kitchen… naked."

I wink at him. "I can, but *maybe*, I don't want to… naked. Keep in mind, we have other people living with us."

"Oh, that won't stop us. I'll just send them to my condo for a few hours. Maria will have a blast cleaning that place."

I grab one of our new black plates and place a piece of Maria's fantastic smelling dish on it. "Okay, then I'm in."

Maeson sticks his fork in my portion.

I slap his hand away. "You have the entire pan, leave mine alone."

He shrugs and continues to devour his section. "Is that your phone ringing or mine?"

I shake my head. "I don't hear anything. You're senile."

"Or deaf." He laughs before leaving my side. "It's yours, woman. You left it on the night stand." He hands it to me. "It's Aria."

Deep breath. Just breathe.

I tap the green button on the screen. I'm too late, she hung up. I call her back, but no answer, so I text her.

Message Sent: *Sorry missed your call. Call me back.*

The phone lights up again. "Hey, Aria."

"Ruby, long time no speak. I'm sorry about that." Aria's voice sounds… happy. Oddly so.

"It's okay. How are you?"

"Great! Wanna do coffee? Starbucks?" She laughs. "I found one close to your place."

"Sure. When?" I hold my breath.

Please don't say next week or some day far into the future.

"Now?"

I check on Maeson who seems to have forgotten about me. The Moussaka has his full attention. "Sure. Give me a few, and I'll pick you up."

"No need. I'm in your area, so I took an Uber."

"Oh, okay. See you soon then."

When we hang up, an eerie chill hits me. She's never sounded so lively, which is a great thing, but peculiar to hear.

I hope she's in a cheerful mood because her life has changed for the better.

"She good?" Meason frowns.

"Yup. She's seems more than good. She even asked to meet for coffee."

"Glad to hear it. When are you going?"

"In a few."

"Alright, lass. Be safe. If you need anything, let me know. I'll be here, gaining a few pounds." The smirk I've come to love reappears.

"You do that." I rise to my tiptoes, leaning toward him, and tap my lips.

His smile deepens as he grabs my nape, forcing my head backwards, and flicks his hot tongue against my exposed skin.

"I love our silent communication." He nips my bottom lip. "Is that what all couples do?"

Is he seriously trying to carry a conversation with me in this position? Let's even the score, shall we?

"I'd like to think it's our special thing, but who knows. I don't have the proper experience in the relationship subject." I grab a fist full of his hair and tug—hard.

Maeson suppresses a groan between gritted teeth. "Me either. But I'd say we have our own unique quirks which make our dynamic work for *us*. Don't you agree?" He adds extra pressure on my neck before biting down on it.

I clench my legs together, fighting the desire pooling between them. "I do."

I know what he's doing. I'm loosing the battle. Must regain control.

I stare into his dark green gaze and grin. "Close your eyes."

"What are you going to do?"

I widen my smile. "Do as I say."

"Aye, my Goddess." He releases me.

I slide my hand over the soft fabric of his pants, stopping to massage his dick, smirking as he growls and pushes against me. "Don't. Tease. Me. Ever. Again." I release my grip and smother his mouth with mine, gliding my tongue across his parted lips.

Before he has a chance to respond, I flip my messy hair back and sashay out of the house, leaving my heavily aroused and stunned *boyfriend* behind.

WHEN I PULL INTO the parking lot, Aria's outside waiting at a table.

A bright smile beams on her face as she waves.

I point to the entrance. "Getting mine. I'll be right out."

In a few minutes, I have a steaming Grande Flat White in one hand and a croissant in the other. "Hey, stranger," I say to Aria as I set down my goodies. "How are you? I've missed you."

Aria lowers her gaze. "I missed you too." She sips her coffee before meeting my eyes. "I'm sorry for what I said. I was jealous. You've done nothing but help me with my bullshit situation, and I've treated you like shit. Please forgive me?"

I glide finger around the white top to my coffee. "There's nothing to forgive, honey. You didn't do anything wrong. I was just worried about you."

"You're the only one who's ever cared, and I couldn't even congratulate you on your great news. That's a shitty thing for a friend to do."

"I don't blame you. I've been there before. There were times I'd get so upset when people were able to laugh and have fun. It was unfair to me, and sadly, I hated them. What happened between us is no different."

"You get me so well. It's been a rough few months. Involving you felt wrong, so I pushed you away. I did what I do best—deal with life alone."

"No worries, Aria. I get it. I really do, but don't worry me like that anymore. Maybe give me a heads up once in a while." I sip on my coffee, rejoicing in the sweet liquid hitting my taste buds.

"I will." Aria's frown turns into a full on grin. "I have news."

"Really? What?"

"I have an out to escape my hell. When the idea hit me, I knew I had the ability to go through with it." She giggles. "I've never been happier in my life. Enough is enough at some point, right?" Aria reaches for my hand.

I take it and squeeze. "I'm loving what I'm hearing, but you need to spill. What's your plan?"

"First, let me ask… do you still have your old condo?"

"Actually, I do. Didn't want to let it go in case things didn't work out with Maeson, or if I need space from the man." I laugh. "Do you need it?"

"If it's okay with you—then, yes. He doesn't know where you live, so he won't find me there." Her eyes sparkle in a way I've never seen before.

"Yes, Aria, yes! Move in whenever you're ready. It's even furnished, so you don't have to worry about a thing."

"Thank you! This means a lot to me. I'll finally be free."

"I'm so happy for you, sweetie. And I'm beyond glad you made this decision on your own. When do you need the key card?"

"Whenever you have it ready. I just… need to gather a few things."

"I can get it today, if you want."

I can't believe what I'm hearing. She's finally leaving that life behind

"That'd be great. I'll meet you at Rose Garden."

"Don't you want me to take you? Why pay for another Uber?"

"Oh…" She sips her coffee, then lights a cigarette. "I have some shopping to do first." She points to the Old Navy a few shops down.

"Okay. Sounds good. I'll text you when I leave the house and meet you at the condo." I stand, opening my arms wide.

Aria smiles and plunges herself into me, squishing my ribs. "I missed you so much."

Tears form at the edges of my eyes as I embrace my fragile friend. "I missed you too, Aria Mikaels."

"I love you. You're the sister I never had and the strongest person I know. Every day I begged to find the power in myself, but failed—until recently."

"What you're doing takes a lot of courage and belief in yourself. That makes you as strong as anyone else going through a rough time."

She releases her hold on me and shakes her head. "Sometimes, I wonder, though… is it strength or taking the pussy way out?"

"The only thing pussy about you, Aria, is you have one. Don't ever doubt yourself again." I smile and give her another hug. "Go shop your heart out. I'll see you later."

"Thanks, Ruby. I mean it."

"I know you do."

23

MAESON

The day Axel, Ruby, and I couldn't wait for has finally arrived. Precious Tomorrows's grand opening.

Our mission is almost complete, and my goal to make Ruby the happiest woman in the world has begun.

Before I meet up with everyone, I have one last thing to do.

A decent man can't show up empty handed to the most important moment in his woman's life.

I might not be many amazing things, but decent I sure am.

My mum raised me better than that.

I have twenty minutes before the brigade begins their search for me, so I hustle out of my office, rushing to the nearest flower shop.

Roses. Red roses for her. For any woman I—

"Fuck." I slam my fist against the steering wheel and hit the gas pedal.

Stop thinking so damn much, you bloody nitwit.

I remove the thought from my mind and focus on my main priority—make sure Ruby has no worries about the opening. She should enjoy the fruits of her labor with no extra bullshit, like I did ten years ago with Rose Garden and Club Royale.

Today is strictly about the strongest woman I know, the children, and the women desperate for the things they're unable to find—safety and peace.

It seems all of the invited guests have arrived—including a very pregnant Molly. Axel is first to notice me, and he graces me with a cocky smirk.

I went overboard with the flowers, but three dozen is all I could carry here.

I couldn't carry them, but that doesn't mean there aren't a few more dozen in our house waiting for her.

"Maeson you're fina—" Ruby stops in her tracks. "What... are all those for?"

I grin. "You, Princess."

Her jaw drops. "Me?" She covers her mouth with her hand.

"Yes, lass, you."

"Why?"

I hand her one bouquet and pull her closer, kissing her plump red lips—the ones I've been craving since she left our bed this morning. "You deserve it, that's why. Today is a huge day for you, love. And I'm here to support you."

Big fat tears brim at the corners of her amber eyes. "Thank... you..." She leans her head against my shoulder, not bothered at all by the roses suffocating us. "You're nothing like the person I thought you were ten months ago..."

"Oh? Better or worse?" I chuckle.

"Better, Maeson. So much better." Her voice cracks and my heart does the same.

"Ditto, babe." With a sigh, I lay my temple against hers and whisper, "You're everything I've searched for but was too afraid to find."

"Ditto," she murmurs back.

Our eyes lock and an unspoken agreement passes between us—*our search is over.*

"Hey, love birds, get moving! I'm massively swollen, and ya'll are making me stand out here in these heels for too damn long." The pregnant one always finds the worst moments to interrupt.

Ruby and I dislodge ourselves from each other and join everyone at the front door. We both smile as Molly hands Ruby a scissor to cut the red ribbon blocking the entrance.

"Are you ready?" I ask Ruby in a hushed tone.

"Yes, but I'm scared."

I tilt my head to the side. "Of what?"

"Failure." She lowers her gaze.

Her lack of confidence awakes my beast and the urge to protect her hits me. I puff up my chest. "With me by your side, there's no bloody chance of that happening."

"I'll hold you to that." A small grin surfaces on her face as she straightens her shoulders and cuts the ribbon.

Everyone claps and cheers as the material hits the ground. Even I find myself joining in on the festivities.

How can I not? We busted our asses to get this done in time.

But wait… Ruby hasn't clapped, cheered, or moved at all.

What is she doing?

She's… kneeling… before the doorway.

"This is for you, little girl… This is where you find peace, freedom, and safety. I promise to never allow anyone to hurt you ever again, and do everything in my power to protect each person who takes sanctuary here." Ruby peers up at the sky. "Thank you Mom and Dad for making my dreams possible. I promise the money you put aside for me will be put to good use." Her shoulders shake as she bows her head.

My inner beast growls, pushing me forward.

Protect. Defend. Stop her from feeling pain.

I wrap my arms around Ruby, helping her to her feet. Mascara stains her face and the sight makes my heart constrict. Before I can say anything to soothe her, she places two fingers over my lips.

Between sniffles she says, "Bitter-sweet. Had to be said. I'm okay now."

Expel what's begging to explode from within.

Can't. Not the time. Instead, I nod.

Molly waddles over to us along with Axel and Jax who seem as affected by Ruby's release as I am.

"I'm so proud of you, sweetie pie. That was beautiful." Molly rubs Ruby's arm as she brushes away her own tears.

"Thank you, honey bunches of oats." The pain on Ruby's face is replaced by a sparkling grin.

These two have the most nauseating nicknames.

I might be shaking my head in disgust, but inside I'm smiling like a wee lad on Christmas morning. "Ready to go in, ladies and gents?"

Axel places an arm around my shoulder. "About time you asked, partner. Let's make this young lady proud by showing her what her dreams look like in reality."

I smirk. "Let's do that, *partner* or maybe it's time I initiate you into our fucked up family and call you *brother*?"

"Brother, huh?" He shrugs as we enter the building we slaved over, turning it into everything Ruby wished for and then some. "Doesn't have a bad ring to it…"

"Then brother it is, Ax."

"GUYS?" MOLLY SAYS IN a higher pitch than usual. "I don't mean to ruin the excitement, but…."

"What is it, Mo?" Ruby's at her side in seconds.

"I'm so sorry, this is your special day…" She inhales harshly. "My water broke an hour ago, and I can't deal with the contractions anymore. They're getting closer and more painful by the minute. Gggrrr." Molly hunches over, grabbing her belly. "Forgive me, Ruby, my son seems to have a mind of his own."

"Oh, my God! You didn't ruin anything, you just made my day even better. Let's get the fuck out of here. My Godson's coming!" Ruby's head snaps in Jax, mine, and Axel's direction. "Boys? Car. Now. Jax? Get a grip! Move your legs." When he continues to stand in place as frozen as a statue, Ruby stomps over and slaps his face. "You're about to be a dad, this isn't the time to piss your lady panties." She rolls her eyes at him before guiding Molly out of the building.

Stunned as ever, *Cinderella*, finally opens his mouth, "Dad… I'm going to be —"

Unable to stand by as he scrambles, I grip the man by the arm and drag him to the car where Axel awaits.

Bloody fucking first-time Dads. They're all the same.

Like you were any different?

Touché.

After putting his mom through fifteen hours of labor, my Godson has arrived, and unfortunately for Jax, he didn't get to watch it happen. The bloody idiot passed out because he stood behind the doctor during Molly's examination. Something about dilation, and seeing her at ten centimeters.

But Ruby, being the warrior she is, stepped in and took over for Jax.

Again, bloody fucking first time Dad's.

When he was wheeled out of the room, I couldn't stop laughing.

Former military guy who traveled to the most dangerous places in the world and watched people get blown up can't handle birth?

That makes logical sense.

Anyway, since the fun and games are over, I was told it's time to meet my newest family member—sweet little Alexander.

I knock on the door and peek my head into Molly's room. "Godfather here to see his namesake Godson," I say in my deepest macho man voice.

"He's here, Mae Mae. Come an' get 'em." Molly's normal chipper tone is weak and tired.

Fifteen hours is a bloody long time.

Slipping past the white curtain, I spot Xander in the bassinet. Stuck to the side of it, there's a paper with the usual information.

Alexander Lachlan Kieran
Born: April 25, 2018
8 lbs. 2 oz.

Big boy. No wonder Mo's exhausted.

"May I?"

Molly smiles. "Of course."

The closer I get to him, the more my fingers shake. Memories wanting to be relived rush to the forefront of my mind, but I force them back.

At least for now.

I steady myself before reaching for the sleeping child and slowly lift him to my chest. The moment he's nestled against me, my nervousness is replaced by a natural sense of expertise I used to know and love.

Cherished.

Staring down at his precious face, I realize how much I *really* miss this. Molly and Jax are two very lucky people to have such a blessing in their lives. Some never get the chance because they can't and others do, but don't give enough fucks to properly care for their children. Luckily, there are enough parents out there who do a great job raising their kids, otherwise we'd have a full on shit show in this world.

"Looks good on you." Molly sighs. "I wish I could've seen you with—"

"Me too." Must. Change. The. Subject. "Where's Ruby and Jax?"

"Ruby went the bathroom to wash up. Poor thing never left my side." She shakes her head. "Unlike my fiancé who's napping behind this other curtain." She points the white material blocking him from our view. "Such a big ass man, yet he couldn't handle it. I thought he was having a heart attack. When he passed out, I was partially relieved. At least he was out of commission and not freaking out the entire time."

I laugh, and Xander's little arms fling upward.

Too loud for the little guy.

Luckily, he didn't fully wake up. I lower my voice and sway him side to side. "How long has he been out?"

"Xander? Or Jax?" She grins.

"Teddy bear."

"Oh, he's been in and out for a while—just like Xander. It seems they're on the same schedule. The whole *'like father, like son'* bit has begun."

"Better early than never right? Jax isn't the worst person to resemble."

"True." Molly slides the curtain aside to reveal a sprawled out Jax. She nudges him. "Honey, wake up. Maeson's here."

He murmurs something unidentifiable, then rolls over.

She repeats her attempt, but with a harder shove. "Wakey, wakey."

"Hhhmm? I'm wake."

I lay Xander in his bassinet and stride over to the other baby, bending low enough so my lips are flush against his ear. "Wake. The. Fuck. Up! You. Bloody. Pussy!"

His eyes pop open. "Fuck you! You have no idea—"

"Don't I?" My gaze meets his, and if it were possible, I'd have real fire blazing in them. Fire hot enough to burn his damn tongue off.

"Sorry, man. That was—"

"Not called for." Molly growls.

"I'm… out of it. Sorry. Honest, Maes."

I shrug and extend an arm to him. "You're forgiven—*this time*—but never again, got it?"

He takes my hand, lifting himself. "Yeah. I don't know what I was thinking, brother."

"Me either, but let's move past it before I change my mind and rough you up in front of your son."

"No, don't. The boy probably thinks I'm weak already, he doesn't need another reason to doubt me." A small smirk surfaces on Jax's lips.

"You're right. But, eventually, he'll realize you're a big softy and seek out the brawn of this family—his Godfather."

"That's okay with me, because together we'll turn my little lad into a real man." He scrubs a hand over his unshaven face. "Ruby still in the shower?" he asks Molly.

"Yeah. Maeson can check on her? I'm too tired to move, and since Jax is finally awake, he can watch Xander while I sleep for a bit."

"Sure. Where is it?"

"Take a right out of this room and it's at the end of the

hallway. I'm sorry, we got the short end of the stick with the least upgraded room."

"No problem, I'll find it. You get some rest. And Jax?" I raise an eyebrow. "Take care of these two. Use that big set of balls you got to protect them with your fucking life, you hear me? No more fainting like a wee lass."

He straightens. "I hear ya."

"Good. If you need anything, let me know." I place a hand on the doorknob, turning it. "I didn't have the option, but remember, there's two of you, so you better support each other every minute of the bloody fucking day because the next few months will be hell. You'll struggle, but you'll get through it with love and patience. Strive to do the best you bloody can because this wee boy is helpless without you and you'd be lost without him. And cherish every moment, no matter how difficult things get."

"We will." Molly wipes at her wet cheeks. "Love you, Mae."

My heart constricts. Three simple words spoken by a woman I consider a sister, pull at my heart strings in a way I never thought possible. I meet her gaze and smile. "Me too, Mo. Me too."

24

Ruby

Molly's labor and delivery was a true eye opener. Weeks later, I'm still reeling from the entire terrifying, yet exhilarating experience. Every time I see or even think of baby Alexander, an unfamiliar longing afflicts me.

Motherhood doesn't scare me, but the possibility of history repeating itself does. With my parents medical history, I could end up like them—unable to watch my child mature into an adult.

I've tried to convince myself the timing is wrong and having a family is a bad idea, but the yearning continues to linger through my mind, body, and soul.

What's the right answer, Mom?

I need you… I wish…

"Ruby, are you hungry? I make something good. Something Greek?" Maria stands in the doorway of the living room with a broad smile and her hands on her hips.

"I'm alright for now, Maria. Thank you."

"Okay. I make something light instead." She wraps a purple apron around her waist before washing her hands. "Why you here alone? Maeson upset you?"

"Oh, no. Not at all. I'm just… thinking."

She tilts her head to the side and frowns. "About what? You tell me. I help. Old ladies give best advice."

"I don't want to bother you with my petty problems."

"No bother! Talk, and I cook." She turns, digging in to the fridge and cupboards. When she faces me, her arms are filled to the max.

I stand. "Let me help you. I'm not a bad sous chef."

She shakes her head. "Sit. Tell me what bother you." She sets everything down in a neat pile, then raises an eyebrow.

"Please don't repeat what we talk about to Maeson."

"Never! I keep your words private."

"Thank you. I'm just not sure how to discuss this subject with him because of what he's gone through." I drop my gaze and stare at the pink socks covering my feet.

Out of nowhere there's a loud bang. I jump to my feet, rushing to Maria's side only to find a fragile—*not so fragile*—Maria gripping her pan.

She smiles sadly. "Baby is the *'thinking'* you doing. You want one? Yes, how can you not! Maeson is good man, and he is"—she clears her throat—"*was* fantastic father."

"That's not… exactly the issue."

"Then what?"

"Whether or not I want to be a mother."

"Don't you dare say this! No! Impossible!" She points to the chair under the kitchen island. "Kathiste. We talk."

Kathiste… I know this word… Dad used to say it often.

'Kathiste, Ruby mou, it's time for breakfast'.

It's funny how certain things remain ingrained in your mind for a lifetime and others float away in an instant. It seems my fathers language is the latter.

Once I do as Maria requested and sit, she continues. "You know I never had baby, right?"

"Yes, I do."

"Do you know why?"

"No…"

"Because God never gave me one. We tried very hard, but it

didn't matter. I cried and cried for my failure… for not be normal."

"It's wasn't your fault, though. Technology wasn't the same then. Maybe if it was…"

"Maybe, no maybe, too late now. My point is people pray day in and out for family, but you don't even want to try? Shame. Such shame. Does Maeson know? It will break his heart."

"No, I didn't get a chance to discuss these new feelings with anyone yet."

"Please, tell me why. I want to understand. I had a different life than you, so I don't see the same opinions."

"Okay. Did Maeson tell you… about me?"

"Not everything. Some." She brings two fingers together, leaving a tiny space between them.

"Life was… hard for me after my parents died, and I'm afraid to have something like that happen to my child. I'm better off not wanting a family."

"Ah! I see. You're scared. But why live in fear? Take chance, and maybe, it turn different for your baby. Learn from your life. Take steps to make it better in case something bad happen to you."

"But nothing's guaranteed no matter what I do."

"I know, child, I know. But have faith in your path. We're meant to go through the bad and good to get to where we should be. It makes us stronger, you know?"

"Yes, I guess it does."

"I'm sure it is that way. Look at me, I'm a stronger lady even though my wishes didn't come true. After so many years, I never give up, then one day Maeson came into our lives. Right before our eyes there was the child we never had. He needed parents when his were far away, and when he… *you know*." Maria's eyes shine with wetness, and she covers her mouth, taking a moment to regain her composure. With her free hand, she reaches for mine and squeezes it lightly. "You see, my point is don't give up and don't not want something because you're scared. Do the opposite, desire it with all of your heart."

"You're right. I think I need more time to figure it out."

"As a young woman, you have plenty of time. Don't rush. Whatever is meant to be will be."

"And what is meant to be?"

I jump out of my seat and spot Maeson's leaning against the wall next to our bedroom, grinning.

"You sneaky, asshole! We could've had a heart attack!"

"It's not fun being scared half to death, is it?" He laughs. "Remember that next time you decide it's a good idea to do it to me."

I roll my eyes. "All you've accomplished is to motivate me more than ever to get you back."

"I'm looking forward to the challenge, lass." Maeson struts over to us. "So, what's going on here? Talking dream meanings? Prophecies? Or whatever you European women gossip about?"

Maria laughs. "Close, Yiós. We talk other things, but not for you to know." She pats his forearm since she can't reach anything higher. "Eat? I making good *stuff*." Maria attempts to Americanize the word *'stuff'* but fails.

She's the cutest woman I've ever met. I wish I could adopt her in place of the grandmother I never had.

"Yes to the food." Maeson plops on to the stool next to me and winks. "I'm starving."

I wrinkle my nose and whisper, "Not in front of her, you nut."

"You're no fun." He wrinkles his nose back at me.

"I'm plenty fun when the time is right."

"Fun later, children." Maria smirks. "I'm no deaf, just old." She places two plates in front of us. Each is filled with French fries and a gyro. "Eat." She places her hands on her hips.

That's light food? What does big meal look like?

Maeson doesn't seem phased by the massive amount of food as he shoves a bunch of fries in his mouth and moans. "Maria's homemade fries are the best. And wait until you try her Gyro, you're going to die."

"Thank you, Yiós. I put all my love into everything I make." She nods in my direction. "Don't forget what we talk about." On her way out of the room, she pats my hand.

"I won't. And thank you, Maria, it helped a lot."

Once she's out of view, Maeson nudges my arm. "What's going on?"

I shrug. "Woman stuff."

"Which I can handle if you haven't noticed." He lifts the Gyro to his lips, biting into it. "Go on, I'm waiting."

"Maybe after we eat?"

Maeson takes two bites in a row. "No problem…"—bite, bite, bite—"I'm a fast eater."

"You're not alone with those fears." Maeson sprawls across our bed. "Why'd you think I'd judge you on your feelings about having children? You have a right to an opinion just as much as the next bloke."

I place my feet on the step stool Maeson bought me and grab on the edge of the mattress, plopping onto it. "Since it seems we're stuck with each other for however long this lasts, I felt like this was something you should know." I give him a sideways smile. "Certain subjects are deal breakers in relationships, and I prefer to express my concerns before we get in too deep." I shrug. "Saves us from extra pain."

Maeson entwines his long thick fingers with mine. "First? Not a deal breaker. I'm not only with you to bear my children. Second? If we want *us* to last, we will no matter how difficult life gets. And if you open your eyes, you'll notice I'm a man who takes his commitments very seriously."

"I did notice, but if you've paid any attention to this girl,"—I point to myself—"she has a hard time trusting. I'll believe in *forever* when I see it. Until then, my motto remains, *'one day at a time'.*"

"Whatever you say, Princess. But I'll prove my loyalty to you one day. I've been fucked with and know what it's like not to have faith in others afterwards, but time helps us forgive—time heals us." He caresses my thumb, then brings it to his lips and licks it.

My eyes roll to the back of my head, and I sigh. "Not yet. There's more to discuss."

"Like what?" Maeson continues to kiss and nip different parts of my body.

"Meeting Xander… did you…"—I drag in a deep breath—"were you… affected?" My desire increases as he lowers himself on top of me, but I place my palm against his chest.

The green in his eyes darken, and he frowns. "Aye. The second I saw him, my life as a father flashed before my eyes. For a second, panic took over, but somehow—*don't ask me how*—I overcame it." Maeson drops his head, leaning his forehead against mine. "Holding him reminded me of the good and the bad associated with fatherhood. The anxiety of having a child and possibly losing them still terrifies me. Which is why I agree with you. We might one day want to have children, but it's too soon for us as a couple who's lived together a short four months. There's no rush to make a final decision. Plus, it's too soon for us as individuals since we have internal battles over the idea."

I close my eyes and release the tightness in my chest. "You're one-hundred-and-ten percent correct, Maeson. Same page."

"Same bloody line, Princess."

Incoming Message: Hey are you busy today? Maybe I can meet Alexander? I'm sorry I didn't want to go earlier, but it was too soon for a baby to have strangers visit. I think now that he's a month old, it should be okay? And I promise I won't touch him and spread my adult germs. Let me know. XoXo Aria

This text would've surprised me over a month ago, but after how much Aria has changed, it doesn't in the least. I type a quick response, telling her I'll confirm with Molly and get back to her.

While I wait to hear back from Mo, I wander out to the backyard where my new black cast iron bistro table set awaits. I place my coffee, cigarettes, and phone on it and settle down on the chair facing the sun.

Everything's coming together, isn't it?

Molly's found her happily ever after with Jax and Alexander. All that's left for her is their wedding, which is planned for next year. Then there's Aria, who seems to have found peace after she left that bastard. Finally, there's me… Maeson and I have been in a great place ever since we moved in together.

I might not have that fairy tale story ending, but it's close enough for my standards. And topping off my chocolate sundae is Precious Tomorrows, which has been running smoothly for a month now.

Buzz. Buzz. Buzz.

My phone illuminates, showing two new notifications. The first one's from Molly.

Incoming Message: *Of course, sweetie pie. Come by anytime you ladies want. Love ya.*

I light a cigarette and smile at the *'love ya'* part. Before she became a mom, she was affectionate, but after? Even more so. And I'm basking in it since I haven't felt this much love in years.

Luckily, she makes returning the affection easy by not pushing and allowing me to go at my own pace. It's also easier because my relationship with her has become closer than some blood related sisters are.

Not so effortless with Maeson, though.

Never has been.

My receptiveness with men is an entirely different story. But with an enormous amount of pride, I can say I've made huge strides in the right direction.

Every day I put myself out there by trying something new — even if it's showing him the smallest sign of trust like… holding his hand when I'm scared or dealing with a panic attack versus me going through it alone.

Every step, no matter how small, is a step forward.

"Damn sure it is!" I cheer myself on aloud.

After taking a few sips of my coffee, I check the second notification I received.

This one's a simple, *'Okay'* from Aria.

Message Sent: *Molly said we can visit anytime. Let me know when's good for you.*

Incoming Message: *Today?*

Message Sent: *Sure. I'm not doing much. Pick you up in a few.*

"**H**E'S BEAUTIFUL." **A**RIA SAYS, from a safe distance away from the baby.

Since we've arrived at Mo's place, Aria has refused to get too close to Xander. She kept saying she was too scared to give him her *germs*. And the way she'd say the word, tempted me to ask her what kind of *germs* she's worried about spreading—maybe I need to know too. But I'll keep my mouth shut for the time being.

"Thanks, Aria." Molly's grin widens as she rocks her son. "Are ya'll sure I can't get either of ya'll something to eat or drink?"

Aria shakes her head. "I'm okay, really."

"Same here." I extend my hands toward Mo, wiggling my fingers.

Molly laughs. "He's all yours. I need to pee, anyways." She places him in my arms. "Be right back."

I settle on the couch with the boy and motion for Aria to come closer.

She flinches. "I'll stay here."

I frown. "Why, Hun? You can't hurt him by standing near us."

"Because…" Her voice cracks. "I'm… not… good with babies." She bows her head, focusing on her shoes.

"I wasn't either, but look at me now. Try?"

"No!"

Her reaction surprises me and the baby. Xander's eyes pop open, but before he has a chance to fuss, I sway him like his mom did before. Within seconds, his scrunched up face relaxes, and he returns to sleeping peacefully.

Once I have him settled, I check on Aria, who's backed into the corner of the room. I raise an eyebrow. "What gives?"

She shrugs. "Don't push, please. A lot's going on, and I think it's taking a toll on me."

"I'm sorry. I didn't mean to. I'll stop."

"Thanks." She gives me a small smile. "He's cute, though. Seeing him makes me want one, then maybe I won't be so alone."

"You're not alone. You have all of us, if only you'd reach out once in a while. How many times a week do I ask you to hang out, and you decline? After a while, I don't know what to do differently to bring you closer to me."

"Yeah. I'm not used to it, and I freak."

I purse my lips. "I know the sentiment closely, which is why I keep trying with you. Others don't understand, and they give up since you keep them at such a long distance. Can't blame them for that, right?"

"No, I can't." Aria sits on the floor. "Were you the same like me?"

"Very much so. Maybe worse? And I probably still am from time to time. However, each day that goes by, I bust my ass to change—*to be stronger*. That's what I've wanted to pass down to you ever since we met. Help, support, and love are all I have to offer my friends. The ones willing to accept those things from me, that is."

"Thank you for being there, even though, I haven't been as receptive as I should be." She fusses with her shoe laces. "Don't give up on me, okay?"

"Hell no! You couldn't pay me to." When Aria's frown changes to a smirk, it's like I've conquered the world. "Chin up, buttercup, we've got a lot of bonding and growing to do yet."

"I'm looking forward to it."

"Me too." Molly says as she enters the living room. "But what are we looking forward to?"

"The bright futures we have ahead of us." I giggle.

"I'm all for that." Molly throws her hand up to the ceiling, waiting for my air high-five.

I complete the move by lifting my free arm and pretend slap hers.

Aria snorts.

"Don't hate." Molly grins and repeats the same gesture for Aria.

She bobs her head side to side. "You're both tools, but I wouldn't mind being one with you guys." Aria laughs as she saves Molly's hand from hanging all on its lonesome.

Best friends. Sisters. This is what it's like to have them.

Finally.

25

MAESON

With Ruby away working at Precious Tomorrows, I decided it's time for a *man's* day. Axel and Jax were on board, so we chose to start of the morning at our usual gym.

Coffee—*made the proper Greek way*—in hand and a bag filled with extra clothes, I enter the building. As expected, it's packed solid. It doesn't matter what time of the day it is, top notch gyms like this are always busy as fuck. Lucky for me, I have connections and never have to wait.

I set my bag down, scouring the place for my friends. Between the motivated women running on the treadmills, the overachieving men attempting to lift weights heavier than they can safely manage, and the blokes pretending to belong here while searching for their next bedmate, they're nowhere in sight.

Either Jax and Ax aren't here yet, or they hit up the locker room first, so I check there. "Bloody hell, I knew you tools would be hiding in here gossiping." I plant my hands on my hips and tap my foot like I've seen women do.

Ax laughs. "Don't you know us by now?"

Jax shakes his head and smirks. "You'd think he would after

all these years." He adds an extra bit of southern charm to his tone, matching Axel's.

I lower my head and bend at the hip, waving an arm in front of me. "Forgive me, ladies, it's been too long, and I've forgotten how things used to be."

"Should we show him mercy?" Jax asks Axel.

Axel huffs. "Fine, but just this one time, J."

My smirk turns into a wide grin, then I find myself laughing like old times.

I've missed this more than I imagined.

"Good to have you back, Maes." Axel punches my shoulder.

I nod. "Good to have us all back."

"Hell yeah!" Jax gives me a sideways smirk and opens his arms wide.

I wrinkle my face and step back. "What are you doing? Bloody fuck! You've turned into a pussy." Against my will, another smile rises to the occasion.

"Bullshit! You know you love my man hugs. Regardless of what you've been taught back home, men *can* hug each other. Now come here you, dumbass." Jax wiggles his fingers as he spreads his arms wider.

"Blah." Yet again, *against my fucking will*, my body walks straight into my brother's arms.

He wraps them around me. "See, big man, that's not so bad, is it?"

"It's worse than I bloody thought."

No, it's not. It's soothing in a 'I miss my family, I miss being held by someone who gives a fuck', and a 'I miss hugs.' way.

"Looky here, Frank, a group of hom —"

My beast rises, and I'm in the stranger's face, gripping him by the neck before he has a chance to finish his sentence. "You're about to have your balls shoved down your throat if you keep talking."

"Hey man, let him go! He's turning purple!" Someone behind me says.

"Poor baby, you can't handle it can you? What happened? All

shit talk, but no action out of you? What a bloody pity, was looking for a challenge."

The man baby shakes his head as he tightens his grip on my hands. "Sss… ooo… rrr… rrr… yyy."

I slam him against the lockers and inch my face closer to his, whispering, "Respect—you give it to get it. But where I come from disrespect gets you special treatment—you give it and end up dead. Wanna die because you're an uneducated motherfucker?"

"Nnn… ooo…"

"Next time? Think before you speak." I shove him once more before storming out of the room.

Air. I need air.

I'm out of the building in seconds, ready to smash something into pieces, but someone's bulky hand grabs my shoulder. I turn only to be met face to face with Jax.

He grins. "Lost your cool, huh?"

"A wee bit."

"I think more than that, but what he said was uncalled for. Shit, if someone were to bully my kid about that nonsense I'd flip."

"You know how it was for us growing up—men were supposed to be a certain way and anything less was unacceptable, but I'm over the old school bull. I'm tired of the expectations. I'm tired of pretending to be this strong man who doesn't have feelings, who can handle everything, and who doesn't need a bloody fucking hug once in a while."

"Me too, buddy, but rise above those losers. What they think means nothing to us, or in your case, it shouldn't. Not at our age, we've been through too much to let silly words get the better of us."

"Yeah…" I lean my head against the brick wall and light a cigarette, inhaling deeply.

Deep breath. You're not that fat kid getting beat up in school anymore. Just breathe. You're not the helpless father watching his daughter cry because her school mates teased her. Let go. Let it all go. You've overcome it all, and then some. You've grown from each experience.

"I know where your head is at, but don't go too deep into memory lane, for both of our sakes."

"Trying not to."

He thrusts his hands into his pockets and kicks a rock against the side of the building. "You better not."

Before I can say anything further, Axel joins us. "You good?" He frowns.

"Aye."

Axel nods, then points at my cigarette. "Got an extra?"

I pull the pack from my pocket, handing it to him.

"Light?"

Slicing my head to the right, I allow a small grin to surface. "Want me to smoke it too?"

Axel laughs. "Nah, I'll handle that." One, two, three puffs later. "So much for our bro day…"

I purse my lips. "I'm sorry, man. My fault for losing a gasket back there. Let's skip this place and do lunch instead?"

"I like that plan. Missed breakfast, so you know I'm starved." Axel rubs his stomach.

Jax slaps his palms together. "Where to then?"

"Babe's Chicken? I could go for some fried ch—" My phone rings, and when I see who is calling, I answer right away. "Ruby? What's up?"

"I'm so sorry to bother you on your man day, but you and Axel need to come in. We have a situation with one of the children."

"Be there in five." I hang up and nod toward Ax. "We're needed at PT."

"Shit. Is it bad?"

"I'm not sure. Ruby said it's something with one of the foster kids."

"Let's go."

I shake my head at Jax. "Sorry. Raincheck?"

"Hell yeah. And soon, alright?"

"Aye, brother." I smile and hold out my hand.

He takes it with a grin. "Maybe next time we go somewhere less… crowded."

"Good idea," Ax says for both of us.

HALF AN HOUR LATER, Axel and I arrive at Precious Tomorrows, and Ruby's waiting outside.

As soon as I park, she rushes to the car. "Guys, it's Anastasia. She's having a hard time. I've tried to calm her down—help her in any way I could, but nothing worked. Maybe one of you can at least try?"

The tears shining in her eyes give way to a painful ache in my chest, and in this moment, I'd do anything for her, except face a crying eleven year old girl.

Achilles heel, meet my downfall.

Ax glares at me and frowns. "I got this. Where is she, Ruby?"

Ruby's reaction to my silence matches Axel's, but she wastes no time, and waves for us to follow her.

Once we get to the girls room, I hang back by the door, watching as Ruby and Axel console the child by her small pink desk.

While they figure things out, I take in the room we designed for her before her arrival. Just a little something to make each child feel more at home.

Anastasia's walls are painted with three different hues of pink—hot pink, magenta, and pastel pink. We were told it's her favorite color, and Ruby thought it'd bring her some happiness if she had a room fitting her personality. Then Axel ordered teddy bears, dolls, figurines, and such for each room.

And what did I do?

The only thing that felt right—I painted a small circle in a color matching the room and put my hand print in it.

A small piece of the love I'll always have for Madison, I left with each of these children.

I might be lost in my musings, but from the corner of my eye I notice a shift in the conversation. *She* moves into my line of sight, pointing to me.

Air rushes out of my lungs, and I struggle to get it back when

I *see* the girl. I knew her name, even read her file, but I haven't met her.

Someone must be fucking with me. Playing the worst kind of prank.

"Maeson, can you please come here?" Ruby asks in a low soothing voice.

I can't speak or move. Upset child or not, you couldn't pay me to go near her. She looks too much like my baby with vibrant green eyes and dark ringlets hanging loose past her shoulders.

"Maes…" Axel blocks my view with his bulky body and murmurs. "Don't focus on her appearance. Just breathe. There might be similarities, but she's not her, okay?"

"Sure about that?" I clench and unclench my hands.

"One-hundred percent." He places a palm over his chest and grins. "Lawyers honor."

"Like you have any left." I brush past him and approach the girl.

Imposter.

No, she's not. She's just a kid who kind of looks like your deceased daughter, that's it.

Impo—

"I like…"—hiccup—"your…"—hiccup—"name." Anastasia graces me a tiny smile.

I straighten, throwing on my straight faced, unfeeling mask, and do what I'm used to doing with strangers—hide my accent. "Thanks." I push my hair back with trembling fingers and turn seeking Axel or Ruby's help, but I find they've left me. *Fucking left me with my worst nightmare.* I can handle Xander, he's a boy who doesn't resemble the past in any shape or form, but *her…* not an easy request to fulfill.

Try. She's crying and needs someone. Her short life hasn't been easy, so don't make it any harder.

I settle on the edge of Anastasia's bed, folding my arms cross my chest. "So…" I'm at a loss for words. This awkwardness drives me crazy—it's not *me*.

The girl shifts in her chair. "So…" Her grin reappears.

Just breathe. Give the kid a chance, no one else has.

"What's upset you so much, Anastasia?"

"Stasia, please." She peers down at her shoes as she taps them together.

"Okay, Stasia, it is."

"Thanks." She peeks up at me. "I'm sorry I bothered everyone."

"It's no bother, at all. We're more concerned about you and the cause of your distress." I clear my throat. "Do you, uh, want to talk about it?"

She bobs her head up and down. "I'm confused a lot and moving made it worse, I think."

I nod. "Moving's a big change for an adult, let alone an eleven year old, but we want you to be happy here. What can I do to make that happen?"

This isn't a business transaction, asshole.

Don't make it sound like one.

Is that how you talked to Madison?

"I don't think you can because all I want is my mom and dad. They left me, though." A tear slides down her cheek and she rubs at the wetness until there is no sign of it. "Sorry."

"For what?" I frown.

"I'm too old to cry. It's embarrassing, but, inside I hurt too much."

I lean forward and whisper. "Don't tell anyone this, but I cry too, and I'm *very* old."

A big fat smile appears on her lips. "No way!"

"Yes, way. See, you're not alone. Don't ever let anyone tell you it's not okay to show your emotions. People can be silly, and you shouldn't allow anyone to convince you to change. Be yourself and meet the standards you want to live by, not others."

"I'll try, but it's hard, you know? I want to fit in. I'm teased because I don't have a family, and nobody wants me to be part of theirs. That's why I get so mad, I wish mine didn't do what they did."

"Fu—*forget*—what they say, they don't know what they're talking about. A family isn't always made up of what we think it's supposed to be. Some have a mother, father, sister, and brother, but others only have friends they can call family. What matters most is surrounding yourself with those who truly love you and would do anything for you."

"I don't have friends either…"

"Give it time, you'll surly make friendships here. More kids are arriving soon and before you know it, you'll be in a new school which gives you an even bigger chance to make friends. But don't do what I did when I was a kid and hide in your room thinking it'll happen naturally, you have to put yourself out there once in a while."

"I guess I can try. Did you eventually?"

"Nope. I struggled, and to this day, I regret it. However, I'm not an expert in that matter or the family aspect, but Ruby is. Why didn't you want to talk to her?"

"Because… ladies make me mad. My mom was the one who… sold me for drugs, not my dad. He cried when those people took me away, but she laughed because she had her next fix. It's hard for me to open up with *them*."

"I understand, Stasia, I do, but Ruby is very different. If you give her a chance, you'll see she's more like you than you think. She's the person I was referring to who has no blood family and only friends to call on." I shake my head, still unable to believe how Anastasia ended up in the system.

Both parents are addicts—one sold her to the black-market, the other called the cops when it was too late to get her back.

Anastasia was found during a sting operation and put into foster care once the investigation was over.

Unfit parents and no other living family brought this young girl here.

Anastasia's eyes widen. "Really? She has no one?"

"Not until recently. That's why I suggest you give her a chance."

She shrugs. "Maybe…"

Don't push the subject.

"What made you think I was the right person to talk to? I'm not exactly the right material for mushy stuff." I fold my arms across my chest.

She points to my arms. "Those."

I look down only to realize I'd forgotten to change before we came here—my skin is exposed—the tattoos are exposed.

Shit.

These should frighten her, not the opposite. Intrigued by her reasoning, I raise an eyebrow. "What about them?"

"My dad has a rose tattoo like that, but only one. He said it resembles how much his love for me blooms. When I saw yours... I thought maybe you're nicer than you look."

I huff. "And how is it that I *look*?"

"Scary." She laughs. "Hulk get mad, scary."

I curl my lip, fighting the urge to laugh with her. "I do not! Most people say I'm handsome, not an angry green monster."

"Ew! Handsome. Blah. You're old!" She sticks a finger in her mouth, pretending to gag.

Like I haven't seen that reaction before.

This time around, I don't fight it and burst into a fit of laughter. "Thanks, *child*, now I'll go cry in a corner because you hurt my feelings." I use my well-practiced pout and move to the other end of the bed, facing my back to Anastasia.

"Fine, I take it back... you're not old."

I sneak a peek at her. "You sure about that?"

"Yes!" She giggles.

"Alright." I slide to my original spot. "Did this old guy meet your expectations, then? Did I make your day a little better?"

"I think so. But maybe, when you have time, you'll come back? I miss my dad less while we talked."

An ache reappears in my chest, yet it feels different—in a soothing way. Maybe it's not an ache but a sign the hole in my heart is healing?

After all this time, I hope it is.

"You got it. Next time I'm here, I'll be sure to visit."

"Thank you." She jumps out of her seat and wraps her arms around me—or tries to.

"You're welcome, Stasia. Can you promise me something?"

"Sure, what?"

"Talk to Ruby. I promise she can help you more than anyone else here."

She puckers her forehead and scrunches her lips. "Fine. I will."

"Good. And before I go, I want to show you something." I walk over to the wall at the right end of the room and touch the bright pink circle. "I put this here. It's my hand."

Anastasia frowns. "Why?"

"I had a daughter long ago, and before she passed away, we painted these in our house. Some circles had her hand and others had mine, then we put our names in them. So to pass on a piece of her memory and my love for her, I put one of these in everyone's room. Think of it as someone in this world *does* care and is willing to protect you."

"That's why you built Precious Tomorrows? For your daughter?" She steps closer to the wall and places her hand over the handprint.

"No, Stasia. I didn't have anything to do with Precious Tomorrows, Ruby did. Her dream and wish is to protect as many kids in the foster care system as possible. She doesn't want another child to suffer like she did."

"Oh."

"She really and truly does care for all of you. If there is one woman in this world to put your faith into, it's Ruby."

"Is that what you did?"

"Yes, with all of my heart, and *that* I don't regret for a second."

She grins from ear to ear. "Then I will to. Thank you for helping me, Mister Maeson."

"At your service, Stasia." I bow my head. "Until next time."

Anastasia waves as I step out of the room and walk right into…

Ruby.

A full on crying Ruby.

"That was beau… ti… ful."

"You were spying on me?"

"A little." She sniffs.

"Did I meet *you're* expectations, Princess?"

Ruby nods and smiles. "You exceeded them, my Prince." She

tucks her arm into mine, pulling me toward the exit sign. "You shouldn't be afraid of being a father again. What I saw today proved to me your heart is bigger than you let on."

"You might be right on the heart thing, but not the fear thing. The idea of losing another person I love that deeply while helplessly watching them go is my worst nightmare. "

"Mine too." She nods. "Mine too."

26

Ruby

Infinite alabaster walls surround me. People mingle in the distance. Children laugh while running up and down this… corridor?

Where am I?

I try to move, but nothing happens. Then how can everyone else?

I flex my fingers—that works. I shift my head side to side—good to go. Last thing, I raise my arms—perfect execution there. So, I can do certain things, just not actually move from my current position. Great.

Something vibrates in the distance. The sound becomes louder and more annoying by the second. I search for the culprit, hoping to end the incessant noise, however there're only these white walls and the people—and they're…

What are they doing exactly?

I squint, focusing on them. They're talking, but their bodies aren't moving at all. Everything about this place is off. Terribly so.

"Hello? Can one of you help me please?"

Nothing.

"Can someone tell me where I am?"

Nothing, again. They don't even glance over. I must be dreaming—I better be. If I'm not, then that means I'm back in the psych ward… No! That's not possible, I've been doing so well. The idea of returning makes my heart pump at full speed. The more I image this blankness as my reality, the more my palms drip with sweat.

This is a dream. Just breathe.

I pat the wall—it's real. I touch my own arm—that's real too. This isn't a dream… No… No, no, no, no, no.

The realization turns my legs into jelly, blurs my vision, and causes my head to spin. Someone sent me back, but why? What did I do wrong?

Deep breath.

If I calm myself enough, I can make better sense of what's happening.

Buuzzzz. Buuzzzz. Buuzzzz. Buuzzzz. Buuzzzz.

"Fuck. Someone stop that sound, please." I wave my hands in the air. "Anyone?"

They must be medicated. We all must be and that's what's causing my illusions.

"Ruby?" A soft disembodied female voice travels down the hallway behind me.

I wrestle with my body to turn around, but damn it all to hell, nothing happens. Instead, I nod. "Yes. It's me."

"Ruby, my sweetheart, you need to wake up." Her voice is music to my ears.

A song I'll never forget.

"Mom?"

"Ruby, you need to wake up!" The tone is definitely my mom's, except this time, it's not loving like before, it's harsh and stern. Exactly like when I used to do something bad.

"I am awake. Can't you see that, Mom?"

Buuzzzz. Buuzzzz. Buuzzzz. Buuzzzz. Buuzzzz.

Gah! Someone end that sound already.

"Ruby!" She shrieks.

I close my eyes. This is a cruel dream. I don't want to hear her voice anymore.

"Ruby, please. Open your eyes, my love. You need to wake up."

"No, I'm done playing these games," I mutter. "You're not real. None of this is."

"She needs you. Ruby, my shining gem, please wake up," The imitator whispers in my ear.

Buuzzzz. Buuzzzz. Buuzzzz. Buuzzzz. Buuzzzz.

"No!" I snap my eyes shut and cover my ears.

Cold, feather light touches brush across my skin. Terror crawls through my veins, but I hold steady, knowing whatever this nightmare is will end soon.

Deep breath. Just breathe. In and out. You know the drill.

The connection ends as abruptly as it began. The coolness invading my area? Gone. A sense of hope fills me, and I open my eyes. Before me stands… my mother.

Teardrops cascade down her beautiful face as she opens her mouth wide. "WAKE UP NOW!" The sound is paralyzing—completely debilitating. Her face contorts, morphing into a new face with black and red skin. It releases an evil laugh and rams into me. "You're too late."

A SCREAM ERUPTS FROM my lungs, and I open my eyes to find Maeson towering over me—not the monster I saw before.

I'm home.

"Lass, what happened? You bloody scared the living shit out of me." Maeson's hands travel up and down my body. "Did you hurt yourself in your sleep? Was it another nightmare?"

I grip the silk sheets beneath me, begging my quivering muscles to relax. "I… think so. Not sure. It was… weird." I sit up and shove my favorite knitted blanket away. "Can I have some water, please?"

He places a soft kiss on my cheek. "Aye."

While he's gone, I attempt to replay my dream, but it's still too fuzzy. Only bits and pieces come to mind—especially that odd vibration noise which wouldn't stop.

Vibrating. My phone.

I scoop it off the wooden nightstand and tap the screen.

Ten missed calls.

No voicemails or texts, though.

I slide across the notification for more details and details I get. Each call's from Aria.

Maeson steps into our bedroom and frowns, tilting his head to the right.

"Aria," I say as I select the call back option and listen to it ring.

He presses his lips together and shakes his head. "Hope she's okay, but I'll get dressed just in case."

The ringing continues until the voicemail kicks in, so I hang up and try again.

"Ruby?" A thick manly southern accent fills my ear. "Don't hang up. You need to get to my house. It's bad." The line goes dead.

A sharp shiver stabs its way down my spine, and I drop my phone.

Moving is impossible, but more necessary than ever. My limbs are numb. My throat is dry. My head is jumbled. I. Can't.

I can and will. Fuck the terror running through your veins.

"Ma… Mae… Maes…" My voice refuses to cooperate.

Deep breath. She's okay. Has to be. Just breathe.

Maeson storms out of the closet, hands filled with clothes. When his eyes meet mine, he drops everything, rushing to me. "I'm coming with you. No argument, got it?"

I blink back tears and nod.

Just breathe. Just breathe. Just breathe.

"If something happened to her again because of that guy, I'll end him. Un-fucking-believable. You moved her out of that place, and somehow, she's back there?" He picks up the clothes, tossing them onto the bed. "Ruby, we need to save her even if that means we lock her in our house." He growls before heading back into the closet, returning with a duffle bag.

My mouth drops at the shady thing. "What is—"

"Don't ask. Come, Princess, we have to leave." Bag in hand, he lifts me into his arms as if I weigh nothing at all and runs out of the house.

SHE'S OKAY. SHE'S OKAY. *She's okay.*

The entire drive up until we arrived that was my mantra.

Maeson squeezes my shaky hand as he steps in front of me. "I'll go in first. You wait at the door."

"No." My lips quiver.

"Stubborn." He rolls his eyes then moves past the entrance.

The stench of rotting food smacks me in the face. I should be used to it by now, but it smells even worse today. Nothing has changed, clutter isn't the word for the mess in this house. The broken cupboards haven't been fixed either.

Why am I surprised?

Once we get Aria out of here, I'll make sure she never comes back. Enough is enough. I believed she had control of the situation, but I was wrong.

Maeson stops short, and I slam into him. "Lass…" He backs up. "Turn around. Go back to the car."

"No. Let me through." I shove against his broad body, but he doesn't budge. I try again with the same outcome. I give up and lay my head against his back, releasing a harsh breath. "How bad?"

"Bad." Maeson forces me back another step. "Go. To. The. Car. Now."

"Don't tell me what to do. Let me see her, please. I can help. I can change her mind."

"No, lass, you can't." He's stiff as a board as he turns to me. His eyes are glossy. His cheeks are wet. "Car. Please. I beg you."

"If you care for me, you'll let me through."

"I do and that's why I'm not."

I scowl. "If you don't move, I'll make you."

"Try all you will, but I refuse to allow it."

"Fine." I kick him in the shin. As soon as he doubles over, I speed past him into the living room, immediately stopping in my tracks.

No. No. No.

Aria's small and fragile body lays limp on the floor with a

syringe sticking out of her arm and an empty bottle of pills next to her. She's...

Ended her pain.

"Ruby, step away. Do not touch her. We need to call the police." Maeson's deep voice penetrates my thoughts.

Disregarding him, I sit by Aria's head and touch her face. A tear slides down my cheek. "Why'd you do this? I promised I'd get you away from him. Why, Aria, why?" The floodgates open and my lungs heave. I want to shake her, and beg her to wake up, but I'm too late. "This is all my fault. I could've done more for you—I fucking should've! I'm so so so sorry." There's movement in the corner of my vision, and I lift my gaze. A man stands at the end of the room.

Before I can say anything, Maeson breezes past me in a flash and puts the guy in choke hold. "What did you do to her you, fucking bastard?" He slams the stranger's head against the wall—*twice.*

"Not me. She. Did." He struggles to breathe. "Came. Home. Found. Her." The man sags against Maeson, crying. "Letter. In. Her. Hand. Read. It." He gags.

Maeson shoves him once more before he storms toward us, searching for the note in question. He spots it in her left hand, carefully lifting it. "What did you do? Read the thing, then put it back so you look innocent? Fucking asshole." He mutters.

I watch in a daze as Maeson opens the small sheet of paper and reads it. His tear filled eyes meet mine, and he gently places it in my palm.

Ruby,

I wanted to tell you, but I was too ashamed. If you're reading this, know that I'm sorry. I couldn't infect more people. I couldn't live this way. By the time I was told I had AIDS, it was too late. Too many complications. Too many people affected. He gave it to me, but neither of us knew he had it, so don't blame him. I came here to tell him, but he's not here. I don't have the energy to go home—the home you gave me for my new start. I was so excited for a second chance. It was only possible because of you and the strength you gave me. You saved me from one fate, but this one... there was no rescue in sight. Please forgive my weakness. I wish I was like you. I wish I could live with this, but how can I when I have to tell someone I have a disease? I can't, that's the problem. This was the only way. I'm to blame. I'm so sorry for making you deal with the aftermath. I love you. You're the sister I never had. You helped me in a way noone ever did. You're my hero. Stay strong, even through this. Stay strong for me... Please.

Aria

Similar to this morning, a vicious, violent, and painful scream pleads to be released. I want to fight it. Be as strong as Aria asked, but I don't know how.

It doesn't feel right to act like I'm fine and pretend someone I care for with all of my heart isn't lying here as lifeless as the cockroaches embedded in this nasty carpet.

I'm done fighting. Done pretending. I let go. I let it *all* out—the pain of loss every loss, the guilt, the shame, and the realization this poor girl had no one but me who truly cared in this world.

I didn't do enough to save her. Aria's pain should've been mine to carry.

"I was too blind to see what she was dealing with. Too stupid to connect the dots when she wouldn't touch Xander. Too self-involved to worry about anyone else but me," I whisper.

"No, love, you weren't. You were living the best you could after what *you've* gone through. None of this is on you." Maeson tucks his arms under my shoulders, pulling me up and away from the room.

I want to look back. See her one more time, but whether I do or not, the horrific vision of her in this room will remain with me forever—along with my parents, my ex, and my foster parents.

The monster from my dream was right. I was too late, and it's all my fault.

27

MAESON

Over the last year, I've witnessed many sides of Ruby, except this one who's broken, shattered, guilt ridden, ashamed, low self-esteem, and down in the gutter.

The loss of her friend Aria took a serious toll on her mentally and physically. In a matter of a week, she's lost an unhealthy amount of weight and won't stop crying. I don't recognize her anymore. My attempts at consoling her haven't worked in the slightest, because she continues to blame herself. And the scary thing is, she's not only relating the events leading to Aria's funeral as her fault but everything else that's happened in her past as well.

The death of her parents—her fault. The death of her ex-boyfriend—her fault. The abuse she and the children at her foster care received—again, her fault. Now she's added one more to the depressing list—Aria's passing.

Part of me wants to shake the guilt out of her or somehow force her back to reality, but unfortunately, the heart wrenching process of grieving is long.

Through my own experiences, I've learned there isn't a right or wrong way to deal with fucking unfathomable life events. All you can do is take one step at a time, then one day at a time, and from there, month by month to until eventually, each year that passes it becomes a distant memory which once upon a time crippled you.

I want to help Ruby get to that point—I need to get her there because no one should live the way she's been.

Pushing the bad shit aside is a Band-Aid, and we all know Band-Aids don't last forever. One day, that sucker will slide off, expelling everything you're hiding from. And when that happen, everyone around you is fucked.

I think that day is approaching for Ruby.

One year ago, I met this feisty woman who brought challenge and excitement back into my life. I thought I'd done the same for her—I thought her pain and fears were dwindling.

But I was wrong.

I should've known her mind and body are still in healing mode. I should've known the smallest event would set her off, let alone what's recently transpired.

I should've protected her better by forcing her out of the house.

It would've been better if she wouldn't of *seen* Aria, and I'd simply told her what happened.

Right?

Either way, it's too late for what ifs. What's done is done. I'll just work one hundred times harder to make her believe none of this was her fault. But how, when all she does is ignore my efforts or shuts me out?

I'll find a way, I always do.

What's shocks me further is she's treating Molly the same way. Unimaginable.

Like I said, this Ruby I don't recognize.

Actually, no one does. And we don't know how to bring her back.

I guess this is how Jax felt when I lost my fucking mind.

I wish there was a simple solution to fixing Ruby, but there isn't. All I can do is keep my promises to her by helping her fully heal this time around.

As I step between my two favorite girls, I caress Ruby's back and kiss her flushed wet cheek. "Princess, let's take our seats."

As expected, she doesn't acknowledge me.

I peer over at Molly, who's also crying. "Mo, honey, please find Jax, and I'll get Ruby seated."

"Okay. Okay," she whispers.

"Love, it's time." With a slight nudge, I direct Ruby to the first row closest to the alter of the church.

Again, she doesn't react to me in the slightest, but at least her body goes in to motion—not much motion, though. Ruby moves like a zombie, her feet shift forward in short drastic steps, and her face expresses zero emotion.

That sassy smile I fell for and pray to see a glimpse of every day has vanished from the few signs of life Ruby gives. Along with that, went everything else, including the fire in her eyes.

The fire which told me she was still fighting.

While the priest speaks, I take Ruby's small cold hands in mine, giving them a reassuring squeeze. "Tha gaol agam ort. Agus bithidh gu brath." The hushed words I haven't used in years, slip from my lips with ease. They feel foreign, yet… *right*. I stare at Ruby, waiting for her to do what I'd normally expect.

Please don't do it. Don't Google. Please don't ruin it.

To my surprise, she doesn't. Instead, her bloodshot and swollen eyes meet mine, and she creases her forehead, but doesn't ask the question I see in her gaze.

Knowing Ruby as well as I do, I am one hundred percent sure not understanding what I said is bugging her.

Maybe this will bring her back to me? Even a little?

I grin deeply and squeeze her hands again, whispering, "To be discussed later, lass. Don't fret."

She gives me a slight nod, then stares back at the priest.

Conversation over. There goes the hope glimmering in my heart.

THE FEW FRIENDS WE invited over for a bite to eat after the funeral crowd around a distraught Ruby. Molly, who's also crying, has Alexander in one arm and rubbing Ruby's back with the other.

How to console? How to fix? How to make the woman who stole my heart and fixed my shattered soul smile again?

I don't know. At least, not right now.

"I need a stiff drink. Please." Ruby's voice cracks.

Molly moves, but I hold up my hand from my spot in the doorway. "I got it."

And the dangerous rollercoaster begins. But I'll be damned before I allow it to happen to her like it did for me.

I pour her half a glass of sweet red wine and add two ice cubes.

That's as stiff as her drink will get on my watch.

When I enter the dining room, sadness billows around me and my stomach drops at the sight of Ruby.

Her hands muffle her sobs as she rocks back and forth. I can imagine her doing the same thing as a scared child, scared teen, and now for the second time as an adult. No one should experience so much loss before they turn thirty.

Jax meets my gaze and shakes his head.

I know what he's thinking — *don't give it to her, she'll turn down the same path you did.'* But the last thing I want to do is cause a fight or make her day worse than it already is. One drink, then tomorrow I'll talk to her about it.

Guide her down a better road.

Against my better judgment, I hand her the glass. "Can I get you anything else?"

She peers up at me through tear filled eyes. "No. Thanks."

"Okay. I'll get the table set." I look back at Jax. "Help?"

He nods. "Right behind ya."

Within a minute, Jax strolls into the kitchen with Xander. "She's worse than I expected."

"Aye, and I have no bloody clue how to make it easier for her. She's lost too many people. When will the suffering end?"

"I hope soon. But helping her out of this is the tough part. Have you had a chance to talk to her alone?"

"Not yet, but I plan to tomorrow."

"Good. Someone has too. And if worse comes to worst, she needs to see a professional. We don't want her turning out like you did."

I roll my eyes. "I wasn't that horrible, don't exaggerate."

He huffs. "Want a play by play, brother?"

Slicing my head to the left, I grab the utensils and plates. "I'm good. My memory's still intact, thank you very much."

"Mine as well, and you don't need to relive it again through Ruby."

"That I wouldn't wish on anyone."

Not even my worst enemy.

28

One month. One long, dreadful, and never ending month has passed since... I lost her and guilt continues to plague my soul.

I hoped with more time, I could wrap my head around each event leading to... *that day*. I thought I'd understand why she made the choice she did, and I would feel less… responsible, but I don't. The regret is worse, the voices in my head are louder, and the knot in my chest keeps growing.

Maeson's constant badgering doesn't help, and neither does Molly's. I've tried blocking their voices out by covering my ears, avoiding them as much as possible, and even spending a few days locked up in my old condo. Nothing helped.

I just want to be left alone. Why can't they comprehend that?

What's even more annoying is every time Maeson sees me with a drink, he goes on and on about not using alcohol to deal.

Like I don't know that?

I don't just *need*, I *want*. Lately, I can't proceed without it, but there's no way in hell I'll admit that to anyone.

How I deal with each loss, each beating, each heartbreak, and each fucking painful thing I go through is my damn business.

I'm sick of their pity. I'm especially tired of seeing it on Maeson's face and hearing it in his voice. How many times do I have to say I'm fine? How many times do I have to plaster on a fake ass smile for him to believe me and leave me alone?

I should leave. Find the space I need somewhere far away.

The condo isn't far enough. He has access to it at anytime.

I grab my empty glass and pour my new found favorite drink—*Tequila*—to the rim. Two good sized shots, and I'm out for the count, which is exactly what I need. I used to beg for a full night without nightmares, but now I plead for a least one hour. Well, I did beg for an hour until I met my friend Teq. He blacks me out completely, unlike my oldie but a goodie, Vodka.

How pathetic have I become?

Very, but I tried to be strong. I even did the whole take deep breaths and just breathes that helped during my worst moments, except this time.

I can't let go long enough to forget. Losing *her* opened the flood gates I'd securely locked deep within my mind. And once it burst, the solidified walls shattered. There's nothing holding back the past I couldn't cope with on my own.

The memories, the visions, and the voices torment me every minute of every damn day. Sometimes, I feel like three—*maybe four*—separate people, and others, I'm my normal self—the new Ruby I'd grown to be with Molly and Maeson's help.

How do I explain that to someone without sounding insane?

I can't. No matter how I slice it, I'll end up back in the looney bin because I'm too weak. Too fucking weak.

That's exactly what you are and it's why you didn't notice Aria's weird behavior. It's the reason you failed as a friend. Your ineptitude caused her death. The poor girl gave you all the signs you'd need to help her, but you were too blind. She even flat out told you she found a way out. What did you think that meant?

"I thought she was talking about moving to the condo. Please leave me alone. Please stop! " I implore my internal enemy.

Her sinister laugh bounces around the inner walls of my skull.

I used to fight the multiple fractions of me, but I don't have the power or desire anymore. What's the point? I've failed too many times to succeed now. So, instead of battling them only to lose, I finish my drink and pour another. I'll just keep at it until darkness takes over, then no one can bother me for a while.

Hello, my dark friend, I feel you. I welcome you...

"OF COURSE ME AND *mom worry about our health. But our minds are our worst adversaries, Ruby. If we let the 'what if's' imbed themselves too deep, we wouldn't live our daily lives. We'd become obsessed over our issues. How would that help us or even you, sweetie? You must learn to live day by day and embrace the good things we have, not the bad," my dad says in his soothing accent.*

"Is that why when I think about losing you both, it's hard to breathe and my head feels all spinny?"

"Yes, Princess. You can't allow your thoughts to take control. No matter what happens to us, we'll always be near. But why are we talking about something that won't happen any time soon?" He smiles deeply.

I shrug. "Because like mom says, I'm a worry wart."

"Well, don't be. You're too young for that nonsense, let us grownups do the worrying. Then when you're old enough you can take over."

"Okay. Mom said the same thing."

"She's a brilliant woman, you should listen to her." He wraps his arms around me and kisses my forehead. "Now, off to bed with you, it's a school night." He stands to leave my bedroom and walks over to the door.

I pull my blanket up to my chin. "Dad, wait."

He turns. "Yes?"

"Mom said when I panic or my thoughts get bad, I should take deep breaths and that will calm me. What do you do to help you?"

"Actually, that helps me too. But the other thing I do is close my eyes and count."

"Like one, two, three counting?"

"Well, yes and no. I count to four then add random numbers until I relax."

"Why? How does that help?"

"Counting randomly takes your mind off of what's bothering you because you're too focused on the numbers." He grins again.

"Oh… Okay, Dad. Thank you."

"You're welcome, my little Princess. I love you and good night."

"I love you more."

He blows me a kiss before shutting the door behind him.

Once I'm alone, my worries start all over again, but this time, I do what my super hero dad does. "One, two, three, four, seventy-five, nineteen, thirty-seven…"

I SQUEEZE MY EYES together, wishing the calming dream would continue. I don't want to be awake, that's when all the bad shit rushes to the forefront of my mind. But reality is, dreams are as fake as those bullshit fairy tales I believed in.

There's no such thing as happily ever after. Maybe an ever after, but the happy part was lost on me and poor Aria.

Misery loves… I think we all know the rest.

Don't seek their company. Leave. Get as far away as possible without them knowing.

Maeson and Molly might miss me for a few days. Sam and Bekka, probably even less. It won't be a big deal if I go. I'll be doing them a favor by releasing them from their worries.

I'm a survivor, and survivors succeed best alone. No one should have to watch me drown in my sorrows. My life, pain, and history is my own to deal with not theirs.

It's time I return to where my downfall began.

I'll either find peace or it'll find me. Either way, I need to disappear. It's the appropriate thing to do. I've been a shitty friend, a shitty girlfriend, and worst of all, I haven't helped anyone at all. My dream to show others, like me, there's a better life out there, was a complete failure. How can anyone trust my advice when it didn't aid Aria in the slightest.

I should've seen the defeat in her eyes the last time we spoke and done something. Forced her to open up.

Shoulda. Coulda. But didn't.

Too fucking late.

Enough. Quit the pity party and get out of here. I lift myself into a sitting position and my vision blurs. But I'm so used to the walls spinning around me, I move past the dizziness and trudge my heavy body into the shower.

Goodbye, stench of Tequila. Hello, rose scented body spray. Help me breeze through airport security.

FIVE HOURS LATER, the sticky-icky Big Apple breeze whips my hair in every direction. I breathe in deeply.

I remember you, but I can't say I've missed you.

Cars honking, people bustling around me, the nauseating smell of roasted nuts and hot dogs combined, and the huge skyscrapers—*yup, no longing sentiment here.*

I might not miss New York City, but I'm glad I went with my gut and took the first available flight. The space is needed. There's no friends to annoy with my issues, but there's plenty of bars who'd love my company.

Time to start this journey.

I grab my small book bag and squeeze past a group of tourists, hopping on to the bus routed for Times Square. If there was one place I loved in this city, it was Times Square, especially during the holidays. I remember my mom and dad taking me there and to the Rockefeller Center for ice skating.

Those were the good days.

The bus stops, and I step off—right into a muddy pothole.

Great. Just great. What's next? Rain? Since I don't have an umbrella?

Annoyance fills me until I spot an unoccupied alley where I can light a cigarette in peace. I inhale, exhale, and repeat until the entire thing turns to ash while contemplating where to go. One place comes to mind, but do I really want to revisit that part of my life?

The fling with the owner was just that, and maybe he doesn't own it anymore?

With my shit luck, he probably does. But it's the only bar with open doors this early.

Fuck it. If I see the man, I'll deal with him at that time. For now, I really need a drink.

I chuck my cigarette butt in the trash can and walk three short blocks to my destination. Ace of Hearts. He sure was the ace of my heart—until he shattered it into tiny smithereens.

The shiny red sign appears into view, and I force my legs to stop, not ready to touch the familiar dark cherry wooden door.

Why did I come back here?

I thought running away from Dallas and returning to Manhattan would make me feel better… yet, an odd sensation of wrong doing nudges me.

Why, though?

I know why, but I refuse to admit it.

You miss him. You miss them all. This is why you're a weakling.

No. My feelings on leaving them behind haven't changed. They're better off without me, and I'm better off without them. I got too close, hoped too much, and wanted more than I deserve. From the start of my life, I should've realized I was the cause of the destruction following my every move. I even warned Maeson about it, but he didn't listen. Now with Aria's death, he'll recognize the truth behind my words.

I have.

An older man opens the entrance to Ace's and smiles as he holds it for me.

"Thanks," I mumble before passing through the door.

The interior hasn't changed. Black leather booths and chairs surround square tables covered by blood red table cloths.

From the first time I stepped foot in this place, I'd always thought it looked like a sex club, and boy was I right. I'd accidentally push through a hidden door by the bathrooms and found myself amid sex of every kind. Swingers galore. Young and older couples alike. It was a sight to be seen for my young nineteen year old eyes.

My peeping Tom moment was over before it started when Angelo grabbed me by my jacket. He was such a buzz kill.

But we did have the most fun with him… back then… when you'd let me out more often.

Back then is the key word. I don't need you anymore. I'm whole again.

Bullshit, you are.

I growl internally before closing off my mind and pick an empty seat at the back end of the bar.

It's not packed by any means, so the mixologist—as they're called here—saunters over to me with a sloppy grin on his face. "Never thought I'd see those golden eyes again, Red."

I shrug. "And here I am, Damien."

He nods and continues to smile. "Here you are, is right. Wait till the boss finds out."

I slap a one hundred dollar bill on the bar top and narrow my eyes. "How about he doesn't, and you get me my usual?"

Damien pretends to seal his lips. "You got it, Red. Scouts honor." He bows as he tucks the money in his pocket. "Extra strong Long Island, true?"

"Yeah." I pick up the familiar large white card laying in front of me. One side is embossed with an Ace of hearts and the other is the drink menu. I focus on the creases in the paper, needing to do anything but watch the man I used to call best friend.

When he slides my drink across the bar, he flicks his head in my direction. "By the way, you look fabulous. Not bad for an aging, mid-twenties girl. You've lost a lot of weight, Red. Still got that ass, though." He laughs as he hands me a black straw.

"Thanks. Life's changed me."

As expected, the reminder turns Damien's fabulous smile into a displeased frown. "I've told you this before, and I'll tell you again—life fucks with us all, and you know that as well as I do, but our paths have been mapped out already. There's nothing we can do about it. Let go of it already, please."

"Was is that easy for you to do? Because last time I checked, you were as fucked up as I was."

"Honestly? I've moved on. Living my days thinking about that dreaded basement wasn't doing me any good. You saved me, and I owe you big time. If it wasn't for what you did... I'd be..." His icy gray eyes flicker, and he snaps his mouth shut.

I take a big gulp of my adult iced tea and raise an eyebrow. "Go on, please enlighten me... you be what?"

In slow motions, he moves his head side to side. "Nothing. Forget I said anything."

I grind my teeth. "No, you don't get to pull that shit with me. Spit. It. Out."

"I'd be suffering all these years later. I'd be a fucking mess… like you." His voice cracks as his eyes meet mine.

With my lips pursed, I stare at the man who I took beatings for. "Those nights aren't the only reason I am the way I am, Damien. So much more has happened since then."

"Then tell me so I can understand. Because from where I stand, you were the strongest kid I knew, and I just don't get how that fierce little girl could let the bad shit control her as an adult. You were my hero and the person who inspired me to be as bad ass as you. Shoot, I even got the same tattoo, hoping it'd give me the same super powers." He grins sheepishly.

An unexpected chuckle escapes me. "Did you really?"

"Yeah. And I think it worked because I'm cured."

"That's hard to believe. When I saw you last, you were bouncing from girl to girl looking for an escape."

"As were you, especially with Angelo. But people change, they grow, and they let go of the past in order to move on."

I cup my empty glass and lower my head. "I'm trying."

"Obviously, not hard enough."

"Like you'd know?" I roll my eyes.

"Explain. I'm all ears."

"Fine. But remember, you asked for it."

I spend the next hour and a half reliving the years Damien missed out on. The years my best friend chose his boss over me.

"Shit, Red. I'm so sorry… I didn't realize…"

"You had no way of knowing, especially after how we left things…"

"Right, that was a dumb decision on my part, but I needed the money badly."

"And I told you, I had it. I told you, I'd take care of you until you got a new job."

"Yeah." He sighs. "I shoulda listened and maybe what

happened after you and Angelo broke up wouldn't of gone down. I could've been *your* savior."

"I didn't need a savior, I needed my best friend. But coulda and shoulda don't matter anymore, Damien. Neither of us knew how my life would turn out."

"True." His gray eyes light up. "So, you were rich the entire time, and you didn't say shit to either of us? What kind of friendship is that? Even worse, you pretended to be broke with Angelo—aka the man you *loved*."

"I had my reasons and don't regret it. When people are clued into wealth, they act differently, and I didn't want that to happen with either of you."

He hands me a third drink. "I get it. You wanted us to care for you as the Red we already knew, not the filthy rich one." He groans. "Man, I wish I listened to you back then. And I wish you woulda told Angelo too. You know the decisions he made—"

"What decisions would those be?" The familiar deep bravado pierces my ears. The man I knew intimately for over a year is directly behind me, close enough to feel his breath on the back of my thin T-shirt.

I freeze and cover my face with my hair.

Damien's grin deepens. "Hey, Ange. I was talking about your new idea to add food to the menu, that's all."

He didn't blow my cover for once, thank the Lord almighty. Now's the perfect moment to skedaddle.

Before my ex can respond or notice me, I grab my book-bag and dash to the bathroom.

If I stay in here long enough, he might end up leaving so I can avoid him completely.

Please don't make me face him again. I can't deal with the embarrassment or the feelings I buried away seven years ago.

29

MAESON

This is a nightmare. It has to be. She's been gone for two weeks, and I haven't a clue of where she is. At first, her cell would ring, then it'd go straight to voicemail, now it seems to be off the grid.

I promised her so many bloody things and haven't kept one, what kind of a man does that make me?

A shitty one at best. Even my pathetic attempts to find her have failed, and my last resort is more appealing as each day goes by—hire Jax's Marine buddy. His investigative skills are beyond impressive, and he has high class connections—ones I needed two weeks ago.

If you wouldn't of made your little runner… run, you wouldn't be in this fucked up predicament.

I knew I was pushing too hard, but my biggest fear was her turning down the wrong path, fucking up the progress she's made.

Good intentions—terrible execution.

Sadly, I'm not the only one in panic mode. Molly's a complete mess. Comforting her with more promises I'm not sure I can keep was my only option. For now, Jax and I appeased her enough to relax and focus on Xander. Jax even talked me up like I was some type of a God. *'Maeson's the fixer, Molly. Trust in him. He takes care of everything.'*

Yeah, I take care of everything all right… Exhibit A, Ruby's missing for too fucking long.

Fixer, my ass.

Speaking of my brother, Jax is calling me. Our connection is so deep, he senses my thoughts. I chuckle and tap the green button on my cell. "What's doing?"

"Any news?"

"None yet, but I need a favor."

"Hit me."

"Get me in touch with your guy. I didn't want to over step the boundary, but she's left me no choice. For all I know, she's dead on the side of a road somewhere. I can't sleep knowing I didn't do everything in my power to find her." My chest tightens and it becomes hard to breathe.

"You sure about this?"

"Aye. Privacy be damned! If she didn't want me to search for her, she should've told me to fuck off forever. But, she didn't, so like I promised her and Molly, I'll keep those I lo… care for… safe."

"I'm with you there, but I also get why she ran off. The poor girl had too much go wrong in her short life. Too much damage and not enough healing. Just remember how to handle things when shit hits the fan, okay? See her decisions through the ones you made when I was losing sleep over you."

"Aye, I remember… I'll never forget." I pause as another pang stabs my heart. "I never said thank you, but since I know how you felt? I am so very grateful to you and sorry I ever made you go through it."

"It's in the past, brother. We've lived and learned. Now, let's worry about the present and bring Ruby back to her family where she belongs, Maes."

"That's the plan."

New York. Her phone last pinged in Manhattan. And lucky for

me, Jax's connection found the last address she was at. How was Ruby's hometown not one of my possible guesses?

I'm such a bloody idiot.

Dumbass or not, I need to figure out what to do with the information I've been given. Do I go after her, or do I let her be? My beast roars at the idea of leaving her in a city filled with the painful reminders of her past. He wants her back.

I want her back. I want her more than I've wanted anything in my life. Except for wanting my daughter back, of course.

She's given me purpose again. She's made me smile more times than I can count. She's made me *feel* on a more than a friendly level. Ruby has taught me so much more than any other woman has. How can I not want my Princess back? I'd be a fool if I thought otherwise.

Done. The decision is made.

New York City, here I come. Maeson Alexander is about to wreak havoc up and down those bloody streets until he finds his...

Other half.

30

Ruby

In the last two and a half weeks, loneliness has dug its claws into my soul. I was so used to being friendless and family-less, I've never realized what it meant to truly be alone until I left Dallas. Now I'm having major doubts.

I was probably better off being smothered by them than drunk and high by myself—as alone one can be at bars and clubs.

My nights were spent in those packed places just so I was surrounded by sounds and not my nightmares. Although, my days… those were harder to deal with—hangovers galore. Somehow I managed. Rinse and repeat has been my motto… one that's getting old.

I should check in with Maeson… or Molly. Yeah, Molly. She's the understanding one.

I grab my old phone and replace the battery I removed. Smartphones are too easy to track and knowing how Maeson thinks, I bought an old school flip phone as a backup. It takes a minute for my iPhone to light up, showing missed texts, calls, and voicemails.

I should listen to these first in case I don't want to call them yet. They might be too mad or even worse, they may never want to see me again.

Molly - *Where are you, honey? Please call me. Let me know you're okay...*

Maeson - *Lass, stop running and come home. We can face this together if you'd give me a chance.*

Molly - *Xander misses you. I miss you. Please come back home.*

Maeson - *I thought we had something... different... something special... I guess I was wrong.*

Sam - *Girl, I'm not gonna sugar coat it... come home. Everyone is going crazy looking for you.*

The missed texts continue to pour in, but I stop reading as something catches my eye. All of them say *'come home'*.

Is that what Dallas is? My home? Could I've really found it this time?

No, you idiot. They are using your weakness against you. Stay where you are... it's fun.

They wouldn't do that... would they? What reason—

My other cell rings. Damien's name flashes on the screen. "What's up?"

"Ahhh, Red. Can you imagine my surprise when I saw your name in Damien's cell? Here I thought the shady woman who abruptly left my bar was just some rando, but come to find out, she's my evasive soul mate."

At the sound of his husky voice, chills crawl up my spine.

Stop.

I was lucky enough to avoid him last time, but I guess deep inside, I knew evading him completely was too good to be true. I open my mouth, then clamp it shut. What I needed to say was spoken the day he left me for the fiancé I never knew he had.

Soulmate, my ass.

"I hear you breathing, sweetheart. Dodge me all you want, but you know how things work with us. We're connected, always will be."

I huff. "We haven't been anything since you made your choice, *Angie*." I grind out the nickname he despises.

"Now, now… Red, things have changed. I was stupid then."

"No argument there, but what's your point?"

"Meet me at Ace's."

"Not happening."

"Don't make me beg. You know what begging does to me."

"Beg or don't, I don't really give a shit. I'm not coming there."

"Fine, have it your way. I'll make you come somewhere else." He chuckles.

I roll my eyes. He hasn't changed one bit. Surprise, surprise. "Goodbye, Angelo." I slam my phone shut and chuck it across the room.

My insides are already torn between the past and the present, seeing him won't help the situation in the slightest. The last thing I need is old feelings showing up while I'm in a relationship — even if it's one I'm not so sure I'm still in.

You should go there and set him straight. Tell him to fuck off face to face. End that chapter with a bang.

Part of me loves the idea, but the other screams — *steer clear*. With my questionable judgement's lately, I'm not surprised which side wins — closure it is.

Maybe if I find peace with minor shit, I can find some type of solstice with the bigger ones?

I'll never know if I don't try. Once I'm done with him, I'll call Maeson and let him know I'm coming… home.

THE SECOND MY FEET cross the threshold, I realize I've made a mistake. With Angelo you don't receive a conclusion, you're inundated by more questions than you started with.

"Red…" His voice used to sound so sexy, but compared to Maeson's, its severely lacking.

Lacking or not, it still affects you.

"Angelo…" I raise an eyebrow, inspecting him. His dirty blonde hair is shorter than I remember, other than that, he's the same tall, lean, and muscular man I knew as a teenager.

"You're more beautiful than ever. I must say you've officially outshined that stunnin' red gem you're named after." His icy blue eyes bore into mine.

I curl my lip. "Lame compliments get you nowhere."

"Since when?"

"Since you fucked up, and I lost faith in your bullshit." I cross my arms against my chest, hoping to appear stronger than I feel.

Angelo slaps a big hand over his heart. "Shit, Red, that hurts. I wasn't the only one with faults." He lowers his gaze. "I'm sorry. That was wrong of me."

Is he kidding? How can he hold my 'faults', as he called them, against me? I was a young abused female who had nothing left to lose, of course I wasn't a perfect girlfriend.

Inside I'm fuming and want to scream, but on the outside, all he sees is calm Ruby—*Red* as he likes to call me. "Faults, huh? Which one are you referring to? Was it all that money you wished I had? I wasn't high enough on your totem pole, which is why you swept me under the rug without a second thought. Oh wait, that wouldn't have been a flaw of mine—it was yours." I purse my lips. My blood pressure's rising. I should calm down, but the broken heart he left me with still hurts. "Maybe it was all the shit I took in that foster home before I met you and hadn't had a chance to deal with it? The past you couldn't bring yourself to help me with because it was too fucking real for you. Was that what caused our downfall?" I tap my chin, looking up at Angelo innocently and a whisper, "No, Angie, it wasn't. We both had imperfections we didn't want to face. Plus, we were too young and too stupid to realize how wrong we were for each other. You gave me an escape for a short time and I gave you…" I shake my head. "I'm not sure what I gave you, but it doesn't matter now, it's in the past."

"I'm sorry. You're right." He smiles sadly and wraps his fingers around mine. "I want to show you something."

I nod, allowing him to take the lead.

He pushes past the hidden entrance of the private swinger area, stopping at the next door which leads to his... pleasure room.

"Remember how much fun we used to have?" He rubs his hard dick over the denim fabric covering it. "I tried to forget, but who can forget Red once he's had her? Got divorced over you. No one was ever good enough. No one made me feel alive like you did. Please, join me again, Ruby Red." He grazes his lips across mine.

Time freezes. Our bodies are flush against each other, but the usual sexual desire I once felt for him isn't there. No chills. No goosebumps. No wetness. Nothing at all.

He's not the man for you. You know who is.

A tiny broken voice—one I haven't heard in ages—over powers the others. She was too weak to speak up... until now.

Find the beast. He fulfills us. He's beautiful. He chose us regardless of our imperfections. This man didn't. He's a fake.

Something's happening to my mouth, something that hasn't happened since Aria passed away. The edges of my lips extend on each side, until a full grin surfaces. I straighten my spine and face the pale blue gaze I no longer hunger for. "Angelo, I'm not Red anymore. I haven't been since I left this place. What you needed from Red, *I* cannot fulfill. And what Red needed... *I* no longer need from you."

Angelo sighs, releasing his hold on the door knob and kneels. "Mistress, you've changed so much, yet I haven't. I miss it. No one else wields your power. No one makes me ruby red like you used to. They're all pathetic replacements who pale in comparison, and I'm in need of more." He reaches for my hand, tugging me closer.

I shake my head and pull away. "I'm sorry, Angelo, time *has* altered me. I'll never be the woman you desire."

Angelo lowers his head as he stands. "I've made many mistakes and leaving you behind was my biggest one. I wish you'd reconsider. I'm a better man—I've grown up a lot." He raises an eyebrow. "Unless... someone else has captured your heart? Is that the case, Red?"

Maeson's smoldering emerald green eyes pop into my head and nod. "There is... or was... I'm not too sure right now. But regardless, you and I won't be happening. Fool me once..."

"I ain't gettin' a second chance. You've made it very clear that I'm not the one to fulfill your desires. I hope you find happiness, if anyone deserves to be properly loved, it's you."

"Thanks, Angelo. That means a lot coming from you."

"So, let me guess, you ran away from him to figure your shit out?"

I laugh. "You know me so well."

"How can I not with the connection we had." Angelo shifts toward the door leading to the bar. "From one friend to another, I want to offer you a piece of advice—fuck running away all the time and face your issues head on. Go get your man before it's too late." He holds the door open, waving me out of the swinger room. "Leave the past behind already. Let go, Red, let go."

"I will, but before I do, there's one last thing involving our past that needs to be resolved."

"Oh? What's that?"

"The day you left me, I was pregnant. I wanted to surprise you, but you broke up with me before I could."

"You're lying! There's no way... we were so careful..."

"Not every time. Remember?"

He swipes a hand across the five o'clock shadow growing on his normally clean shaven face and groans. "I do."

"I believed you when you said the chances of it happening were low. I was so young and stupid." I shake my head.

"It appears, I was too." He lowers his gaze to the hardwood floor. "So... I've had a kid in this world for all these years, and you haven't told me? I would've stepped up. No matter what ridiculous choices I made, I always loved you. Shit, I still do. I'd do anything for you. Our relationship wasn't just about that room where Mistress Red did her thing, it was Ruby and Angelo living their day to day too."

"Don't go there. What we had wasn't anything more than a superficial connection. You fulfilled your needs and wants on a transactional level. I was the idiot who fell in love only to find out I didn't meet *all* of your requirements. I was devastated when you chose someone else. Your decision affected mine shortly after. I settled with the wrong person. Your actions caused me more pain than the beatings I endured. Because of you, our baby…" My shoulders tremble as a sob breaks free.

"Our baby, what?" When I don't answer, he drops to his knees and clutches my hands. "Please, tell me. What happened?"

"I tried to be strong and move past my love for you, but… it was too late. My pregnancy ended at eleven weeks."

"No! No! No!" He smothers his face against my belly. "Why was I so fuckin' self-involved? I knew my heart belonged to you, but status mattered more. We could've had a family—we could've been happy. Instead… Fuck! I'm so sorry."

Anger grips my soul as the memories I locked away break free. I used to imagine how this conversation would go, and how I'd make him pay. I wanted him to hurt as much as I did. I wanted him to beg for forgiveness. I yearned to bruise his skin from head to toe.

Too many men took advantage of me. Between my disgusting foster father and my pathetic exes Angelo and Ray, my mind, body, and soul never had a chance to heal. The build up of mistakes, regrets, and frustrations has reached their eruption point.

It's explosion time. Get the retribution we deserve. Two of them beat us to a pulp. The other only needed us for our skills. They fucked us for kicks. I've been dormant for far too long, let me out. Release the pain. You're happier when I take control.

"Stand!"

His eyes widen and his jaw drops. "Mistress?"

"I said, stand!"

He rushes to his feet.

"You have one minute to prep." I turn, striding past him and into the bar.

When Damien notices me, he grins. "She's back. I knew it wouldn't take long."

"She's always been here." I tap my temple. "I just temporarily put her away."

"Same. It seems the Dom in me needs a release from time to time. No one since Angelo?"

"My ex forced to me into submission, remember? And my new guy… he doesn't know."

He drops the plastic cup in his hand. "How can I forget… I just thought after… you took your rightful place."

"Not yet, but today, I will."

"Business or pleasure?"

"Business. Settling my dues."

He nods. "Past debts must be paid. Will you tell Maeson?"

"For sure."

"Will you tell him *everything*? Including how this is part of who you are and it's your therapy?"

"Yeah. I need to be whole again."

"You definitely need to heal. It's time." He hands me a small towel. "In case things get messy."

"Thanks."

"I'M SO HAPPY TO see you, Mistress. I promise to be good." He reaches for me.

I slap his hand. "Kneel! You've forgotten your place. Lessons must be learned."

"Yes, I've failed you. I've failed our child. I've—"

"Shut your mouth! Enough with the bullshit. Why are you here, Angelo?"

"Forgiveness. I seek forgiveness."

"Why am I here, Angelo?"

"Atonement. Redemption. Compensation. Release."

"Right. Let's begin. Rules?"

"I don't touch you. No sex. No attachment. Use my safe word."

"Ready?"

"May I ask a question first?"

I nod.

"Is this the end for us or the start of something new?"

"End. The finale to our story."

"Okay." He lowers his gaze. "Red."

"Hands."

"Tighter, please." He begs as I wrap the rope around his wrists and fasten it to the bedpost.

"Begin the count." My body tingles with a sense of power I haven't felt in too damn long. I miss this part of me.

Being a Dom to a consensual Sub was the perfect release. The role gave me the control I sought, and in turn, I gave someone the pleasure they needed. It was a win win for both parties. Sadly, I lost my true self when I met Ray, but that changes today.

Red is back for good.

"Three!"

I tighten my hold on the black belt and flick my wrist, cracking the smooth leather against the pale skin of his back. "Again?"

"Yes, Mistress."

As we continue, my heart pounds at top speed and my breathing has intensified to an unmanageable point. Imagines flash before my eyes, ones I never wanted to see again. The restraint I had—gone, and I find myself unable to distinguish between what's reality and what's not. "Free me of the past! Free me of the memories!"

My submissive groans. "Only you can do that."

Who does he think he is? Punish him!

Black and white spots invade my vision. "I didn't tell you to speak!" I pull my arm back, then propel it forward at maximum speed.

When the belt connects with Angelo's body, he jumps. "Yellow!"

It takes me a moment to register what he just said, but once I do, I toss the belt aside and drop to my knees. "I'm so sorry. I lost myself."

"I spoke out of turn. It was my fault." He stands and holds his arms out.

I reach up and untie him. "No, it's mine. We shouldn't of done this. I'm too angry... too hurt. My mind isn't in the right place, and I saw you as an opportunity to heal, but I was wrong."

He shakes his head. "I pushed your buttons on purpose. A

selfish part of me knew how our last interaction would end, but I didn't care because I missed you too much."

"Did I hurt you?"

"No. But you would've if we didn't stop."

"Yeah." I peer down at the floor. "I should go."

"You won't find peace or freedom here, but we both know where you will." He helps me to my feet and wraps his arms around my body. "Follow your heart, Red."

Yes! Follow the path leading to... Him. Reunite us. Become whole. Then you can forgive the others.

31

MAESON

Bloody hell, this hotel's a shit hole. Why wouldn't she stay somewhere safer?

Because her mind's clouded as fuck. Don't act like you forgot how bad those days where.

True.

While I was down and out, I couldn't care less if I was sleeping on a filthy street or a plush mattress.

"Sir, you need to move your car or pay the meter," A middle aged woman says through the open window.

I shake my head. "I apologize officer, I thought I'd only be a minute. I'll take care of it now."

She nods and smiles. "Not from around here, huh?"

"No, not at all." I grin as I realize I didn't hide my accent from a stranger.

"Welcome. Just know this isn't the best neighborhood to experience what the Big Apple has to offer. Find who you're looking for and get outta here before you get into trouble." She taps the door before walking back to her car.

As soon as she disappears, I look for the nearest meter and spot it at the corner of the block. I pay the thing, grabbing the ticket it spits out and place it on the dashboard of my car.

With that taken care of, I head back to the hotel and wait for Ruby by the entrance.

The first time I went in there, they refused to give me any information because they thought I was a cop. *'We ain't narks 'round here'* the guy at front desk said. The dirty fuck was lucky I kept myself in check and didn't bash his head in the wall.

But it is what it is. Fighting isn't in the cards today, so I'll just wait around until she shows up.

Could be hours or days, but this is one woman who's worth it.

After two hours of complete boredom, a petite figure steps out of the alley. I'd recognize her anywhere. "Princess," I groan with relief.

Ruby eyes widen.

I smile deeply and take a few steps closer to her, opening my arms wide.

Ruby's staggered steps don't slow her down as she rushes into my hold.

Neither of us speak while we embrace like we haven't seen each other in years.

I don't know how she's truly feeling, but I for one am beyond grateful to see her beautiful face. The poor girl has been to hell and back, so no matter how sunken in her eyes and cheeks are or how thin she's become, she'll always be my Princess.

Eventually, when she's back to normal, I'll plump her back up.

I smother my face against her neck. "I've missed you, lass."

"And I you," she slurs. "How did you find me?"

My gut sinks. Early evening, and she's drunk—not a good sign. "I have my ways. You should know that by now."

"True. Expected you to show up at some point. Not surprised. Waited for it actually…"

"Well, here I am to whisk you back home where you won't be all alone. You shouldn't have run away to begin with, but I get why you did. I ran too."

"It was too much being there, and I didn't know how else to deal." Tears brim at the edges of her amber eyes.

I shake my head and place a finger on her lips. "You don't have to explain anything to anyone. You're an adult who can make her own decisions. My only concern is, are you finally ready to accept my help and support?"

A faint smile graces her lips as she nods.

A chuckle escapes me. "Then let's get out of this shitty neighborhood and go home already."

"Wait. Not yet. One more thing to do. Please."

"Oh? What's that?"

"I want to visit my parent's graves. Need to feel close to them."

"Your request is my demand, lass." I peer up at the hotel. "Anything you need up there? Or can we skedaddle?"

She laughs. "You're so old."

"And you love it."

"Sure do. And yup, a few things up there. Be right back." She hands me her purse before rushing to the entrance. In two minutes she's back carrying a small bag. "Okay, ready."

The moment we settle into my rental, relief and pure contentment washes over me. "Lead the way." I lay a hand on her thigh. "I can't wait to meet your parents. I hope they like me."

She giggles, sounding like the old Ruby I've missed so dearly. "I was just thinking the same thing. But how can they not? You're an old rich guy who won't leave my side even when I treat you like dog crap."

"Isn't that the truth." I attempt to pout, but it turns into a defected smile.

"But you stick around 'cause I'm amaze balls, and no one compares." Her infectious giggles reappear.

There you are, Princess. Flee the suffocating shadows and come back to me once and for all.

"That's one statement I can't disagree with. And since you're so grand, do you mind setting up the GPS?"

"Sure thing, Mae Mae." She grabs my phone, tapping away on the screen, then places it on the dashboard. "All done."

"Thanks."

As a mechanical voice guides us to the cemetery, questions inundate my mind. But I'm worried if I ask them now, she'll find another reason to run again. So, I give myself a minute to think before I say something stupid.

Minute's up, and I open my stubborn mouth. "How was your visit here? Do anything fun? See any old friends?"

Ruby stills. "It was okay. And yeah… I met up with some people I used to know." Her phone beeps and she pulls out a flip phone — *which I've never seen before* — and reads the message on the screen.

I look over and yes, snoop. The words are as clear as day and my mind goes blank, but my beast roars.

I'll always love you, Red. If you ever change your mind, you know where to find me.

Say what?

Who the bloody fuck is *Red*, and why is my *Ruby* getting love messages from another man?

I force myself to settle down and calmly caress her arm. "Is everything alright? You look as if you've seen a ghost."

She snaps her phone shut. "Um. Yeah." Ruby peers at the window. "There's something I need to tell you, but we're almost at the cemetery, so can it wait until after?" Her words are less slurred than before.

I'm assuming the dreaded message sobered her right up. "Sure. I'm ready to listen whenever you're ready to talk." I tilt my head, smiling as she faces me.

There's nothing for me get pissed about if she's willing to be honest.

WATCHING RUBY AS SHE spoke to her late parents tore at my heart strings. She broke down more than once while telling them everything they've missed out on.

When I attempted to help her, she waved me away. It took her about an hour and a half to spill her soul, but I would've stood there for days if it brought Ruby some sort of peace. And I think it did because she hasn't stopped smiling since we left.

"Pull into this lot." Ruby points to the right where there's an abandoned building. "There's a lot I need to explain before we go home, and I need you to listen with an open mind." She frowns. "Please?"

As much as her words worry me, I nod. "Go ahead. This is a judgement free zone." I park the car, cutting the engine.

She releases a heavy sigh. "Where do I start?"

"Well, I know the beginning, the end is unknown, so how about the middle?"

"Okay. While I was here, I went to see two old friends. One is Damien, he lived in the same foster home as me. So, I went to the bar he worked at when I lived here, hoping he was still there and sure enough, he was. We reconnected which gave me a chance to let go of some of the hurt he caused me when he chose someone else over our friendship—*our bond*." Her eyes become glassy.

I frown. "That's harmless, love, why do you look so upset?"

She shakes her head. "The bar Damien works at is owned by an ex of mine… the second friend I mentioned. His name is Angelo. He… ugh… I don't even know how to say the words… how to explain."

"Just come out an' say it, love. Rip off the Band-Aid."

"We were… I was… his Dom." Ruby's cheeks turn red and her bright amber eyes shoot to the floor of the car.

"Dom… as in… *'Mistress you own me'* kind of deal?" I raise an eyebrow, truly intrigued and not in the slightest disturbed.

She peeks up at me, smirking. "As a matter of fact, yes. Angelo wanted to be dominated in every way, and I needed to dominate—to hurt, to own, and to finally tell someone what the fuck to do. So, when he propositioned me, I accepted. In time, it had turned into more than just a business deal, we were stupid and got attached. Then, as if on cue, I ended up getting hurt." Ruby rolls her eyes. "He chose a *normal* girl over me and that was it. I left the bar and never turned back… well, until recently."

"And now that you've seen him, how do things stand?" I wanted to throw up thinking the bloody question, and since I've gone and asked it, I think I might.

"The same as when he left me, except he's single now. But I'm not the woman for him, and he's not the man for me. All he did was remind me of the past I don't want to relive." She shrugs. "Being around him made me realize how much I missed you and how right *you* are for me."

No matter how stupid it looks, I grin from ear to ear. "You know I've been told I have that special *'once you've gone Maeson, you don't go back'* affect on women, so how you feel is completely understandable."

Ruby slaps my shoulder and laughs. "Conceited much?"

"Hell yeah! You should know that by now."

"You're right, I do. I guess I had a lapse in memory."

"Aye, that Angelo bloke must've messed your whole mind up."

She shakes her head and rolls her eyes. "Oh, please. Don't start with the jealous commentary now."

"Fine, fine. But I do have a few legitimate questions left."

"Okay, go for it." She clasps her hands together, placing them firmly on her lap.

"What did he call you when you guys where… together?"

"Red."

"Why?"

"He used to say he wanted me to turn his skin ruby red—pun intended. So, he started calling me Red. Eventually, the nickname stuck and everyone who knew me used the name as well."

I process, dissect, and then snap my drooping mouth shut. This broken woman, I thought I knew, is so much more mysterious than she's ever let on. She has a past life I would've never imagined anyone going through. "Who knew my firecracker girl was once known as Red, the provider of all your desires." I chuckle.

"Ugh. Don't say that name, it's horrendous."

"Why not? I kind of like it." I wink at her. "And the name suits you, even makes you sound sexy."

"Jealous Maeson thinks a name another man called me is sexy? Tell me it isn't so."

"Oh jealous I am and always will be. But we all have ex-somethings, so how can I hold that against you?" I squeeze her hand. "I can't, shouldn't, and won't."

"That's big of you, Maeson. And thank you for not making me feel like shit about what I used to do."

"Not in my nature, especially when I think a powerful woman is a sexy one." I start the car, needing to get back on the road before we miss our flight home. "I always knew there was a lioness deep within you. If my foggy memory serves me right, I recollect meeting her a few times, but sadly, never fully unleashed. I think it's time you release her."

Ruby pats my leg as she licks her lips. "You sure your beast can handle a *ravenous* lioness?"

Revving the engine, I show off my dimples, knowing how wet they make her. "Never doubt my *tenacious* beast, my love. He's much more powerful than you could ever imagine."

She arches an eyebrow and curls her plump top lip. "We'll see about that, *old man.*"

"Old or not, Princess, I'll always keep up. Cut me off at the knees, and I'll find a way to regain my footing. That, my dear, is how much purpose you've given my life."

That's how deeply my heart has fallen for you.

A BRUTAL SEPTEMBER HEATWAVE descends upon us, leaving us limp and bedraggled. Neither Ruby nor I wanted to leave the air-conditioned house, but somehow, we've managed to find a semi-normal day to day routine. Besides the heat, Ruby needed time to adjust, and I've done my best to give it to her.

Things aren't the same, though. Ruby's tense around Molly and seems to be avoiding her. She's even staying away from Precious Tomorrows. She said she won't go near it because she feels like a fake and won't return until she's fully recovered.

Recovered from what I haven't the slightest idea.

It's like pulling teeth trying to find out what's bothering Ruby, but I've learned not to push and wait for her to open up.

At this point, her behavior worries me. She's not struggling with the loss of Aria, this Ruby's affected by something else altogether. I'm trying not to think the worst, but she's sleeping more than usual, avoiding everyone, and has a hard time remembering things. How can I not to assume she's hiding something big?

It's been a few weeks of keeping my mouth shut and not prying into her private business, but whatever she's still battling has caused enough destruction. I need to involve myself before things reach an irreparable point.

Enough is enough.

I don't need to be a professional to notice she is in major need of help. I'm willing to bet all my money, down to the last penny, something is out of her control, and she's too afraid to admit it. The signs of my worst fear are everywhere and the problem I'm facing is... how do I approach her and avoid her bolting on me again?

I'll try tonight, and hopefully, not fail... like before.

If I want to be the man by her side, the one protecting her — *from harm she's causing herself* — I need to prove I give a bloody fuck...

Even if it means I'll lose her in the process.

32

Ruby

I grip the dreaded thing, steading my shaky hand and tip the bottle to my lips. Warmth fills my mouth and slides down my throat with a burn I've come to enjoy. An instantaneous rush fuels my body with enough courage to step out of this bathroom and meet Maeson's green eyes head on.

Every single time I think I have the strength to stop, the miserable part of me inundates my mind with shame, forcing me to believe I'm better off with the delirium this liquid provides.

'It helps you feel less, forget more, and makes you happier. Don't you see that? You've been hiding it so well, no one will ever know. So, why stop now? If you end the euphoria, you'll struggle. Do you want to feel pain again? No, you don't. Just once more. Then end the addiction.' Each pep talk was the same, and my weak mind would concede.

One more time turned into another and another, then so on for way too long. Now I'm stuck lying to everyone, pretending nothing's wrong.

My stupidity landed me in this position, and I have no clue how to ask for help. Alcohol has its grip on me and won't let go no matter how hard I beg for the release.

The blame is all mine. Not Aria's death or my pitiful past. There's no excuse good enough for the situation I'm in.

Adding to my shame, Maeson wants me to face everyone at Precious Tomorrows. How can I when I'm the biggest hypocrite? I tell people struggling to always be stronger and fight through their problems, yet what do I do?

I run away, drink like a fish, and hide from those I love.

If I open up to Maeson or Molly, they'll never forgive me for the choices I've made. Shit, Molly'd hate me, and probably, never let me see Xander again.

Rightfully so. Who wants an alcoholic around their kid? I wouldn't.

Which is why I've done everything I could to stay away. Especially, from that sweet baby boy.

"Lass, are you ready?"

Inwardly, I sigh. "Yup. One sec." I finish brushing my teeth for the third time, then inspect the room for any possible evidence left behind. As soon as I open the door, Maeson's blocking the opening, towering over me.

His eyes blaze with an indescribable emotion as he seems to be doing a careful examination of his own. After a moment, his top lip twitches and a smile appears. "You look beautiful, love."

I lower my gaze, bowing my head. "Thanks. I actually tried today." My words come out sarcastic, yet there's honesty laced within them—it really has been a long time since I've truly tried to appear presentable.

"Whether you try or not, you'll always be a beauty in my eyes." He kisses my forehead. "Never forget that."

His kindness reminds me there's still people in this world who care for me, and I smile. "I won't."

Maeson clasps his hand with mine, entwining our fingers. "Promise?"

Here he goes with the *'promise'* thing again. Ever since we came home over a month ago, he's had this thing if we say promise after something, it means we're being honest, and we have to keep true to our word.

The first time he asked, I didn't want to worry him further, so… I promised since it seemed important to him.

Today's no different. "I promise, Maeson."

"Good. Now are you ready to go? Those kids are excited to finally see you."

My stomach drops. The desire to pull away from Maeson and disappear again takes over. I freeze, needing a second to regain my confidence.

Maeson squeezes my hand and pulls me into him. "You can go out in to the world and live a normal life again. Nobody's judging you. I swear it. Everyone loves you, Ruby."

The nod, not truly convinced, but his words are enough to get me out of the house.

"Ruby, look what I made today!" A young boy smiles proudly as he holds up a bright finger painted paper.

His excitement makes me grin. "Wow! It's fabulous and must be framed."

The boy giggles. "It's not that good."

"Oh, yes it is! Have more faith in yourself, little man." I bend, reaching for the homemade painting. "I'll have it hung in the hallway for everyone to admire."

"Okay. Thanks, Ruby!"

I wink. "De nada, mi amigo."

His eyes widen. "You know my language?"

"Un poco."

"I can teach you more… if you want." He peers behind his shoulder. "No one else here knows. It sucks."

Wetness gathers at the corners of my eyes. "Well, once you teach me, you won't be alone. We can practice every time I'm here. How's that sound?"

In an instant, his frown turns upside down. "I'd like that a lot."

"Then it's a deal." I wave the boys artwork in the air. "And make me more of these to show off. Don't give up on your talent, okay?"

He nods. "Never!"

A few of his friends waiting at the end of the hallway call his name.

"I have to go." He tackles me with a tight hug before running off to meet his buddies.

When they're out of sight, I slip into my empty and lonely office. Maeson was called away for who knows how long, and I've visited with every floor already, so I'm not sure what else to do… other than find a drin—

"Hey, stranger." A warm and inviting southern voice pierces my heart.

No matter how difficult it is, I force myself to meet her crystal blue eyes. "Hey, Mo." I press my lips together as a meager attempt to smile.

"Quit tryin' so hard, Rubster, I know you're still hurting. Be fake with everyone else, but not me. And don't forget I'm a mom now, I don't miss a little fucking detail." She steps closer, pulling my body into hers.

I lay my head on her shoulder and let my body shag, releasing the ever growing knots underneath my muscles. "I'm sorry."

She pats my back. "Don't be, silly. You've been through a lot recently, let alone what you went through before moving here. I get it, you needed space."

"That I did."

Molly laughs as she motions me toward the empty chairs in front of my desk. When we sit, she sighs. "I hope you've found some type of serenity while you were away, but never do that shit again. For you to completely heal, you need time. And when I say time, I mean the real and true kind for yourself—not out getting wasted. You've got to make peace with the bad crap in life before you find the good hiding underneath. And if you don't find a way to do that, you'll end up hating yourself and everyone around you forever."

I fidget in my seat, afraid she'll notice how bad my recent choices have gotten. "How am I supposed to do that when history keeps repeating its self? I try so hard to let go and forget what's happened in my life, but I can't escape it. I don't have many options left."

Molly shakes her head. "Girl, we always have options if you'd open your damn eyes, or even ask someone to help you see the light. If you don't want to hash it out with me or Maeson, seek a professional opinion. There's no shame in that. Look at our poor girl, Aria, she walked the path you're on and where did that get her?" She pats my trembling leg. "Don't be one of those pity seeking, *I need help, but won't ask for it*, shattered soul's walking this earth, it never ends well."

"I don't want to be, but I guess I'm too ashamed. Made too many mistakes…"

She raises an eyebrow. "Who hasn't? What makes yours more unforgivable than the next guy?"

I shrug. "I guess there isn't a difference."

"Then stop being so hard on yourself and move the hell on. Accept the decisions you've made, fix your fuck ups, then let them go. And for your sake, do it soon. I need my best friend back. Shit, you need you back."

"You're right. I just need some time to figure things out."

"Take every minute you need because like I said, time is the only thing that can heal you at this point." Molly stands. "Speaking of time, my butt needs to get into gear and pick up my son from daycare."

"Okay." I lift my shaky body to embrace my friend and whisper, "I've missed you."

"Me too."

After I spent a few hours catching up on emails and voicemails, Maeson finally makes an appearance. Despite his broody demeanor, he's smiling.

"Hey, you," I say awkwardly.

"Hey, yourself." He continues to grin.

"What are you so happy about?" I arch an eyebrow.

"Seeing you behind that desk is what." He moves further into my office. "How was your first day back?"

"Not too bad. It feels right being here again. How was your

day? Regardless of your smile, your body radiates a pissed off vibe."

"Eh, lass." He shrugs. "Nothing you need to worry about."

"Hmmm. Are you sure?"

"Och, of course. You ready to leave?"

"I guess so. Where to?"

"My secret garden, love. We need to spend some quality time together. We've much to discuss, don't you think?"

I roll my eyes. "Don't you ever get tired of talking?"

"With you? Never."

"Okay, then let's go."

THE DRIVE TO MAESON'S *secret garden*, also known as his backyard, was a short and quiet one. And we're still sitting in silence as we lay on the hammock.

I don't know what to say or how to open the discussion about what I'm hiding. A big part of me hopes he'll start off soon, so I don't say something I'll regret.

As if he's read my mind, he sighs. "Where to begin?" He taps his lips with a finger. "First, I want you to know I've missed *you*—my sassy lass, and I'm in dire need of her. So much has happened in a short time, but I want—*need*—to help you somehow."

I bit down on my bottom lip, hoping the pain will halt my tears from slipping down my cheeks. "I miss her too, Maeson, but I've fallen into this deep dark hole I don't know how to climb out of. How did you escape it?"

"Slowly. It took me a long time to heal, love. Which is why we have to take control as quickly as possible. You need your life back into your own hands and away from the demons. If my stubborn ass can do it, you can too." He kisses my now swollen lip and whispers, "Stop hurting yourself. When you damage my Ruby, you're damaging me too. You don't want me in that darkness with you, do you?"

"Hell no! Then we'll both be fucked." I laugh.

He grins. "I've missed that sound."

"It sounds foreign to me too." I close my eyes and squeeze his hand. "Where do I start—how do I repair…"

"I'm not an expert, but I'd say start with less or no more drinking to give yourself a chance to clear your clouded mind. Stiff drinks only provide an escape from reality for a short time and your main goal should be to move forward. If you don't, you might end up being stuck in status quo forever, or worse end up… gone forever." He shakes his head. "Fuck. I can't even imagine…"

I touch his overgrown beard and stare into his fiery green eyes. "Then don't imagine it, because I won't let that happen."

It's to late, and you know it.

"I sure as fuck won't either." He winks. "I'll commit you to the finest facility there is before I allow you to cause any more harm to yourself." Maeson sits up. "Starting tomorrow we'll work on bettering each other, not just you. I *will* keep my promises to you, and I *can* be the rock you need. Or I *will* die trying, lass." He smothers my mouth with a sloppy kiss, then slides his tongue across my lips. "I've fallen for you, Princess. Fallen hard."

The rawness in his voice guts me.

I have to tell him how bad it really is. But I can't ruin this moment with my nonsense. I'll end the addictions on my own.

I rub my face against his thick beard, releasing a low moan. "You're not the only one…"

"Then don't ever leave me again. *Please* talk to me before things escalate, and you decide to do something crazy. We're a team. We'll always be as long as you keep me in your inner circle." He grins. "How else can I protect you from the big, bad, and uglies?"

"It's not your job to be my knight in shining armor, but for your peace of mind, I'll try harder to be more of an open book." I shrug. "I guess if I can't freely talk to *my significant other* , then who else do I really have?"

Maeson chuckles. "Don't let Molly hear you say that, she'd stab both of us."

"Oh crap. You're right. But I was thinking along the lines of a day to day confidant. My parents were everything to each other and that's what I want with… you." I bite down on my lip and stare up at him.

To my disappointment, he doesn't respond. Instead, shuts his eyes and lays his head back.

As much as I want to question his reaction, I don't and simply welcome the silence. I've said too much, and it seems, Maeson needs time to process my way too heart-rending declaration.

After a few minutes, he clears his throat. "Ruby, for us to get to the place your parents and mine were at, we need to have complete trust in each other."

"Are you suggesting we don't have that?"

"Aye, I am. There are things you're hiding from me. I waited for you to tell me yourself, but that has yet to happen. How can you be the Yin to my Yang or vice versa when bullshit like secrets sit between us? I've ripped my soul wide open for you… yet… you continue to hold back."

I shield my face with an arm, hoping to hide the flush burning my cheeks. "I have no clue what secrets you're talking about… I told you… everything."

"Lies." He wraps his long fingers around my arm and moves it out of the way. Then he curls one of those lengthy digits under my chin, forcing me to face him. "Listen to me carefully. Over the years I've learned many lessons and one of them…" He peers deep into my eyes as if he's reaching for something inside of me. "Is to accept the dark and plaguing parts of your past and present. Embrace what was and cannot be changed, before you can truly walk alongside what is light and free. You need to acknowledge every fragment of your shattered soul because it's the only way you'll move forward in life. And I'm afraid until that happens, what *you* consider to be perfection will never exist."

Before I speak, I allow the truth in his words to embed themselves in to my brain.

Perfection is something I've never envisioned, but something close would be nice to finally have.

But is it possible for me?

Am I capable of finding true happiness? If so, how?

Follow his advice, put in the hard work, and don't give up when shit hits the fan, that's how.

"Alcohol." I whisper.

"What?" Maeson eyes me curiously.

I lower my gaze. "How bad the need for it is what I've been hiding."

"As in you can't stop? Need it in your bloodstream every minute of the day? That bad?"

"Yes."

"I told you I noticed you were drinking more than usual, but I didn't think it was at an addiction level." He growls. The sound is deep, guttural—angry. "Why did you let it get out of hand? Why didn't you ask for help?"

"I was hurting too much and wanted to stop feeling, even if it was for a little while. Then it turned into an all day need."

"That's why you've been shaking this entire time! Your need is at dangerous level. And you drove drunk how many times? You could've killed someone!" He shakes his head. "Fuck, I sound like a nagging parent. I don't mean to, Ruby, but I care about you… I fucking lov—"

"Shut your mouth." I press a finger to his thick lips. "Nag all you want. I can handle that, but do not finish your sentence… *Please.*"

Maeson rolls his eyes. "And why shouldn't I? Too much to *feel*?" He slides his legs off of the hammock and grinds his shoes into the dirt.

"N… No…"

"Then what?" He rubs the back of his neck.

"I don't deserve it. Not yet. Only when I'm better."

"Do you even want to get better? Or is this some bullshit run around?"

"Not at all. I need to change… I have to. I don't want to end up like…" I grab his arm. "Please, believe me."

He peers back at me. "Oh, I do, lass. But believing is also seeing, and I've yet to *see* anything. You've run and hid behind something at every turn. You've given me no evidence, and I've blindly followed you hoping you're *different* than the rest of the women out there." He sighs. "Why can't you *see* my devotion to you—my belief in you? It's been there since the first night we met. No matter how hard I fought it and refused to acknowledge the emotion… *the feeling*… it's there and won't go away."

A tear slides down my cheek. "I do know. I do see. I'm just afraid more than I've ever been."

"You think I'm not? Life is scary as fuck to begin with, then add watching the people you adore struggle? Been there, done that, and now, I'm repeating the cycle with you. So, aye… I'm scared too, but I'm here to stay even when you leave me behind at every chance you get."

"I'm sorry. So sorry." My face burns as tears continue to flow from my eyes. "What can I do…"

"You can let me help. Truly help you. It'll be hard, but the recovery will be worth it in the end. I promise. You'll be able to breathe again. You'll be able to smile without feeling bad for doing so. You'll learn to depend on your own defenses and not a substance." Maeson shifts to face me fully. His eyes are as tear filled as mine. "Just say yes, Princess. *Please.*" He leans forward to caress my wet cheek.

After all this time, the effect Maeson has on me still amazes me. For the last few months there's been a tightness in every muscle of my body I couldn't get rid of, yet with one of his soft touches, the tension melts away.

I breathe in deeply, holding it in for two-seconds before I release the build up of doubts, fear, and angst. Is this what clarity looks and feels like?

No silly, this is your first step toward it. Don't get ahead of yourself.

Meeting his eyes, I frown. "What if I fail?"

"Not possible if I'm by your side." Maeson smiles, but it doesn't extend very far across his face. "Princess, let me in. I can aid you in letting go."

The conviction glowing in his gaze gives me the strength I seek. With a small nod, I grin. "Alright, Maeson, help and guide me toward what is light and free. I'm ready."

We're all ready—Ruby, Princess, Red, Mistress, and Lioness as one.

33

MAESON

Woman with their damn 'potty' breaks. Ruby disappeared into the bathroom at least fifteen minutes ago, and there's still no sign of her.

It can't take that long to freshen up, right? Unless… bringing her here was a bad idea. She seemed ready.

After six months of serious rehab, Ruby's back to her usual vibrant self. When she first started, back in September, none of us thought she'd make it through. But with the deeply imbedded perseverance I knew she had, she walked away a success. Even the staff and doctors were amazed by her strength and desire to recover.

In the end, she'd done it all on her own, just like every other struggle she's dealt with in the past.

Yet, you still worry?

I do, because one thing I've learned from the life I've lived is, a person in recovery isn't truly ever out of the woods. It takes years—*even a lifetime*—to overcome their addiction.

Although, I am cautiously optimistic. Each day she continues to laugh and enjoy life, the better her chances are. Once and for all, she seems *free*.

Most likely, I'm worrying for no reason, but I'd prefer to know for sure.

I search for Molly and Jax between the mass of people crowding the bar, but I don't see them.

They're probably out there dancing like they should be.

I'll leave those two alone. Their first real night out since baby Alexander was born shouldn't be ruined because my over protective beast's acting up.

That means, I'm left with one choice—go after Ruby myself.

I put my drink down and trudge through the club in search of my girl. Just thinking of Ruby brings forth an image of her dancing around the kitchen naked. A smile forces its way to my lips, and I release a long satisfying breath.

As I open the door to the bathroom, I spot Ashlie and freeze. "What the fuck are you doing here?" The unexpected sight of her brings on a panic I haven't felt in years. I lunge for her, but check myself mid-strike.

Steady, Beast. Remain levelheaded. It's the only way with this one.

"I… I…" She covers her mouth and nods to an open stall.

"What the bloody hell is wrong?" My hands tremble. "Where's Ruby?" Fear creeps further up my spine with each second passing by.

Ash-fucking-lie bolts for the door, but I grab her arm, forcing her to face me. "What's in that fucking stall, damn it?"

"She… she's in… there." The fucking woman stutters, like a blubbering child.

I shove her out of the way, rushing to the stall.

I'm immobilized.

My brain short circuits.

My heart stops.

My lungs cease to function.

Ruby.

My Ruby.

Princess.

My Princess.

She's slumped over the toilet.

I drop to my knees and attempt to lift her. "Princess?" Gently, I tap to her face.

Nothing happens. Her body's as lifeless as it appears.

With cautious maneuvers, I lift her and secure my grip before moving out of the stall.

When I lay Ruby on the tile floor, the bitch in front of me whimpers.

"What'd you do to her? You wanted her out of the picture so bad, you had to hurt her?" I snarl.

She shakes her head.

"Speak, you fucking monster!"

"I found her. Wanted to talk. Apologize. I didn't mean to… cause trouble."

"And I'm supposed to believe that shit? Does this look like you didn't cause trouble? Fuck you, Ashlie! Do us both a favor and stay the hell out of our lives."

Forget her. Focus on your soul mate. She needs you.

My beast howls as another attempt to revive Ruby fails.

He wants to be released. He wants to hurt the dreaded woman weeping before his presence. But we both know she's not worth the aggravation. Ruby's survival is the only thing that matters.

"Sssooorrryyy!" She grabs the doorknob.

Does she really think she can escape the scene that easily?

"Don't you bloody fucking move! Call the cops! Now!"

As she scrambles with her phone, I take a second to examine Ruby's entire body. There's no external damage, no blood—a needle.

What?

There's a needle sticking out of her arm.

She overdosed? But where did she get the drugs from…

In the distance, I hear Ashlie's panicked voice. "Come fast! She's not breathing! Please! Right. Royale. Yes."

I look up, emanating pure hatred in her direction. "You left me with our sick child. You never came to see her. You let her die. Now you hurt someone else I—Go! Get. The. Fuck. Out. Of. Here!"

She nods and runs out of the room.

When the door slams behind her, I surrender to the rollercoaster of emotions pleading to explode. Releasing what

I've held in for too many bloody fucking years, I joining my beast in a gut-wrenching roar until I have no voice left.

She may have acted innocent and would claim otherwise, but deep down, I know she did this on purpose.

She *will* pay for what she's done.

I'll make sure of it, but right now isn't the time. Ruby comes first.

"Ruby? Baby? Please wake up!" I caress her beautiful face, kiss it, and cup it between my hands. "What will I do without you?" For the third time, I attempt the little bit of CPR I know and exhale against her lips, supplying her lungs with as much oxygen as possible. I'll give her my last breath, if she'd just wake up. "Why'd you let her get that close to you? Did you want it? Did she force you? Please, open your eyes."

Fuck, this cannot be happening. This has to be one of those hellish nightmares you try to fight off, but can't wake up from.

Tears slide down my face. I don't wipe them away and pretend to be a strong man. I don't stop them from trickling down my face and onto Ruby's pale cheeks. "Princess... I'm losing you, aren't I? Please don't leave me all alone. You weren't the only one afraid of being left behind. You weren't the only one scared of never finding someone who truly cherished you — someone who wouldn't break your heart. I just never told you. I should've. Don't know why I didn't. I did the same thing with Madison. Didn't tell her how much I loved her, how much she meant to me, how she was my always and forever shining star, and how she was my... Princess... just like you." There's too much darkness surrounding us. It's crushing me under its weight, and I can't catch my breath.

Deep breath. Just breathe.

Not enough. Need more air. "Princess, as long as we have each other, we'll never be alone. Just stay with me, Please."

It feels as if she's gone already.

Her body is too limp, too unmoving. Her skin is too pale.

"We have so much to live for. Don't leave me, lass." My heart pounds against my ribs.

I didn't get a chance to tell you how I really feel. How I've felt since that first night we met. I should've shouted it from the rooftops. I should've bulldozed past my insecurities and told you…

"I love you, Ruby. You'll forever be my soulmate. You're my beginning, middle, and end. You're my happily ever after."

Thank you so much for reading the second book in Ruby and Maeson's story! I truly hope you enjoyed it, but their story is isn't over just yet.

Awkward familiarities of *'The Beginning'* are behind us, and now that we've moved past *'The Middle'* section of this trilogy, please join me for *'The End'* we're all waiting for.

Please stay tuned for the final installment in the Shattered Souls Trilogy which is titled —
TIME HEALS.

Until then, my dear readers, remember to…
Take a deep breath and just breathe!

Please don't forget to leave a review with the retailer you purchased your copy from to let me know what you thought!

As always, thank you for your continued support!

Thank You!

To my forever, my Pumpkin, I love you with every molecule in my body. You're my rock, the shoulder I cry on (but most often fall asleep on), and my knight in shining armor. We've been through so much, yet your belief in us has never wavered. My love for you could never be explained or written on a piece of paper because it's so grand, it'd take years upon years from me to do so. I adore and cherish our bond to the moon and back a million times over.

Nikki, Costi, Mom, and Dad—I love you so much! You're all everything to me, and because of you, I smile every single day. No matter how sad I am you've shown me I'm never alone.

To my entire family, I love you! Your support helped me pursue this dream of mine. Thank you!

I must thank a dear friend and partner in novel writing crime, Author Kate Smith. You've stood by me through thick and thin when writing Barely Breathing, and this time was no different. You've kept my muse afloat by being my sounding board day in and day out. I am forever grateful for friendship!

Sasha, Kierstan, Stormie, Carolee, Kassandra, and Vivi thank you for believing in me and being the best street team ever! Your feedback and support made me good cry on multiple occasions. I am forever grateful to all of you for giving me a chance when no one else would.

Thank you to my amazing Readers! My gratitude is immeasurable!

Lastly, but most importantly, my sweet and beautiful baby girl, Serafina. You're the miracle Daddy and I prayed for day in and day out for eight years. You've brighten our lives and filled our hearts with love that expands to the moon and back for eternity. We thank God everyday for giving us the best gift we could ever ask for—You! And I thank you for being the amazing daughter all mommies wish for!

We love you, Inna Bubulina!

About The Author

When I'm not at my full-time job or spending precious time with my daughter and husband, I'll often be found writing on my phone, iPad, or laptop. During my war with infertility, writing became an outlet to express my feelings, and escape a difficult situation. My struggles fueled the inspiration to write stories about people who hold on strong during their own times of adversity.

My goal is to remind my readers that no matter what they're going through, it too shall pass. Find the strength hidden deep within your soul for it will help you endure the hardest of times.

As many of my favorite authors did for me, perhaps I can provide a small getaway from plaguing troubles.

Spread Love. Spread Hope. Spread Kindness.

*I love to hear from my readers, so
please feel free to contact me on the
following social media:*

FACEBOOK - AUTHOR KATERINA BRAY

www.facebook.com/authorkaterinabray

INSTAGRAM - KATERINABRAY

www.instgram.com/katerinabray

WEBSITE

www.katerinabray.com

TWITTER - @KATERINABRAY

www.twitter.com/katerinabray

SHATTERED SOULS TRILOGY

TIME HEALS

Coming Soon!

www.ingramcontent.com/pod-product-compliance
Lightning Source LLC
Chambersburg PA
CBHW010509100726
47902CB00011B/2141